Wher_____ _____

Will...

By: Sue Lacey

Acknowledgements and
grateful thanks to my family
for their technical assistance
with this book.

The characters and events in
this book are purely fictional and
the work of the author's
imagination.

ISBN-13: 9798644714421

Sue Lacey was born in 1948 in Kent. As a child she spent much of her time alone with her head in a book. Books became her friends and, along with her love of animals and in particular, dogs and horses, she would lock herself away in her own little world.

When the family moved to Cornwall she was just a few weeks from taking GCE exams, but felt out of place in the new school, and so, at fifteen, chose to leave and take up the offer of a job on a farm where she was in her element.

Six years later she moved to Cambridgeshire, where she married in 1973, becoming a family with one son. Further education had not occurred to her until she watched with pride as her son received his degree. Beginning a journey through evening classes to achieve both GCSE and A Level English, she then ventured on, with limited expectations, to attempt an English and History Degree, finally being awarded this at the age of sixty, but it took nearly another ten years before she realised that perhaps it was time to put it to use. She has now done just that by publishing her first two novels, and this is a sequel to the second book, 'Where am I?'

Other books by Sue Lacey include:
'What Lies Behind Closed Doors'
'Where Am I?'
(All available on Amazon Kindle.)

To all my faithful readers who have encouraged me to keep writing, and a particular thank you to Jonathan Marshall for representing 'Steve' on the cover photo.

Chapter One.

Those of you who have first read the story of my much earlier ordeals, or should I say my earlier adventures as that is what they eventually became, will know now that my name is Melanie Cook, Mel to most people.

Though perhaps this may seem a strange way to begin my latest story this is not at all the case as the ordeal I spoke of from my earlier story began with me finding myself in a dark, damp place, apparently trapped, and with such loss of memory which left me with no idea where I was, why I was there, but worse still with no knowledge even of who I was! As you can imagine, this was a drastically terrifying time and led to events and encounters that now, looking back on them, still make me shudder at the thoughts.

Up until that time, as I did eventually come to remember and bring back to reality, I had been just an ordinary girl, brought up in a small village in Kent by my parents alongside my older sister Jennifer. Later my sister married Alan West, eventually moving to Halewood near Liverpool, and after finishing college, I went on to the

University College London (UCL) to do a degree in psychology. It just so happened that it was during the final term of our course, a group of us girls went into the city on a hen night. It was towards the end of the evening that I met Jake Murden, if 'met' is the right word for calling someone a 'flash git', just before tripping and falling, somewhat tipsy on the floor, almost at his feet!

To fully understand how this came about and just how this was to lead into our eventual engagement, it would ideally be beneficial for the reader to have first read my previous book, but suffice it to say that it was my relationship with him which turned out to be the catalyst for that traumatic ordeal of which I've just spoken, and worse still finding myself as I did accused of murdering my dear Jake.

As you can image, this had the effect of taking things from bad to worse, much more than worse; more from worse to unbelievably unbearable for me, plain boring little old me, who had always led such a humdrum life to that point. One minute there I was, engaged to the man of my dreams (which had nothing to do with him being drastically rich and handsome by the way), and the next minute there I was lost, scared and in pain, going through a true nightmare from which I couldn't escape, just to learn that I was apparently responsible for his death! Somehow I knew this couldn't be right. I didn't believe for a moment that I'd be capable of doing something like that, but perhaps I was wrong. After all, if I didn't remember right back when this all began who I was, or where I was, then how would I ever be sure... how could I ever prove this to anyone? On my own I very much doubt I would ever have done.

But there I go, getting ahead of myself. This all began with me finding myself in that dark, damp and frightening place I mentioned at the beginning. This eventually turned out to be an obscure cave in the Peak District of Derbyshire. It seems I'd been knocked unconscious before being dumped in there, and then the entrance supposedly sealed with dynamite. Luckily for me those responsible for doing this had not checked to see they'd achieved their aim satisfactorily, and it was this and this alone which is the only reason I am still alive to remind my readers of all the ups and downs that became my life in the period following this.

Perhaps it is misleading and drastically unfair for me to put the incompetence of these people down as the only reason I survived. They may certainly have made it just possible for me to escape my rock tomb, but this was by no means the end of my nightmare. Even after as near a superhuman effort as I could manage in my escape, I had to undertake an awful trek across unknown territory, even coping with some unsavoury character who, so I thought, was happy to offer me a lift (which turned out to be in return for certain favours, which I quickly declined!).

Even so, even after reaching civilisation, my nightmare was only just beginning as this was when I first became aware of the police hunt for me in connection with Jake's death! According to a newspaper report I had been with him just before he died but not been seen since. It was assumed I'd killed him then disappeared, giving cause for suspicion to fall on me.

Following my escape from my 'tomb', I soon found out just how unfit I was to cope with the nightmare which now hung over me like a big black cloud. Having struggled to reach civilisation just to learn of the allegations against me, I realised I badly needed help from somewhere or someone if I was ever to prove my innocence (assuming I was actually innocent). Not just that, but I soon realised how unprepared I was to face the difficulties and dangers which lay ahead of me during this time. I'd not realised until then the true extent of my naivety in so many ways, having always led such a comfortable, well protected life until this point.

Now I needed a whole new sort of protection, and someone to teach me how to cope with so many things I'd never had to deal with previously. The answer to my prayer came in the most unlikely form of a rough sleeper by the name of Steve Lockett. I'd not come across the likes of this man before. I knew there were always dozens of people, more often than not on drugs, to be seen tucked into dirty old sleeping bags in shop doorways etc. in places such as London, but Steve was different. Right from the first time we met I knew he was different in so many ways. He was never on drugs, always (well, as often as possible!), as clean and tidy as his lifestyle allowed, and was always a perfect gentleman throughout our time together. Perfect that is if getting his kicks out of making fun of me counts as perfect gentlemanly behaviour, and often at the expense of my dignity! One instance that springs to mind in particular was an occasion when he took the liberty of actually milking a farmer's cow and then finding it hysterically funny that I hadn't considered it coming out warm! When he managed to stop laughing he asked if I really thought you got 'refrigerated cows'!

When we first met he'd already seen the details of Jake's murder in a discarded newspaper, and was therefore also aware of my situation, yet instead of handing me in to the police in the hope of a reward, chose to take me under his wing and guide me through the difficult and often dangerous times ahead, right up until my name was cleared and the true culprit was dealt with. These certainly proved to be a truly unbelievable mix of ups and downs, spread over what felt like a lifetime, yet actually not much more than three to four months, but during which time I became totally dependent on Steve and, for most of the time anyway, he had the effect of making me feel perfectly safe just by being around.

Even so, although there were odd occasions when I would casually pass a remark and find I got an unexpected and almost frightening response, there was one occasion when I asked for the terrible consequences which I suffered by completely ignoring his instructions to stay where he left me and allowing him the privacy he asked for. Being too inquisitive for my own good, I'd followed him. To my surprise he visited a cemetery and was visibly distraught crouched between two graves. When I thought he was out of sight I'd crept over to read the names on the stones, just to find they were his sister Claire, and his wife Elizabeth with his two year old son Sean. What I'd not counted on was Steve coming back to find me there, even less had I counted on the sheer rage he unleashed on me when he did! I really felt I was about to be killed that night.

To save myself I had taken off alone, battered, bruised and scared, to cope alone for nearly a month. Through this time I went through such a mix of emotions. I was lost and lonely except for a new friend Sally who was kind enough to help me deal with my situation. All this time I found myself more desperate by the day to be back with Steve. I longed for him to come in search of me, I knew I was lost without him, yet part of me was still dreading what would happen if he did find me. Of course I needn't have worried on that score; it seemed he'd been searching for me in the hope of a reconciliation. Things were a bit awkward for a while but, though he still wouldn't expand on what had been the cause of his family tragedy, all dying as they did on the same day, he was so full of apologies and remorse for his behaviour toward me, that I was just thankful to be safely tucked back under his wing where I knew I belonged.

From then on we journeyed along together toward our goal, gradually heading for where it had all begun, Jake's house. It was there that I saw Steve at his absolute terrifying worst, and learnt the whole story of just what had driven him to the point of holding a knife to the throat of Jake's murderer, with every intention of killing him!

It turned out that Steve had been a sergeant in the paras for some years, and had earned the respect of both officers and men. One of the youngest of these was a young lad who he had taken a special interest in during training. It turned out that this young soldier had caught another sergeant by the name of Morgan beating up a prisoner and had been viciously killed by the sergeant himself to keep him quiet, and the blame put onto the prisoner who he also killed to prevent detection. This turned out to be the very same man who had gone AWOL from the army, and had wheedled his way into Jake's business before killing him with the intention of taking it over and gaining from Jake's good fortune!

Understandably, already suffering from PTSD brought on by a particularly stressful stretch of time served without leave, just to find that, just as his plane was touching down at Brize Norton, his sister Claire, wife Elizabeth, and baby son Sean were all killed in an unfortunate car accident on their way to meet him, it was not surprising to find that all this combined at this point, leading him to lose all control, only being saved from the police firearms guns by a captain from his regiment and, somewhere deep inside, his truly good heart.

Chapter Two.

It was clear that the dear, gentle and fun loving Steve I had come to rely on for so long was now in desperate need of help to bring him back from the brink to which he'd found himself. As it was explained to me, he had been offered counselling from the army before his discharge, but at that point just couldn't face it, and so had chosen to take the honourable discharge and spend the next two years living rough, determined he could find his own way through it alone. Of course, though for so long he'd fooled himself into believing this approach was working, in reality all he was achieving was to push it to the back of his mind and pretend it had never happened. In truth he had just tucked himself safely away from everyone and everything, avoiding having dealings with anyone or anything which would risk bringing him back into the real world. The saying goes, 'what you don't see, won't hurt you', but it was easy to see that this was a man who had seen so much more than one could be expected to, and it was all that he had seen that had given him every reason to want to dig himself into a proverbial hole and hide away from the world for a time. It probably was the wrong way to deal with it but, though to most it could look a cowardly way out, to me I can't help thinking it must have taken real courage to go it alone.

I truly believe that when we first met and he took it into his head to 'adopt' me as a helpless case in need of guidance, this had been the first time in those two years that he'd been called on to actually think of somebody else, or to have need to call on some of his particular abilities. So in that small way perhaps we both managed to help one another in some respects.

Until the incident in the cemetery I felt safer and more cared for than I believe I ever had in my life. But then at that point it took stupid, clumsy me to stir up the painful memories of what had happened to his family. Then, just as we were recovering from that awful incident and I was beginning to put all my trust back in him once more, I had to watch as he stood holding a knife to the man Morgan's throat, intent on revenge for what that man had done, while a line of armed response police stood ready to fire if he'd not dropped the knife! Had it not been for the quick reaction of the army captain who had come with them there is no doubt in my mind that Steve would have carried out his threat or been shot, perhaps both.

Following this the captain from his old regiment had taken Steve away for many months of complete counselling and rehabilitation in a specialist centre run for those from the forces. As it was explained to me, just at that point Steve had totally lost control of his actions, and having been trained to kill without hesitation when the need arose, was going to need a great deal of expert help to bring him back to a state where he'd be safe to return to ordinary society without risk to anyone. Of course I was questioned as to whether or not he'd ever shown any aggression toward me, but of course I said no, never!

It seems that normally anyone going through this process would not be given access to civilians until toward the end, but apparently Steve had made it clear that he wanted occasional access to me or he'd refuse to co-operate, and so after the first few weeks were up I was asked if I would agree to visit from time to time, strictly monitored I might add! I didn't mind that though as I was already feeling lost without him around. I'd had to drift back into my old, pre-Steve, life, and I just couldn't settle. As a temporary measure until I found something better, Jake's younger brother Andy had been glad to find me employment at what was now his business. Actually I felt he always looked on me as a sort of big sister even though I'd been out with him a few times before he introduced me to his brother Jake, and long before Steve had enlightened me to him being bisexual! Not that that bothered me I suppose, but

I still can't understand how I hadn't worked this out on my own. Somehow I'm sure he felt closer to me since the traumatic events of the day Steve had saved him from suffering the same fate as Jake.

I must admit that the first time I visited Steve was a little uncomfortable. Neither of us really knew what to say, especially as we were being 'helped' along by a quietly spoken counsellor by the name of Paul who was doing his best to steer us in what he thought was a safe direction. The big problem with that was of course that we had seldom seen the need to be so guarded in our conversation, and this had the effect of leaving us struggling to find barely any conversation for most of the time. To be fair, I do believe even the poor counsellor was at a loss to know just how to encourage Steve to make any meaningful conversation at all. By the time I visited for the fourth time I think he'd decided I was in little danger from what was clearly becoming a very downhearted, almost brain dead Steve. It was during this visit that Paul was called away for a few minutes, leaving us alone for the first time.

Perhaps wrongly, but I really didn't care, my patience gave way to impatience and I got up and went across the room to Steve, looked him straight in the eye and said,

"For God's sake Steve, get up! Don't just sit there like a dummy... you're really beginning to scare me now. Do something, shout at me, get up and hold me, anything. I can't take much more of this, it's just not you. You've got to find a way to get through this. You're not on your own, I'm with you... I'll be with you as long as you want me to, but please just come back to me, or I'm walking out that door now and you won't see me again!"

For a second or two he just sat and stared up at me with a blank expression on his face. I thought I'd blown it now, and was just heading toward the door when he stood up and blocked my way. Without a word he held out his arms, and without another word from me I found myself back where I'd wanted to be for so long, wrapped up in those strong, comforting arms. Now I knew he was going to be ok. It may take time but 'my' Steve was still there, deep inside, just needing time to find his way out.

By the time the counsellor came back he was amazed, and probably a little concerned to find us sitting side by side, holding hands and chatting (well, I suppose I was doing most of the chatting!), and could barely believe the very much more animated version of his patient he now saw. It seems he'd seen Steve go from something resembling a raging bull to an almost zombie like character, but this was a side he'd apparently not seen so far. I honestly think for a moment he thought I'd slipped him some sort of drug! This truly was the point at which all those around him could see that perhaps there really was hope for him making a good recovery after all.

What was going to happen from that moment on I couldn't say, but I felt that the real Steve was in there, perhaps still a little lost in a deep fog of emotions, but none the less I felt he had turned a corner, and I was going to be there around that corner, waiting for him when he found his way out! It seemed that he did, at last, have the will to fight his way back.

Chapter Three.

From that first breakthrough it was as if Steve had truly seen the light at the end of the tunnel as it were. I believe I understood this more than some as this was how I'd felt myself, not so many months ago. I had known just what it was to feel lost in the dark, not truly even knowing who you are as this was in many ways how I had felt that awful time when I'd found myself in a dark 'rock tomb', with no memory even of who I was! Had it not been for Steve taking me under his wing and helping me get both my memory and my life back again, I genuinely don't think I'd have got through it as I did.

Through those months we were together he had taught me a strength I never knew I had. He had taught me how to stand up for myself and cope with things I would never have done before. Now I felt I had truly grown up and was able to go on and make a good life for myself, but what sort of life would it be without Steve? As I have said, he had taught me how to cope better, but still he had been there by my side for so long, to catch me if I fell as it were, and that was why I felt there was always going to be the risk of me slipping back into the old wimpish, childish ways of my early life. I'd always thought my life with Jake had been good in as much as being with him had given me a position in life, but in that position I feel I was always more ornament than use! Very rarely did any serious challenges come my way but that didn't bother me back then. I can see now that that was not how most of the real world works.

On the other hand, from the first day I met Steve I had been faced with the terrible challenge of evading a charge of murder, and had absolutely no idea how to deal with this or the dangers it was to put in my way. It was for this that I was so grateful to Steve for helping me find the unknown inner strength I never knew I had. Without him to fall back on the worry was whether I could keep that strength going alone?

It was at this point that the counsellor in charge of his care, Paul, invited me into his office on my way out.

"Please come in and take a seat Miss Cook. I wonder if you'd mind me discussing your relationship with Sgt. Lockett, Steve I should say."

I sat rather pensively on the chair across the desk from him, wondering what it was he wanted to know, and more importantly, what I was going to say to him! I wish too that he would stop shuffling paper and actually look at me! Actually, I felt just a little bit sorry for the poor chap because I could tell he wasn't quite sure how to tackle the task ahead of him. It didn't take me many seconds to fathom out just what it was he wanted to find out. Should I put him out of his misery or just watch him squirm? I think I know which Steve would do, so I decided to do likewise and just sit quietly and enjoy the entertainment of seeing how he would work up to it (mean, aren't I?).

I suppose that finding the funny side of an otherwise serious situation is one of the many coping strategies I picked up from Steve along the way without realising. Many was the time I would panic over something, just to find Steve lighten the stress by making a joke of it, usually at my expense. So this is what I was doing right now. Poor chap, though about the same age as Steve, he seemed so much younger and more inexperienced, due of course to Steve's years of service in the forces I suppose.

Eventually, after a bit more paper shuffling and clearing his throat, he looked across the desk at me, not quite straight in the eye, and said,

"I know you spent quite some time together since you first met. Can you explain to me just how, and to what point, your relationship developed please? For instance, did you know Steve from before your, um, adventure together?"

"No, I didn't meet him until someone tried to kill me by knocking me out and dumping me in a cave. It wasn't till I escaped from there that I found I'd been wrongly accused of murder, and that was when I met Steve. If it hadn't been for him I probably would never have proved my innocence, or even survived long enough to try."

"So you spent quite some time together then," he said, checking his notes. "Were you with others, or was it just the two of you during that time?"

"We did meet others from time to time, but most of the time it was just the two of us." I could tell what it was he was getting at but had no intention of making it too easy for him, so I just waited while he shuffled a few more papers! (After all, I'd not just achieved a degree in psychology not to know how he was thinking right now.)

"So Miss Cook, do you mind me asking, just how close did your friendship become during that time?"

"Oh very close really I suppose. He knew so much more than me, so I was keen to learn anything he could teach me, and make the most of every minute we spent together. We had some very special moments together I would say,"

I sat back and watched him squirm even more as he tried to figure out how to get the answer he was looking for, but I wasn't going to make it that easy... after all, I had learnt at the foot of the master when it came to embarrassing people, and just for once it wasn't me on the receiving end! Oh yes, I do believe I was beginning to see just how much fun Steve got from doing just this.

"So… um… would you say that during the time you spent together Steve ever acted in a manner which you would consider threatening or," he hesitated briefly, "or inappropriately toward you?"

Poor chap. I know I was stringing him along just to see how far I could take it, but I also know there was undoubtedly a serious side to his line of questioning, so just what should I say? Well, there was about three occasions when he grabbed me from behind with his hand over my mouth …, but that was to stop me screaming after all. Then of course he did viciously attack me at his wife's graveside …, but under the circumstances that was entirely my fault.

Of course there was the really scary bit at the end when he trussed me up like a turkey, threw me at the feet of his nemesis, and offered to cut my throat there and then with that damn great army knife of his!

But no, I assured Paul, he had never been in the least threatening towards me, and as for acting 'inappropriately', that would be wishful thinking on my part, but I knew Steve would only ever look on me as a friend, or at most a younger sister, and that was enough for me, just as long as he was always around to make me feel safe. Perhaps this was a strange way to look at things right now as in my heart I knew that somehow, just for now, it was perhaps my presence which was helping to make him feel safe. It was obvious that he was more than able to take care of himself physically of course as he spent much of his time at the centre working on his fitness levels (not that I ever thought he was other than fit before!), but whilst he was still working on the difficult job of getting himself equally strong mentally, it did seem that he was more than glad to lean on me for a while by way of a psychological crutch, and I was pleased I could be there for him as he'd been for me when I needed it most.

Whatever our separate needs at this point it seemed we both felt the need to stick together, no doubt out of habit after the length of time we'd spent together since we met, and our mutual understanding of each other's pasts. Just what the future held for us both neither of us knew right now, but it did seem that, whatever it was, we would be facing it together.

Chapter Four.

And then one day it happened! I arrived a little late for my usual visit to the centre to find Steve striding impatiently up and down the entrance hall looking like a caged lion waiting to be released!

"Where were you? I've been waiting for ages, you said you'd be here by ten and its ten forty-five now."

"I'm sorry. Does a few minutes make much difference? It's not as if you're going anywhere is it?" I said, feeling a little peeved at being scolded like a child.

"That's just the point. I am going somewhere, or at least I can if I have somewhere to go. They've decided I'm safe to turn loose, and I reckon poor Paul has had enough of my company to last a lifetime!"

For a second or two I just stood looking almost in disbelief, and was about to speak when he went on,

"Well... do you want my company or should I find some other poor mug to put up with me? They'll only let me go if I have a keeper to see I behave, and I said you would. Was I right or would you rather run off and leave me here to rot!"

What could I say? I'd always hoped that when the day came he would still want us to stay together. I just wanted to throw my arms around him and never let go, but Paul had always warned me not to expect too much from him; he may still just want me as that crutch to lean on until he could go it alone, a sort of 'get out of jail free' card as it were.

"Ok, if no one else will put up with you I suppose I'll have to," I said, trying my hardest to keep the broad grin I was fighting back from spreading across my face. "Do we need to go and check out with Paul or anyone before we go? And have you got your gear all packed?"

I was beginning to feel like a mother collecting her kid from boarding school for the holidays! Before I could get further, rather like that impatient school kid, Steve pointed me to the heap of stuff on the floor near the office door (amongst which I recognised his old rucksack which he'd carried since the day we met).

"Oh ok. Paul did want a quick word before we go, but don't let him talk you out of it or I'm out of here if I have to fight my way out!"

I believe he meant it too! The staff had been good to him while he was here but, knowing him as I do, I think he'd had as much help as he could take now and was desperate to break free. At this point I pity anyone who tried to stop him now he'd made up his mind to leave. I wasted no more time as I could see he was getting impatient to get through the door. My chat with Paul was, luckily, a short one. He was just wanting to be sure I was prepared to take Steve on and felt I could cope. I quickly reassured him I was glad to do so, and that, having coped with him at his worst I had no concerns now since he'd had the complete rehab package he'd not accepted before.

"Now, you're not expecting any big romantic future with him are you? I believe you were quite right that time when you told me Steve looks on you as a friend he trusts or a sister, nothing more than that. I don't want you to expect more and get hurt Mel."

No, I reassured him, but failed to say what went through my head, that a girl can't be blamed for hoping, can she?

"Ok, as long as you're happy to put up with him (said with the first genuine grin I'd seen since we met), but you must promise to bring him back or get in touch if you have the slightest concern over his behaviour. You mustn't put yourself or anyone else in danger from him now, will you? You know as well as any just how violent he can be under pressure."

"Don't worry on that score Paul. I'll see he's not under any pressure, and yes, I promise I'll contact you straight away if I have any concerns I can't deal with. To be honest I feel he'll be under more pressure if he has to stay here much longer. Not that you and your team haven't worked miracles with him, but he was always a free spirit and hated being tied down anywhere for too long."

As he got up from his chair to see me out of the office he hesitated for a second, "So where will you go when you leave here? Do you have a place to take him to?"

To be quite honest that thought hadn't occurred to me until now. Though I'd not really got round to asking them I assured him that, as I'd been back living with my parents since my ordeal, even though I'd inherited Jakes house in Richmond which I just couldn't bring myself to go back to, and because it was within easy travelling distance to visit Steve, they were more than happy to accommodate us both while we decide what to do next and were expecting this as soon as he was ready. Actually I had never thought this far ahead, and so had not even considered asking them. Even so, though they'd never met him they were well aware of the part he'd played in saving me from the awful fate I'd been facing, so I lied through my teeth and told him they were expecting him! They had been staying in a small villa they had part ownership of in Spain, but had rushed home immediately when Jenny had rung them with the news, first that Jake had been murdered and I had vanished, then that the police suspected me of being the culprit!

"And do you have transport to get there?" he asked.

I was ok on that score as Andy had 'rescued' the car Jake had bought me from the garage at the house. I didn't have the need of it to get to the office, but it was a lifesaver to get me here to see Steve. As we passed back out into the entrance hall where an even more impatient Steve was waiting, Paul went across to say his goodbyes and I took the opportunity to excuse myself on the pretext of needing the ladies before driving home! Actually I had decided that the least I could do was to ring and warn my parents he was coming. I so hoped this wouldn't come as too much of a shock to them, lacking any great warning. I was pleased that it was Mum who answered the phone. I knew that if Dad had any objections she could always talk him round, all I needed to do was convince her.

"Mum, I need to ask you something. I was wondering ..."

"Yes dear, you were wondering what?"

Oh well, here goes nothing! I took a deep breath and dived straight in,

"Well you see, I've been to visit Steve and..."

"Come on Mel, don't keep me in suspense. He's not ill is he? Or left there?"

"No Mum, nothing like that. Just the opposite. He's fighting, well perhaps not fighting, fit; but they have said he can leave now."

"That's good to hear dear. So where is he going next? Has he got a home to go to?"

Dear Mum, already thinking of his welfare.

"Well you see Mum, Paul says he can only go if he has somewhere to stay and someone to keep an eye on him, so ..."

"So you said you'd be happy to do that? And does this mean you're bringing him home with you? When?"

"Well yes, as long as you and Dad don't mind? And as for when, we'll be leaving in a few minutes."

Much to my relief Mum took the news as if I was bringing her a huge lottery win! To say she was excited was an understatement, and even Dad, listening in on the conversation was, in his own reserved way, obviously thrilled at the prospect of at last meeting this anomaly of a man who had saved his youngest from a fate worse than death. Just what they'd make of him, in the flesh as it were, I really wasn't sure. Then of course, I couldn't help wondering what he would make of them either come to that. Oh well, I'd committed myself to undertake his immediate future, and that's what I'd do, even if we had to find somewhere else to stay. I knew even at this point that he'd said he didn't want to settle in one place for good, but we'll certainly have to for now. He would need Paul's approval to finally sign him off first. Until then he must stay within driving distance for regular visits to the centre, so all I could do was pray he would get on ok with my parents… and them with him of course!

When I re-joined Steve and Paul it was obvious that they'd had a good heart to heart. Steve had calmed down, probably as he now knew Paul was genuinely going to let him go, and was giving him a warm handshake and thanking him and the large group of staff who had gathered to say goodbye. In the time he'd stayed here Steve had made a big impression and many friends. Knowing him the way I do this certainly came as no surprise to me.

As Paul took hold of my hand to shake it he held it for a second longer and said a sincere thank you for my help with Steve's recovery. As he said this he caught Steve's eye out of the corner of his and was about to let go of my hand quickly (obviously still a little cautious of this 'madman' he'd spent months with), when Steve looked across with the old saucy grin and said,

"For Christ's sake man, grab hold of her and give her the hug, you know you want to. She's earn't it ain't she?"

So that was just what Paul did, whether from his own free will or because he felt he'd been given an order, I couldn't say. By this time, with the help of some of the staff, we were soon outside loading Steve's gear into the car, waving a last farewell to the ever growing crowd, and heading off for the Kent countryside.

As we drove further away from the place he'd spent so many months at I'm sure I heard Steve let out a deep sigh of relief. Much as I know he appreciated the help he'd received and the great need he'd had for it, he had spent the previous two years or so out there on his own; as he said during our time together, he was always happiest as a free spirit with nothing to tie him down. Now I was faced with the prospect of just how to manage whatever was to come next! Could I manage? I'd promised Paul I'd stay with him until we could guarantee he could cope. Steve himself had said that he wanted us to, as he put it, 'make a go of it together', but just what he'd meant back then I wasn't absolutely sure. Oh yes, I knew what I'd hoped he meant, but I still can't help thinking he looked on me as a sort of sister cum comfort blanket to lean on and keep him safe!

I glanced across at him as we got nearer to my parents' home, feeling a little anxious as to whether I was doing the right thing bringing him there. After all, knowing Mum the way I do I can't help thinking she might smother the poor man. She still treats me like a kid so I dread to think just how she'll be with her 'hero' who saved me from being murdered! Well, you know what mothers are like and mine's no exception.

"You're looking worried Mel. What's up?" he always could read my mind, "Is there a problem with me staying at your parents, because I don't have to you know, I can find a b&b, a hostel, or come to that, there's bound to be an allotment shed somewhere," he added with a grin.

"Don't be daft, of course you're coming home with me. Besides, Mum would throw me out if I go home without you. Just be patient with her; she can be a bit inclined to flap about when there's anything different going on but ..." I glanced across at him out the corner of my eye to see him trying to hold back an obvious fit of laughter, "what've I said that's so funny?"

"It's just that now I can see where you get it from, like mother like daughter eh?"

I had to throw him a disapproving glare but he was probably quite right; besides which it was so good to see a bit more of the old Steve coming back. I knew at this point that if his wicked sense of humour was still intact everything else would follow given time, the only question was just how much time?

I really owed this man so much that I knew I could never properly repay him but, for what it's worth, I would certainly give it my best shot, and just maybe we'd have a bit of fun along the way. After all, during the months we'd spent together life had been a real roller coaster. We'd gone through moments of worry on my behalf, always turned around by the way this man by my side now had of making light of things, often seeing the funny side of my reactions. We had shared many truly funny moments and laughter. But then of course, there had also been some of the most terrifying moments of my life, yet for most of the time , whatever happened, I'd somehow always felt I could trust Steve to deal with any situation. Now it was my turn to return the favour, my turn to be the capable one, and I was not about to mess it up.

"Now what are you thinking about miss?" Steve threw me a quizzical sideways glance.

"Oh, nothing much. Just wondering what it'll be like now? You know, living a normal life after so long."

Normal? What did I mean by that? I doubt life with Steve around could ever be normal!

Chapter Five.

As we rounded the corner of the road I saw Mum peering out of the window, eagerly awaiting her first sight of the car arriving. Before we had barely pulled up on the drive both her and Dad were outside ready to greet the 'conquering hero', as they saw Steve! Whilst Dad was glad to give him a warm handshake and manly pat on the back, Mum threw caution to the wind and threw her arms round him (or what she could reach of him with her grand height of five foot one to his six foot two!), and welcomed him like the proverbial prodigal son!

Talk about parents' capacity to embarrass their offspring … I wouldn't have been surprised if he'd changed his mind about staying and dashed back to the centre right then and there. Instead of that he seemed happy to accept her over-warm greeting, so graciously that I wondered if I'd accidentally brought the wrong man home with me! By the time I could pry her off of him Dad was unloading his gear from the boot and was ready to carry it into the hall, leaving me to suffer further embarrassment from Mum asking in what she thought was a quiet whisper,

"I've made up the bed in the spare room for Steve. Is that alright dear? Only, after you'd spent all that time together I wasn't sure if you …, well you know?"

"Mum! Shush, you'll embarrass him. Yes, that's fine, and no, we haven't 'well you know', thank you!"

Though I could hear Dad talking to him as they went in the door, I couldn't help but catch the fleeting grin thrown in my direction. Thank goodness Mum didn't or, though what I'd told her was the truth, she would never have believed me. Although she must have accepted that such things go on, as when I was engaged to dear Jake and living together until his untimely death, I had been perfectly truthful on that score when I'd reassured Paul that Steve had never made any advances to me in that way. Far from it; I know he was still grieving for his beloved wife Beth who had died in that awful accident alongside his son and his sister. No, we had become extremely close, both as it were, desperate for a way out of our separate problems, but had somehow formed an unusually unique companionship which had held us up through hard times and sustained our sense of humour to do so in so many of them.

After showing him to his room (somewhat more comfortable than poor old Bill's shed floor), I decided to rescue Steve from the clutches of my adoring parents and take him out to acquaint him with the immediate neighbourhood. We are lucky enough to live in a particularly attractive area of the country. As a child I would spend many happy hours roaming the nearby woods and parkland, usually back then with my little dog as my close companion. Now I no longer have my little friend, but find myself in the company of a totally different companion in this man by my side!

Mostly we just walked in silence with me wondering just what was passing through his mind, but not daring to ask. On the odd occasion he stopped and turned to me, but it felt as if the words wouldn't come. And if they had... what would he say? I chose not to question him, but just squeezed his hand and then keep hold of it as we walked on in silence. Though we'd seen one another on regular occasions it felt as if we had never really been able to speak openly to one another. I felt there was still so much left unsaid between us, and I'm sure Steve felt the same. Perhaps this was not yet the right time for any deep and meaningful discussions. Hopefully there would be plenty of time for that when he'd had chance to settle in and unwind. Of course the words 'settling in' didn't quite sound like words that sat comfortably with the name Steve Lockett!

I did wonder if I'd done the right thing bringing him home. Would he be able to settle here, at least until he was given the all clear from the rehab centre. It seemed I needn't have worried about that after all. By the time Mum had filled him to bursting with her signature casserole, and Dad had poured him a glass of his finest malt whisky to wash it down while I helped with washing up, I don't think I'd ever seen Steve so relaxed! In fact it was not so late into the evening I decided to suggest an early night after what had been quite an exhausting day for us both. Mum and Dad said it would not be so long before they turned in too, so we went on up to see Steve had all he needed. I quite expected to see him leave all his things packed into his old rucksack, but to my surprise he actually started unpacking his few clothes and distributing them between the wardrobe and the drawers with the obvious neatness learnt from years of military discipline. I watched this with a not so well disguised sense of amusement before he looked round and asked,

"Now what? What do you reckon is so funny now?"

"It's just that I never knew you were so well organised before ..." I just managed to duck before a neatly rolled pair of socks hit me! "Is there anything you need?"

"No thanks, or perhaps some water would be good if you wouldn't mind."

I went down to fetch this, deciding on a small jug rather than just one glassful, thanked my parents for making him so welcome, and returned back upstairs jug in hand to find his door closed.

Predicament! Should I knock or just walk in? I listened for a few seconds to see if I could gain a clue as to what was going on inside! Damn it, this is stupid. We'd lived together, closely together (in a strictly platonic way of course) for some months. Why should I suddenly feel intimidated by this man now? Perhaps it's because there is a subtle change in him brought about by the rehab no doubt. Yes, I think I like the changes I see in him, but they still leave me a little unsure just what to expect of him.

Choosing not to knock I just opened the door and was somewhat amazed at the sight before me. On our return from our walk he had changed into his old jogging bottoms and t shirt for comfort, and now there he was, stretched out on top of the bed fast asleep! I stood looking at him for a second or two but decided not to wake him, he looked so peaceful. So I took a cover from the foot of the bed and laid it carefully over him. Putting the jug and glass on the bedside table, I looked at him lying there so peacefully, then left the room closing the door as quietly as I could behind me.

The fact that my room was next door to Steve's somehow gave me a warm, comforting feeling as I wriggled into my bed that night, which struck me as decidedly odd. After all, this was my room, my bed, and where I'd been happy sleeping for all the years I was growing up there. Somehow the knowledge that I had, in some small way, helped to bring Steve back to the man he truly was, and was now able to continue to support him in the coming days, months … perhaps even years, in some small way repaying him for the support he'd given me when I needed it most, I believe contributed to my feeling of satisfaction and complete relaxation that night. I switched off the light, rolled over, and was asleep almost as my head hit the pillow!

The next morning I was woken up by Mum coming quietly into my room with a cup of tea for me.

"Good morning dear. Did you sleep well?" but before I had chance to answer, going on, "I was wondering if Steve likes a cup of tea or coffee, but I listened at his door and couldn't hear any signs of life, so wonder if he's still asleep. Do you think he's alright dear?"

"Yes Mum, I'm sure he is. He was shattered last night. So much so that by the time I took the water jug up to him he was out cold on top of the bed, so I just covered him up and left him. Don't worry though, I'll stick my head around the door and see if he wants a drink."

I put my dressing gown on and went along to Steve's door. Wondering if he was still asleep I tapped quietly… no reply. I tried a little louder. Surely he can't still be asleep. Still no answer, so I opened the door very quietly and peeped in, and remembering how tired he'd been last night, assuming I'd find him still out cold as I'd left him. I certainly wasn't expecting the sight confronting me now! The room was empty, the bed made to look unslept in (or on as was the case here!), and there was no sign of Steve at all! Panic set in. Where was he, had he gone for good? Should I phone Paul?

As hard as I tried to calm myself I could feel I was losing it. He'd only got here yesterday and I'd lost him already. A thought crossed my mind, what about his clothes and his rucksack? He'd put them all in the wardrobe last night. I rushed across to it and was just opening the door when I was startled by a voice from behind me causing me to spin round,

"I know we've slept in some strange places but you don't think I slept in the wardrobe do you?"

"Anything's possible knowing you," I retorted, "but where have you been? Mum was going to bring you up a drink but she didn't want to wake you."

"Yes I know. I've just seen her on my way in. I told her I'll wait till I've had a shower and have one with breakfast."

I looked at him in sheer bewilderment, trying desperately to make sense of what he'd just said before asking,

"On your way in; in from where? Where've you been at this time of the morning?"

"Funny, that's the same question your Mum asked. You really are so alike you know," that wicked smile was directed at me before I was allowed an answer to my question, "I've just popped out for a little jog to work up an appetite for that amazing breakfast I can smell cooking. Now if you don't mind, I'd better get on and have that shower or are you offering to come and scrub my back!"

Little did he know just how much I was tempted by this offer, but I really don't think Mum and Dad would approve, so I declined the offer, lying through my teeth by saying I couldn't think of anything worse than sharing a shower with a hot sweaty bloke, so to hurry up before Dad gets all the bacon. Having armed him with a suitable towel I beat a retreat downstairs to help Mum in the kitchen. Of course, by then she had everything in hand making me somewhat redundant, so all I could do was lay the table. It seemed Mum had been as surprised as me to be confronted by Steve coming in the backdoor just as she was expecting to take him up a hot drink.

"It quite startled me," she said, "just for a second I thought we had an intruder, but he tells me he's used to going for a jog first thing. The door was already unlocked where your father had been out to get his specs out of the car, but I've told him we have a spare key if he wants to go out early another day, so to lock the door and take it with him. I believe he's gone for a shower now. Has he got everything he needs dear, and did you give him a towel??"

I assured her he did (except for someone to scrub his back).and it wasn't so many minutes before a clean, fresh Steve was sitting round the table with us, tucking into a good hearty breakfast and chatting away as if he'd always been part of the family. As I watched him I couldn't help being reminded just how often I've seen him fit so easily into any company he's with at any time.

Even so, I couldn't help noticing that, having nothing much to pass the time, he began to look a little fidgety and on edge just after lunch, so suggested I should take him to look around our little town. Not being much above a mile and the weather being quite settled we left the car at home and walked there.

"Are you sure you're ok Steve, I mean staying here with my parents?" I couldn't help feeling a bit like his jailer, not wanting him to feel 'confined to barracks' as it were, almost like one of those awful people who keep wild animals in cages!

He threw me a quizzical look giving my question thought before allowing his expression to soften along with his voice.

"Of course I'm ok. Why shouldn't I be? Your parents are fantastic, especially letting you bring home any old waif or stray you come across ... and besides which, your Dad's single malt ain't bad either."

"Oh I see, that's all you've come here for is it? Here's me thinking you're here to get yourself fit and all you really want is Mum's food and Dad's whisky?" and as we walked on I found myself telling him how frightened I'd felt earlier when he'd gone out so early without telling me.

"Actually," he said with a grin, "I did just peep round your door to tell you but you were still out cold. Sorry about that but I've got into the habit of an early morning jog to get myself fit. Been doing it for some time now while I was cooped up in that damn centre. The thing is you see, I can keep my body fit and healthy, but I'm afraid it seems it's up to you keep my mind fit!"

"And how I wonder do you suggest I do that if you're going to disappear like that without a word to anyone? Just warn me in future if you're planning on vanishing again! And by the way, you're not just 'any old waif or stray.'"

"That's good of you to say that. Perhaps you should come with me in future to keep an eye on me!"

"I might just do that," I found myself saying, but as I was to learn to my cost, perhaps accepting this challenge was not the most sensible idea for one who had spent these last few, post Steve, months at a far more relaxed pace!

Chapter Six.

True to his word I was woken the next morning, early the next morning at that, by a tap on my bedroom door and an eager looking, wide-awake looking Steve peeping in at me! Surely it wasn't time to get up yet, or so I thought, but apparently he was dressed and ready to go already.

"Whatever's the time? Couldn't you sleep?" I rolled over and peered, bleary eyed at the clock by the bed. "Hell, it's still only quarter to six! Why not go later; after breakfast even?"

"Because it's not good for your digestion to run on a full stomach, that's why. Now hurry up and get yourself out of that pit and get some clothes on or I'll chuck this jug of water over you."

I'd not noticed he was holding the jug he'd taken with him last night. Reluctantly I dragged myself from under my nice warm duvet. Seeing he was still in the doorway I told him to go away and let me shower and dress in peace.

"I'll give you five minutes to get something on, but you're as well to shower when we get back or you'll need a second one anyway," and then he was gone.

By the time I was dressed and downstairs, Steve was already outside in the garden doing assorted stretching exercises, and insisted I join in before we set off. To be honest, these alone were more exercise than I was used to since being home. I couldn't help thinking back to the months we'd spent together, where Steve had had to all but carry me at times, but had gradually achieved the 'almost' impossible, by getting me fitter than I'd ever been before that time. Now I knew I was back to my old unfit days of the time before we met. Well, I figure a little gentle exercise might not be a bad thing, after all I must admit to having felt so much better for it back then ... eventually!

Gentle exercise though was not what Steve had in mind. That first morning nearly finished me off, but that was just the first of many to come. The man was obsessed, or so it seemed, and appeared to think it his duty to push me back to what he saw as a suitable level of athleticism for some reason. There I was thinking it was my job to nurse him gently back to health, yet here he was taking 'command' again of me, like it or not! Should I just go along with it to keep him happy, or should I refuse to co-operate? At the end of the second week we had to go to the centre to allow Paul to check up on his progress, perhaps I should ask his advice? On the other hand I didn't want to do anything to compromise his chances of completing his rehab course, certainly not now he'd made it this far. Then of course it could just be that I was being a wimp!

On the morning of our first visit back to the centre I was actually allowed a lie in as it seemed my 'trainer' decided that waiting for me, firstly to get up, and secondly to keep up sufficiently to be ready in time for our drive, would be a waste of time. Mum fed us a hearty breakfast (perhaps feeling this would ensure that Steve would be sure to come back later), and waved us off on our journey as if we were travelling to the other side of the globe. We had only gone a short distance before Steve asked me to stop the car,

"Shift over and let me have a drive will you? Its ages since I last had chance to get behind the wheel."

A little reluctantly, as he got out and came round to my side, I climbed across to the passenger seat. As he climbed into the driver's seat a thought crossed my mind,

"I suppose you do have a driving licence don't you?" to which he just shrugged his shoulders, gave me a particularly wicked grin, and said with a laugh,

"I reckon if I can drive a tank I can handle this little tin can easy enough!"

Before I could say there's not so many cars in the desert, he slammed his foot down and we roared off up the road with me just glad I put my seatbelt on, and praying we wouldn't get pulled up by the police! I couldn't help thinking how much he reminded me of a kid at Christmas with a new toy, and was about to say that to him, but then thought just in time to stop myself. He had never got a chance to have the pleasure of seeing his little son, Sean, alive, let alone opening presents on his only two Christmas's. What a jumble of emotions this man must be carrying around inside his head. It's not surprising that he'd needed such a long course of therapy to come to terms with it all. Is it even possible to do so I wonder? Hopefully the answer to this is yes, but either way I am committed to stand by his side and help in any small way I can. After all he did for me this goes without saying. Besides, I know now that my feelings for him are so much deeper than I can ever hope his will be for me, but I will be content just to be around him for as long as he'll let me. Right now I can only dream of him ever reciprocating my feelings and if that never happens at least we do seem to enjoy one another's company and the laughs we get from it!

Our visits to the centre continued weekly to start with. After the first month Paul seemed quite happy to cut this down to once a month. Each time he would spend some time talking to Steve, then a while with me to check up on how I was coping with the situation. Invariably he would want to ask if Steve was behaving and holding his temper under control.

"Are your parents still happy to have him there Mel? Are you sure he isn't upsetting them in any way?"

"No Paul, he's fine. You certainly don't need to worry about Mum and Dad. He has them well and truly wrapped around his little finger. You know what a creep he is. As for temper, he's as gentle as a pussy cat with them, especially Mum. I think she'd divorce Dad and marry him like a shot if he asked."

This idea put a smile on his face nearly as much as my description of the strict exercise regime I feel I'm being exposed to! He was quick to explain how this was not Steve being fanatical or unreasonable; this was just a good sign of the original Steve returning. As he explained to me, Steve had originally joined the army to break away from the humdrum life he'd been leading and so, as soon as his younger brothers were old enough to cope, sought to challenge himself and thrown himself heart and soul into his new career. He had quickly been promoted on the grounds that he had the ability to motivate and lead the younger men, making his priority to work on their fitness levels. According to Paul, Steve had already started taking over his centre staff before leaving, so this was an extremely good sign.

"Oh, I'm so glad you think so," I said with a sigh, "It's fine for you. You don't get dragged out of bed at some unearthly hour, then expected to keep up with the likes of him before breakfast!"

"The time you'll need to worry is when he gets you climbing over scramble nets, parachuting out of helicopters, or doing hand to hand combat; oh, and can you shoot Mel?"

"He wouldn't ...would he? You are pulling my leg now, aren't you Paul? No, of course he wouldn't. You're getting as bad as him now. I never know what to believe from either of you"

"Sorry Mel, I couldn't resist it. You should have seen your face though. Did you really think I did mean it?"

"After spending so long with him I'd never put anything past him, and I'm beginning to realise you're not as quiet and sensible as you first appeared either."

For the first time I was feeling truly relaxed talking openly to him. He was now becoming a friend to us both and not just Steve's carer, but still I couldn't help wondering just how much of the true man behind the sergeant's stripes he really sees? Still I can't help feeling that, perhaps though not entirely in the way I wish it could be, maybe I have seen deeper into that man's inner psyche than poor Paul ever could stand a chance of doing. After all we went through together over those months, it was me alone who had been so closely caught up with his reactions beyond the occasional sudden flash which had died out as quickly as it appeared. These I had admitted to. No, it was the ones I had kept to myself that I would keep firmly hidden deep in my mind. I think the worst of these being the violence with which he'd attacked me at his wife's graveside in Ely. That will remain hidden there for fear of making things worse for Steve.

Then of course there was the lead up to the final showdown with the man Morgan, the man who had murdered one of Steve's young recruits and then gone on to murder my poor Jake! Yes, I am aware that there were police marksmen and the army captain there right at the end, but they had not seen the sudden change in the way Steve had treated me in the time immediately leading up to that, and the way he'd trussed me up and held a knife at my throat in front of Morgan. I know he was really using this as a means to get to Morgan, but I have never in my life been so terrified! I genuinely felt he would have slit my throat if that was what it took to get to that man. Though I know he was desperately trying to keep himself together I can now see that the trauma that had thrust the effects of PTSD onto him would have been more than any lesser man would have been able to fight. As far as Paul or anyone else is concerned though, this is another detail that will remain forever pushed to the back of my mind. I figure that 'my' Steve has been punished enough, and now needed a chance to bring some peace into his life.

I knew that thinking of him as 'my Steve' was something I must stop myself doing before I got hurt, but how else should I look on someone who had seen me through such an ordeal, possibly even saved my life? All I could do was be there for him now and hope in some small way to return the favour.

It was on about our third visit to the centre that Paul had left his door very slightly ajar, just enough for part of the conversation between them to be overheard (especially by someone as nosey as me!). Paul asked him,

"So Steve, how are you getting on living with Mel now? I mean, how would you describe your relationship?"

Steve thought for a brief moment to consider the question before answering,

"That's an odd question, seeing as you gave me no choice in the matter," but then went on to say, "No, we're fine. We understand each other. We're like best mates, brother and sister even."

So there you have it, 'best mates, brother and sister,' no more than that. I knew then that I must accept that and not expect or ask for more or I'd perhaps risk losing him altogether, and that I wasn't prepared to do.

Anyway, pushing such thoughts firmly to the back of my mind, we continued in much the same vein for the next three months, me being dragged from my bed at those unearthly times for those exhausting jogs, always as I was told, for my own benefit, though I had my doubts about that! Actually, though I wouldn't give Steve the satisfaction of telling him, I should admit to finding it just a little easier as time went on, though I can't imagine ever being able to keep up with him, but then when I get left too far behind he just uses it as a chance to fit in the odd dozen or so press-ups or other exercises so as not to waste time or cool down too much. He does have this annoying habit of waiting until I come struggling along thinking I've caught up at last, of patting me on the back, telling me 'well done', and then taking off again! All I can say though about all this working out of his body is that it is not just bringing that part of him back into shape, but at the same time it is clearly also releasing his mind from the trauma of before and getting that back into an equal level of fitness. For that reason alone, or perhaps because I'd become accustom to following him anyway, or perhaps just because I knew that following him was what I most want to do with my life from now on, I know I must push myself to the best level of fitness I can achieve.

It became clear that the little things in life were beginning to mean a lot to him. For instance, just being behind the wheel of the car, having the freedom to choose when to come and go (though somehow he always did his utmost to 'come' in time for Mum's dinners!), and enjoying the beauty of the wooded countryside of Kent. Some days we would go off in the morning armed with sandwiches and a flask, and walk to the top of my favourite hill where we would sit leaning on a tree and looking out over a vast stretch of the county. I was so pleased to see he got as much out of this as I always had right from when I was a child. It was on one of these occasions that he was driving home through a neighbouring village that we stopped for me to call in at a shop for a couple of things Mum had asked me to collect. I had to wait briefly while two women and the shop keeper finished discussing what must have been a particularly juicy piece of gossip, apparently not seeming aware of me standing behind them waiting to be served.

By the time I did manage to extract myself from this shop and back to the car I found it empty! Steve had obviously wandered off without telling me where he was going. I figured that he surely couldn't have gone so far in the time I'd been gone but just for a minute or two I must admit to just a brief feeling of panic! Of course I needn't have worried after all. Just as I was frantically looking in every direction like a mother who has lost a kid, I heard him shout from behind me, in the direction of the village garage.

"Hey Mel, come and see what I've found."

Before I had chance to ask what was so exciting he had rushed over and practically dragged me towards the rear of the garage.

"There, look Mel, what do you think of that? Isn't she a beauty?"

I looked in the direction he was pointing, down the side of the garage workshop. All I could see was a couple of old wrecks, obviously ones on their way to the scrap yard, and behind them a tatty looking camper van, probably heading the same way. I could see nothing I would call a 'beauty'.

"Well, what do you think?" he asked impatiently, "It would be perfect wouldn't it? Think of the fun we could have travelling around in her."

It became clear to me that the 'her' he was talking about was the tatty camper van. Surely not, did he really mean this or was he yet again pulling my leg? With Steve it's hard to tell, but the look of enthusiasm on his face told me that on this occasion he really did mean it. I genuinely couldn't see the beauty he must have seen in this vehicle (though have to admit to being quite curious about just what sort of 'fun' he had in mind!).

I had been aware for a week or two leading up to this that he was beginning to feel his old restlessness beginning to sneak up on him. I suppose this was to be expected after spending a good two years moving around and living rough. I had hoped he might overcome this and decide to settle down, preferably somewhere not too far away, somewhere I could see him on a regular basis, but now he was talking of going off travelling in this clapped out old van! Now wait … he'd said 'we' not 'I', so his idea was for us both to go, like a couple of old gypsies in this scruffy looking vehicle. The thought of being 'on the run' as we'd been before (only without police or murderers after us!), did appeal to me too. We had had some pretty good times during that period because of the way Steve had of always (well, nearly always) making it an adventure, and keeping me safe.

"Just think Mel, we could go anywhere we fancy this time. No destination, no restrictions."

His enthusiasm was infectious. I found myself agreeing to the plan to take off into the wild blue yonder, but couldn't help pointing out something I felt was pretty obvious,

"Yes Steve, I love the idea, but why that old wreck? We could have a nice new one."

"I suppose we could, but it wouldn't be as much fun. It would stick out like a sore thumb. We'd always have to worry about it being vandalised or stolen. Besides, this one I could buy, a flashy new one you would have to pay for."

I could see he would hate being a 'kept man', and although having my reservations, I could see his old spirit of adventure driving him on.

"Ok, let's go and have a closer look," I said, "Do you even know if it runs?"

"No, but if not I reckon I can get it going again."

I somehow knew he probably could too. Was there really no end to this man's talents? Nothing he didn't know how to do?

Chapter Seven.

Having done a deal with the owner of the garage who honestly was more than surprised to find anyone interested in the vehicle, Steve persuaded him to agree to let us have it if he could get it going, just to get it off the premises. Using the garage hoist and tools, Steve spent the next two weeks lifting out the engine, striping it down and putting it back in. To the great surprise of the garage man, as soon as Steve turned the key the engine started first time! I do believe he would have taken on Steve then and there, but that was not going to happen. Steve was in no mood to be tied down now he could taste freedom looming up in his direction.

Tatty as this camper seemed it was soon sitting on my parents drive and far from upsetting them seeing such an eyesore there, Dad was enthusiastically out with Steve being shown how to keep the engine up to a good working order! As Mum said to me, she had never seen Dad do more than put petrol in the car,

"I don't think he even knows how to open the bonnet," she laughed as we watched from the safe proximity of the living room window. It had been good to see the relationship that had built up between my parents and Steve. He'd almost become like a son to them, and I could tell he was as happy in their company as they were in his. I had wondered how they would take the news of our plans to 'go on the run' again, as it were, but I believe they did at least have the comfort of knowing he had kept me safe before, and I was financially secure in case of any emergency due to having inherited Jakes house and a share in his business, so had accepted our news graciously.

He threw himself body and soul into the task of renovating the 'old girl' as he called her. His first job once he got 'her' there, now that the engine was running satisfactorily, was to tidy up the bodywork. One thing Dad did have tucked away in his garage was plenty of car shampoo which Jenny and I had given him for Christmas presents over a few years. It was still there because he'd found it so much easier to take his car through a car wash! By the time he'd gone round it with some cutting compound to hide the odd scratches and bring up the true colours of red and white, painted the wheels, and given it a last coat of polish, you wouldn't recognise this as the same vehicle! Ok, it (or should I say 'she') was still an old and pretty tatty looking vehicle, but nothing like the one he'd first shown me that day. Meanwhile even Mum had played a part. She had made herself busy on her sewing machine, reupholstering the cushions which doubled up into a double bed when the table was folded down, making the inside so much cleaner looking than it had been before.

The day after he finished working on the van Steve had to go for what he hoped was to be his final appointment with Paul. It was going to seem strange not seeing him or any of the staff at the centre again, or at least not if he gets the all clear and then continues to 'behave' as it were. By way of showing the progress he had made Steve suggested driving there in the van to show off his handiwork.

"We should give the old girl a name," he said as we set off that morning, "How about Annie?" As he said it he threw me a grin and added, "Seems I've heard the name Annie Lockett before I reckon!"

Just one of the assorted names he'd used for me to help with my disguise last year. So that's what 'she' became, 'Annie van'! He couldn't wait to drag Paul out to see his handiwork and was like a kid with a new toy explaining how he'd gone about bringing it round to its present condition. He did have to admit to the bodywork not being quite 'as new', but both were typical men when it came to sticking their heads under the bonnet to look at his technical skill in that department.

As usual on our visits, it wasn't long before Steve had attracted quite a crowd gathered round to admire his work. While this was going on Paul led me back inside on the pretext of a coffee. It was quickly apparent to me that he had something of importance he needed to say, beside which I was gasping for that drink, so I was glad to go with him. As we sat in his office I wondered what was coming. After a few seconds, as I expected, he began to tell me what was on his mind.

"You see Mel, when Steve was brought in here last year we were told by his regiment that his mother was desperate to know what had happened to him. It seems that, following his sister and wife's funeral he just disappeared. She's not heard from him since. I did try a few times to suggest he should ring her to let her know he was safe, but he wouldn't hear of it. In fact he threatened to leave if anyone spoke to her."

"That's awful, why ever do you think he was so set on not telling her? She must have been beside herself with worry," I suppose I'd always assumed his family must have known how he was living until now.

It seemed from what Paul had understood was that, as Steve had blamed himself for his families demise, he'd felt that those that were left were better off without him. Nothing anyone could do or say had been able to shake him on this belief.

"So I wondered Mel, do you think there is any way you can persuade him to at least phone Mrs Lockett at some point, just to stop the poor woman any more heartache."

He was about to go on when Steve entered the room, full of smiles and enthusiasm, wanting to tell Paul of our planned 'escape' as he put it, and wanting to know if he was at last to get, as he put it, his discharge papers! This brought a grin to Paul's face, but he realised that it wouldn't do to prolong Steve's agony any longer, and so that was just what he did. Steve 'promised to be a good boy' in the future, and I promised to bring him straight back if he wasn't! As before there was a crowd outside waiting to say their farewells, and under the cover of the commotion, I promised Paul I would do my very best to make him contact his mother.

It so happened that we had taken a picnic with us that morning with the intention of 'strolling' (or as near a stroll as he ever does!), up to our favourite place at the top of the hill we'd always loved best for its spectacular view. As we climbed to the top and spread our small rug to sit on I couldn't help worrying in my head just how I would go about tackling the problem Paul had set me. Just how should I go about persuading him to contact his mother? I knew that if he was too determined my interference could upset him, and I didn't know how he would take it finding Paul had asked me to try anyway. Knowing him as I did I also knew he could be unpredictable in his reaction, even to the point of being dangerous! Unpredictability I could handle, but dangerous …

well, I wasn't so sure about that. After his reaction before when he had felt I was interfering with his private grief over the loss of his family, anything could happen. I had absolutely no way of knowing how he would react, but I knew I must try.

I suppose I took the cowards way and decided to at least wait until we'd eaten. I don't know if it's true but they always say food mellows the mind, so that's what we did. There was no doubt that, during the time Steve had been with us, his appetite had certainly improved! Probably this was due to Mum's cooking, so I did wonder just how we would cope with having to feed ourselves once we left here, but just for now we sat quietly tucking into all she had packed. When we had finished and packed up our rubbish to take to the bin down in the car park, we just stretched out on the rug and enjoyed the view. It was at this point that it seemed the opportunity arose to tackle him on the subject of his mother.

"Steve, I …" I hesitated.

"You what? I had a feeling you had something to say. What is it Mel? Have you decided not to come with me?"

He rolled over and looked me straight in the eye. Oh hell, I wish he hadn't done that. How can I look into that face, knowing I'm about to upset him when that's the last thing I want to do? I couldn't back out now so, whatever the outcome, I must be determined and refuse to accept defeat,

"Of course not, I mean of course I want to come with you. It's just ..." I took a deep breath as if about to dive into deep water, "It's just that Paul told me you've refused to contact your mother."

Straight away I could feel the change of atmosphere. It was as if the pleasant sunshine had been swept away by a black, threatening storm cloud. All I could do was wait for the explosion I felt must be coming at me. I wondered if I should get up and run, or at the least get out of arms reach. But then, as I found myself backing away, I thought back to the time after he'd attacked me last year, and of the promise he'd made when we got back together, that he'd never do that again, so I stood my ground, looked him straight in the eye and said in the most determined voice I could muster,

"Well, don't you think you owe her the right to know you're at least alive? You're her son for goodness sake. She must be worried out of her mind poor woman. I know my Mum was last year when I went missing, and she had Dad to support her. Your poor Mum doesn't even have your Dad to help her does she? Just put yourself in her shoes for once and stop being so damn selfish or I ..."

Before I had chance to carry on my tirade, because that's what it was becoming in my aim at self-defence, I dared look up into his face to see just a glimmer of amusement shining in those big brown eyes. Any other time I would have probably hit him for laughing at me, but right now I was just relieved to see the black mist lifting from his expression.

"Well? Are you going to do as I'm asking or not?" I was almost frightening myself with my own ferocity, but felt I had to carry on while I had him on the retreat as it were.

"I will think about it Mel, but it's not as straight forward as you seem to think. In spite of what everyone says, I tell you now she won't want to speak to me, let alone see me."

As he said this the amused glint I'd seen a second before died like the embers of a fire after water is thrown on them.

"She may just want to know I'm alive, but whatever everyone thinks I know it was because of me they all died, and how could I expect her not to hold that against me? All the counselling in the world won't bring them back or alter the fact they'd still be here if it wasn't for me. At least with the killing of young Private Martin there was somebody responsible, someone to hold to account. With my family there's only me. Can't you see that Mel?"

"I do see why you think that Steve, but you're wrong. An accident like that could have happened to anyone at any time. There's no way you or anyone else could have predicted or prevented it. Please try not to hold yourself responsible, you must know they would hate to see you feeling this way."

All he said in reply to this was, "How?"

I dragged a promise from him right there and then that our first call on our travels in 'Annie' would be to visit his mother. I had to help him find a way to forgive himself, even if there was nothing to forgive himself for, and a way to help him move on. I hoped I was right in guessing that the best way to help him find out 'how' was to start with his mother.

Even so, though I could sense him fighting with his emotions, I knew that after so long feeling this way, and in spite of all the counselling over the last few months, I could easily lose this battle. I could see he was torn between wanting to believe me yet being almost scared to do so. In all the time I'd known Steve this was the nearest I've ever seen him to being scared of anything, and I knew I must find a way to win this battle with him. This I accomplished in the end by insisting that if he didn't agree to it he was on his own.

"I'll pack your stuff and you can go, but I won't come with you if you don't say you'll do this for me."

He had bent down to pick up the rug, but as I said that he stood up and faced me with a worried expression on his face,

"You don't mean that do you Mel?"

"Yes I mean every word. Either you agree to visit your mother or you're on your own."

I was relieved to find he agreed to this as I don't think I could have watched him drive off alone.

That evening we spent a pleasant evening relaxing in Mum and Dad's company following what could, knowing my culinary skills, be thought of as our 'last supper'! Mum had flapped about before this checking to see we had all we needed to equip Annie, and that I had plenty of clean socks and undies (typical of most Mums). Little did she know we were trying to travel light, so after her back was turned, some were returned to whence they'd come! Dad and Steve made it their duty to see that none of Dad's single malt went to waste after a short drive down to the village to top up the petrol tank.

It wasn't too late before we chose to turn in for the night. Mum had asked how far we had planned to go tomorrow and Steve had taken me by surprise and told her we were heading just past Cambridge! Good, I thought, he really was going to stick to his promise. All I could do now was pray things would go well between them and he would find some comfort from the realisation that none of his family held him responsible for anything that had happened. We climbed the stairs in silence, but as we reached his bedroom door he turned to me, took hold of my hand, and squeezing it gently said,

"You're sure you want to leave your home and go on the run again Mel? After all, you're not wanted by the police anymore, and you have such lovely parents and a comfortable home here. After all, I don't have anything to offer you that you haven't got or can't afford yourself now."

"Oh no you don't, if you think you're getting rid of me that easily you can think again. Someone has to see you keep your promise to see your poor Mum, and that you carry on behaving yourself, so it looks like I'm stuck with the job and you're stuck with me!"

His expression relaxed into one of relief. "Off you go then and get a good night's sleep, we've got a long day ahead of us tomorrow," and so saying he leant over and gave me a quick peck on the cheek as you would a child! As I did as I was bid and trotted off to bed, I couldn't help reflecting on what a maddening way he had with him. He somehow has a way of making me feel like a small child, yet at other times like a real grown up woman, which I am really, but not when I'm around him. The problem right at that minute was the effect that peck on the cheek had. You see, Steve is to me like chocolate ... a small piece is never enough!

As I climbed into bed and pulled the duvet up around me to keep in the warmth, I couldn't help reflecting on those times we spent tucked into our respective sleeping bags and huddled up back to back to keep out the cold yet, for my part at least, gradually over time wondering how much warmer it would have been to actually share his much larger one! Oh well, I must stop letting my mind run wild and do as I was bid … get a good night's sleep.

Chapter Eight.

I was pleased to find that the next morning I was excused the daily exercise. In fact, by the time I'd showered, dressed and descended to the kitchen I was surprised to find Steve was actually there and had taken over breakfast duty. He had banished Mum to the living room and told her that he felt that cooking today's breakfast was the least he could do after accepting her hospitality for so long. Though Mum was more of a scrambled egg on toast fan, Dad was more than ready to sample Steve's full repertoire with great relish. As we sat together eating I could tell that Mum for one was more than pleased to find that if I was going off travelling again, at least she could be satisfied that I'd not go hungry in his company. She had tried to persuade us to pack a mass of food into Annie, but as we explained to her, though we did have a tiny fridge (well, more of a glorified cool box really), it would be easy enough to buy food as we go so as to be sure it is always fresh.

After breakfast it was time to leave. Dad gave me a warm hug and told me to call if there was ever anything we needed. He gave Steve a little rolled up pack of spanners and the like, a warm handshake and a pat on the back. Steve promised him he'd take good care of me. Mum hugged both of us as if we were about to fly to the moon, made us promise to keep in touch, and handed us a large flask of tea for the journey. Eventually we were able to peel ourselves away from them, climb into Annie van, and wave them a last farewell as we set off once again on our travels to … who knows where!

As it appeared Steve had finally agreed to my demands to visit his mother first, we set off on the road leading to the Dartford Tunnel, around the M25, and then off up the M11. So far, so good, I told myself. Even so I could tell by the way his expression was slowly changing from that of one of a released prisoner (not that he ever felt tied down at my home), but now was showing signs of apprehension, but I just hoped I was right and that all would be well once we arrived there.

Meanwhile we decided to stop for a short break at the services close to Stansted Airport, almost the same place where we had been given a lift to on our journey down last year. He said he was in need of a coffee, but I felt this was just a delaying tactic really! Anyway, whilst he ordered the drinks, I went next door to the petrol station and bought the biggest bunch of flowers they had. I'm really not knowledgeable about flowers, but I have to admit they were really beautiful. Though I could see he was still somewhat apprehensive at the prospect of the reception to expect, I believe even he could see that these flowers just might make a small difference. Well, I figured they would give him something to hide behind if he really felt the need!

Back at the van again I could tell his mind was on anything but the driving, and so I suggested it was my turn to do a stint behind the wheel. To my surprise he agreed, and we were soon away again, heading up past the Cambridge turn off and following the signs for Ely. I had no clear idea exactly where to go so had to take directions from Steve. Expecting to pass through Ely, I was taken by surprise when he pointed me in the direction of a turning into a little village a couple of miles or so before reaching it. Being a bright day weather-wise it was clear to see the spire of the magnificent Ely Cathedral in the distance, and I couldn't help remembering his promise to take me inside one day, but also the way we had never actually achieved this. Instead of this my memories of Ely still hang on that terrible day when I'd upset him to a point that had led him to attack me with such violence that I felt he would kill me. Had I done as he had bid me of course, leaving him to grieve for his family in peace, this would never have happened, but I'd ignored this request, came between him and his grief, and basically asked for everything I got that day. Hopefully the months of counselling and rehabilitation he's been through will have helped him to come to terms with his loss, if this is at all possible following such a dreadful event.

We'd not gone far into the village when Steve said to turn left down a small side road, then to stop. I looked round at him and asked which house was his mother's. For a second or two he just sat in silence, obviously still having doubts about this.

"Come on Steve, stop dithering. After all, the worst she can do is tell you to clear off, but I really can't see that happening."

"I don't know Mel, but I warn you now that the first sign of her not wanting me there and I'm out of here."

Only when I agreed to this plan did he point me in the direction of a house up in the corner of the cul-de-sac. I parked as I was told, off the drive … ready to drive off if the need arose! As he climbed out I handed him the flowers and asked if I should go with him, but was told to wait by the van, presumably to make a quick getaway if he felt the need.

I watched as he walked up the drive to the front door, flowers in hand, and knocked rather pensively on it. It was a brief second or two before there was any sign of it opening, during which I do believe he would have considered making his escape had I not been between him and the van! And then the door did open revealing a lady, I would estimate in her mid to late fifties, her hair was dark with signs of encroaching greyish showing through, and about my height.

"Yes, can I help … "at which point she stopped, stared up into Steve's face in sheer disbelief for a second (almost long enough I thought for him to chicken out), before bursting into floods of tears and throwing her arms around him, "Is this really you? Steve, my dear, dear Steve."

While they held one another and cried, I crept up quietly and relieved him of the flowers to allow him to have both hands free. Any doubts he may have had about the reception he could expect from his mother were well and truly gone. Though I was very much an onlooker at that point, I couldn't prevent myself crying too, just to see the sheer relief and love pouring out of mother and son was something I'll never forget.

After some minutes there on the doorstep, Steve (wiping the tears from his eyes!), loosened his grip on his mother for long enough to notice me standing there, flowers in hand, and said with a smile,

"Mum, this is Melanie. Oh, and these are for you," pointing at the flowers.

"It's lovely to meet you Mrs Lockett. Please just call me Mel."

As I handed them to her she took them, gave them to Steve to hold, put her arms around me and, hoping he couldn't hear her, whispered in my ear, "Thank you dear, they are beautiful but you've brought me something far more valuable than flowers. You've brought me my son."

That was it … now we were all in tears!

"Well, come inside both of you. Don't let's stand out here making a spectacle of ourselves for the neighbours to see. Is that really your vehicle?" Steve grinned at her and managed a nod through his, still teary face, and asked, "Would it be ok if we stay for a couple of days Mum?"

"Of course you can my darling boy. I couldn't bear it if you left too soon."

While he went to move Annie onto the drive Mrs Lockett ushered me inside away from the prying eyes we could already feel were watching.

"Oh my dear, there's so much I want to ask, but I don't know where to start. I've not heard or seen anything of him for a good two years, not even to let me know he was still alive. Is he alright? Where has he been all this time and what's he been doing?"

I realised she was desperate for answers to all her questions but I was worried that if she pushed him too far, too soon, this might be too overwhelming for him. I decided to have a quiet word with her and act as a sort of mediator if I could. Whilst he was still parking the van on the drive and getting together our overnight bags I explained very briefly that he'd been living rough for most of the time, but had just completed a lengthy course of rehabilitation with the army. I stressed what Paul had said that it was best not to push him too hard, but just to allow him to work his way through it in his own time. I was pleased to find that Mrs Lockett quickly understood this, and so did just that, leaving Steve to tell her as much or as little as he was ready to.

By the time he'd fetched our bags and locked up Annie (though who would want to pinch her I can't imagine!), the three of us sat with cups of tea and cake, wondering just where to start the conversation. In the end it was Mrs Lockett who got things underway by asking where we met. She asked Steve,

"So tell me dear, was Mel in the army with you?"

Well, that certainly broke the ice! Steve looked round at me and exploded into a fit of hysterical laughter, causing me to throw him a dirty look, and his mother to sit, bewildered as to what she had said that was so funny.

Eventually, when he could contain his laughter for long enough, he wiped away his tears (this time of laughter) and explained that,

"No Mum, Mel wasn't in the army. They wouldn't have her, she'd never make the grade bless her."

Before I got chance to throw something at him, especially as my cuppa was nearest thing to hand and I was too well brought up to do such a thing in someone else's house, he went on to explain to

72

her about how I'd been framed for a murder last year, and that that was what had brought us together with him helping me prove my innocence. It seemed that she remembered seeing something on the news from time to time about it, but of course nothing mentioned Steve or his part in it. Certainly nothing was said or shown about how the conclusion was reached (thank goodness for that, I thought!). Obviously this, to her, had been just another news story, and in no way connected to her missing son.

After some time Mrs Lockett went to take the tea things to the kitchen and I was quietly amused at the way Steve leapt to his feet to help. I couldn't help being even more amused when I overheard her asking in a quiet and rather embarrassed way whether she should put me in Tom's room or do we share his! I can't help admitting to straining my ears in the hope of hearing him give the answer I truly would love to have heard, but not to be.

"No Mum, it's not like that. We're really close friends; after all we spent the biggest part of last year together, and I think we've come to rely on one another. But I'm not ready to replace Beth, not for some time if at all."

I'd hoped our friendship had helped repair that deep wound to his heart, but somehow I could see I'd never be able to take the place of his beloved wife. The tragedy of her loss was too much for him to overcome, and it was obvious that I couldn't hope to match up with her in any way.

Oh well, just keep hoping, they do say dreams really can come true, but somehow I think not in this case. Meanwhile I was allotted the room belonging to Steve's brother Tom. It was an obvious man's room, plain walls except for a few pictures of assorted sports cars, with a comfortable looking bed with navy blue bedding and curtains to match. I believe I'd been allotted this room for its ensuite shower room, but have to own up to being pleased to find it was also right next to Steve's own room. You see, I had been so accustomed to having him close, that it had got to be something of a comfort blanket, just knowing he was there. I keep telling myself I must be more confident ... well, I am really, at least I am when I have to be; but there's something about being around the likes of Steve that makes me just want to follow him around like a lost puppy, and make the most of every touch and every word (kind or otherwise!) he might condescend to throw my way! It's so much easier to stand back and let him look after me after all!

The next morning I awoke to a gentle tap on my door. This didn't sound like the usual early morning call I'd been used to since having Steve around, but then perhaps he didn't want to disturb his mum. Just for a brief minute I thought of putting my head under the pillow and ignoring him, but then he might knock harder and wake Mrs Lockett. The knock came again, just as quietly but accompanied by a gentle female voice. Oh dear, it seems I'd been ignoring Mrs Lockett's knock and not her sons.

"Come in," I answered and, peering bleary eyed at the clock, realised that the time was quarter to eight and she had brought me a cup of tea. "So sorry, I didn't mean to ignore you. I must have been well asleep to still be in here at this time. Normally I've been dragged out long before this time..."

"I know, by that son of mine to go running I imagine!" She said this with a smile of pure love beaming out from her that sent a glow of satisfaction right through me. "He went off half an hour ago and wanted to wake you, but I wouldn't let him. Perhaps I thought that if you stayed here he would have reason to come back and not just keep running!"

Of course, the thought crossed my mind that it might also give him reason to do just that, just disappear again knowing I was in safe hands, but then if that was in his mind he could have done so some time ago. It gave me a warm glow to feel that she had obviously decided that Steve cared enough about me to come back, and knowing that, in our own separate ways, we shared a genuine (dare I use the word?) love for him. Though we'd not long met I had so much I wanted to ask her about her son, and I knew she had the same need to quiz me about the missing period of his life.

"Would you mind if I asked you something Mrs Lockett? I know we've only just met but even after spending so long with Steve over the last year there's still so much puzzling me about him and what happened."

Putting the cup down on the bedside table Mrs Lockett perched on the edge of the bed and gave a huge sigh before asking,

"Did he tell you anything about the awful tragedy with Claire, Beth and dear little Sean?"

I told her that I had learnt about it, but was careful not to mention the incident at the cemetery. It was easy to see the pain in her eyes talking about it, and even more so when she said how upset she'd been when he disappeared directly after the funeral.

"We were all devastated by what happened, but the picture of Steve in his dress uniform carrying little Sean's coffin from the hearse to the grave tore me apart. He wouldn't let anybody help him you know. As soon as the coffins were lowered into the graves and the vicar had finished the service Steve made everyone leave. He even sent the gravediggers away insisting he didn't need their help. He got quite aggressive you know."

Yes, I knew just how aggressive he could get, but she didn't need to know that. She went on to tell me that he didn't come home until everyone had given up and gone to bed except for her, but she had fallen asleep in the chair. When she woke up in the early hours and found his bed empty she was frantic with worry. She had looked around and found his uniform screwed up and covered in mud, thrown in a heap outside by the bins, and just his rucksack and old combat clothes gone.

"I tried so often to get information from his regiment, but they'd not heard from him either. They promised to get him to contact me if they heard from him, but said it would be down to him to decide. Apparently he's just been in a rehabilitation centre for some time, but it was still for him to decide if he wanted to see me. You say you've been with him for a lot of the time? Why wouldn't he come sooner, or at least let me visit him there? Do you know?"

I explained to her about how he'd decided to accept the rehab he'd been offered by the army, and that I'd been pleased to visit him. As I told her, it wasn't until this was over that Paul had told me that he'd refused to contact her. She was obviously hurt at first until I went on to explain what I now know to be the truth.

"You see, he was so sure you and the rest of the family held him responsible for what happened. He thought that if they hadn't been going to meet him that day they would still be alive."

Poor Mrs Lockett was obviously shattered by this piece of information. She just couldn't believe her ears … Surely he couldn't have been carrying such pain and guilt alone for so long?

"You wouldn't believe what a jibbering wreck he was standing outside your door yesterday! I practically had to push him up the path and threaten him not to run. I think he expected you to slam the door in his face."

"I'm so glad we had this chat Mel. Disturbing as it is to think poor Steve has been bearing that burden alone for so long, at least now we can rebuild our relationship if he'll let me."

I assured her that I believe this would be as important to him as it would be to her. After she left my room and I sat drinking my tea I couldn't help hoping that our chat had, in some small way, helped to heal the suffering this poor lady had been going through for so long. It was clear to see the deep love she felt for her son, a love so obviously reciprocated by him, and yet the horrific circumstances of that day had torn them apart. I couldn't help thinking just how much they could have helped one another had Steve not taken off so suddenly.

A while after this I met Steve coming out of his room after a shower, obviously on his way down for breakfast.

"Jammy beggar, laying around in bed till all hours. Thought you'd like to see round my neighbourhood, but Mum said I shouldn't wake you. Did you sleep Ok?"

"Yes thanks, did you?" I couldn't resist throwing back at him. Giving me a slightly puzzled look he answered,

"Yes, of course. Why? Shouldn't I have done?"

I couldn't help grinning but resisted the temptation to ask why he'd made such a fuss about coming here in the first place. The expression on his face was enough to tell me he knew what I was getting at without the need for me to put it into words.

"Ok, clever clogs, just for once I'll own up to you knowing best."

"That's good of you kind sir," I said sarcastically.

As we sat round the table eating breakfast I couldn't help noticing the love radiating across from mother to son. It was all she could do to take her eyes from him for long enough to lift her toast from the plate. It was just as evident that Steve, now he'd allowed himself to accept that he never was held responsible for what had happened, had gladly accepted all the outpouring of love coming his way, and willingly returned this to her. This was a side of Steve I'd never seen. I'd seen the rough sleeper living on his wits, I'd seen the gentle side of the man who had watched over and guided me safely through my ordeal. I'd even seen the true, capable but sometimes frightening but well trained soldier. But Steve as a gentle, loving and happy son … this was a new and wonderful side to him.

Chapter Nine.

We had been with Mrs Lockett for nearly a week when she asked Steve if it would be alright with him if his brothers, Tom and James, came to visit. It seemed a strange request to have to make, but she had genuinely worked so hard to understand the way he'd been suffering over the time since his disappearance, and was concerned not to do anything to make him feel uncomfortable. Much to her relief he had said it would be good to see them. Though I wasn't enthusiastic to get back to our morning jogs, it did give me chance to talk to Steve away from his mother. Having heard that I was about to soon find myself bombarded by three versions of Steve I was keen to learn a little about them first.

"So are you all alike?" I managed to get out between puffing like an engine!

"Hell no! Neither of them are as handsome or clever as me!"

I didn't know whether to just accept his sarcastic grin or give him a rude answer. As it happened I didn't get chance to do either before he went on to tell me that Tom was a solicitor, and was married with two daughters. He lived somewhere up country (though Steve couldn't recall exactly where!). James was just turned thirty and unmarried. Apparently he had tried out for the army, but not made the standard. Steve reckoned army life was too hard for 'Mum's baby'. He was now working not far from here as a car salesman.

When the day came for them to visit I was a little apprehensive, but at the same time curious to meet the whole family. Tom had phoned the previous evening to say that his wife, Margaret, was unable to come with him as one of the girls was feeling unwell.

"Perhaps next time, or we are planning on travelling around the country so we may be able to visit them sometime." Steve told his mother. "We're not sure yet just where we will go."

"Oh, you don't intend to stay around here or settle down at all?" she asked, looking just a little disappointed.

"Sorry Mum, but settling in one place is not for me, well not just yet anyway. I've been too used to being a free spirit to settle down for a while. But don't worry, I promise to keep in touch now. Anyway, if I don't I reckon I'll have Mel to deal with … and you know she can be real scary when she doesn't get her own way!!"

Scary or otherwise, I assured her that all the time I was around I'd make sure he never left her without some knowledge of how he was and, at the very least, roughly where he was from time to time. I certainly had no plans to let him out of my sight, even if I hadn't promised Paul I would watch over him. Having said this to her reminded me that I'd promised to phone Paul as soon as possible to tell him how the reunion with his mother had gone, and so I took the opportunity to do just that while Steve walked into the village with Mrs Lockett. When I reported the successful reunion Paul was delighted. As he said, this was a really important breakthrough in Steve's rehab, and one he thought would prove to be a make or break moment.

"You wouldn't believe what a big wimp he was when it came to knocking on the door, but now he's seen his mother's reaction he's clearly just a big softy at heart!"

The thought of Steve as a 'big softy' made Paul laugh. He said that he could think of many ways to describe Steve, but that wasn't the one that sprang to mind. I took the opportunity to tell him about Steve's idea to go travelling again soon and I was pleased to hear he wasn't in the least surprised about that. As he said, somehow he couldn't imagine him ever being totally domesticated. I had to agree with him there, but just hoped I'd be able to keep up with him, or more importantly, that he would want me to.

I had just put my phone down from talking to Paul when I heard the back door open and a voice I'd not heard before call out,

"Hi Mum, I'm home. Where are you and where's that old reprobate? Thought you'd have the red carpet out for us all coming home at...," He came to a sudden stop as I appeared round the kitchen door. "Oh, sorry. I mean, I didn't know ..., I'm Jamie by the way." As he walked across the room and held out his hand.

He clearly had no idea who I was or what I was doing here in his mother's house, but I could tell he was beginning to realise I had something to do with Steve. I introduced myself and quickly reassured him I was not a burglar.

"Your Mum and Steve have just popped down to the village for supplies. She obviously knows you all well enough to know it takes a lot to feed you all at once!"

"You could say that. Nice to meet you Mel. How is Steve? Have you been together long, or is that being too nosey? You're not married are you?"

I quickly reassured him that we were not. I was about to give him a brief rundown of our relationship when yet another, slightly older chap walked in. Jamie took great pleasure in introducing me to Tom. Tom was clearly far more reserved but extremely polite, and showed none of the signs of the inquisitive nature of his younger sibling. The one thing that struck me about both brothers was that they shared the same blue eyes and blonde hair, so unlike Steve's dark hair and piercing dark brown eyes. Very odd I thought, but then in our family my sister has always had curly hair whilst mine is poker straight, so these thing do happen. Anyway, Mrs Lockett's hair is not blonde, more a sort of mousy brown colour, so perhaps their father was dark.

"Put the kettle on then kid," Tom said to his younger brother, "It's been a hell of a drive down this morning. Road works all the way down. Seemed to take forever today." Then looking round at me he asked, "Any idea who parked that old wreck on Mum's drive?" to which I had no choice but to tell him it was Steve's.

"Don't tell me that's what he's been living in all this time?"

"Oh no, nothing so luxurious I'm afraid. He's just been living rough. In fact when we first met he was sleeping in some old chaps shed on an allotment," well I couldn't lie now could I?

It seemed both brothers had a totally different view to Steve's missing years. While Jamie seemed to get quite a laugh out of the whole idea of him bunking down in a shed, Tom was clearly quite distressed at the thought. It was abundantly clear who was the joker in this family, though I have to admit that Steve, though serious minded like Tom when necessary, also had a fair share of Jamie's humour when the circumstances allowed. It was heart-warming to sense the affection they both so obviously had for their elder brother. Whilst not too sure if it was my place to speak on Steve's behalf I decided it could possibly save him the embarrassment of having to keep repeating all he'd already told his mother, and so before he arrived back from the shops I gave them just enough information to save him going over the whole story again. Neither were in the least surprised when I explained how he'd come to my rescue.

"He's always been a soft touch for anyone in need of a knight in shiny armour," laughed Jamie.

"Well, I never thought of it quite like that, but we had only been together barely an hour when I nearly got mugged by three druggies, and I have to say he came to my rescue in a rather spectacular way."

Jamie was quick to ask how he'd dealt with three of them and burst into hysterical laughter when I told him Steve knocked them all out and dumped them all in a large shop skip. Even Tom could see the funny side of this, and I reckon I could have kept them entertained for some time with so many of our escapades from last year had Steve and their mother not walked in just then. It was heart-warming to watch the way he was greeted by them both almost like the proverbial prodigal son, or in this case brother, and to listen to the free and easy way they chatted together as we all sat drinking coffee. Clearly they had been a very close family, and it struck me how hard the events of the past couple of years must have hit them, especially as it soon became apparent that Steve, though so obviously loved as a brother, was clearly seen by the other two almost in the role of surrogate father since their real one died. All three were happy to joke and lark about quite freely, but it was clear to see that it was Steve who would keep, as it were, a firm hand on the reins to keep them in check when he felt the need was there.

Mrs Lockett took the opportunity whilst we drank coffee to put forward the suggestion that it would be good to visit the cemetery 'as a family', now all three brothers were there together at last,

"After all, we've not been together, and I believe both Claire and Beth would want to know we were all together and supporting one another at last."

As we walked into the cemetery I felt myself hanging back, reluctant and almost scared to walk toward the two graves ahead of our group. Though my mind was telling me I was perfectly safe, surrounded as I was by the whole family, the vision of our previous visit here was still painfully burnt into my subconscious. As we got closer I stopped and, closing my eyes for a brief second, swore I could feel my head hit the stone, and being held down by Steve's boot on my neck to punish me for poking my nose into his private grief. I can still feel the terror which drove me to take off alone for weeks. But I knew things were different this time with the whole family there. Even so I still hung back away from Steve and watched as he walked forward with Mrs Lockett, bending to place the flowers, half on each grave.

Noticing my reluctance to approach, Tom beckoned me to stand closer with him and Jamie.

"Come on Mel, don't stand on your own. Steve wouldn't want you to feel left out."

I wished I could have been as sure of that, but then none of them knew of what had happened the last time we visited, or even that we had done so. Somewhat timidly I stepped forward, surreptitiously placing myself between the two brothers.

"It's good to have all come here together," Tom explained, "as Jamie brings Mum regularly. I always come when I visit Mum, but Steve hasn't been since the funeral, and that was an awful day for him."

I chose not to enlighten him. As Steve and his mother turned back toward us I was aware of him catching a glimpse of me, probably looking a bit like a rabbit caught in car headlights, and I could tell immediately that he knew what I was thinking. Leaving his mother to come across and speak to his brothers, he surreptitiously took my arm and manoeuvred me just far enough away to take my hand gently in his and whisper in my ear,

"I'm so sorry Mel. I wish I could go back and undo what I did that day. I know how much I hurt you, and I see how scared you still feel now, but all

I can do is beg you to try to forgive me, and try to trust me again. Please Mel, just give me a chance to try?"

He looked at me with such a pathetic expression that right there and then, family or no family, all I wanted to do was to throw my arms around him to comfort him! No, this wasn't the time or the place for that, so all I could do was to squeeze his hand and reassure him that there was nothing to forgive … it had all been a big misunderstanding, and was now forgotten. I don't believe he was entirely convinced, but accepted my answer as the only one on offer.

It seemed that none of the family had noticed our little private moment, or perhaps they just guessed Steve was explaining to me about what had happened that day they thought was the last time he'd been there. Either way nothing was said, and when Steve said he would just like an hour to take me into Ely so that I might see the cathedral, I must admit to feeling relieved that they all seemed happy to go back home to their mother's house and not come along too, especially after Steve offered to bring back a couple of bottles of wine to have with our dinner later.

He was certainly right before when he'd told me what an amazing building the cathedral was. I found myself standing right in the centre of it, looking up in wonderment at its towering magnificence. How such places were built so long ago never ceases to amaze me. As there was no one else about after another couple left, we took a seat on a pew near the front, and as we sat in silence I was aware that Steve's eyes were closed, and I believe I could sense a genuine feeling of peace sweep over him the like of which I'd not seen before. Though I'd never considered myself particularly religious there was certainly something about the atmosphere in here that gave me a feeling of peace, but somehow it seemed to have an even deeper effect on him. It was clear that something had touched his very being so deeply that, just for that few minutes, I hardly dare breathe let alone speak, and so all I could do was to sit quietly next to him and wait for him to make the first move.

Then, without warning or explanation, he got to his feet and suggested that perhaps we should now go to get the wine we'd promised to take home. By the time we arrived back Mrs Lockett, with a little help from Jamie, had a good meal ready for us. Once again I found myself fascinated by listening to the way the three brothers filled the room with such animated chatter. Knowing how little chance they had had to catch up properly I insisted on them carrying on over another drink while I helped their mother with the washing up. I could see by her expression just how much it meant to her to see her boys all together again at last.

"Mel, this idea of him wanting to go off again. Are you sure he'll be alright? I mean, do the counsellors think he's recovered from what happened before dear?"

If only she'd known the half of what had happened before, I thought. All she knew was that he'd had PTSD, which as far as she understood just meant depression. The fact that he'd turned aggressive and completely out of control had never been explained to her, and I most certainly was not about to upset the poor lady more than she had been in the past two years. So I assured her that, yes, not to worry about him. He's a reformed character since the rehab and just had got so used to keeping on the move that he still felt the need to do so.

"Eventually," I assured her, hoping I sounded convincing, "I'm sure he'll find somewhere he really feels is right for him. Until he does I promise to keep my eye on him," once again hoping I was going to get that chance!

As we passed back through the hall to re-join the men I noticed a wedding photo on the wall showing what was obviously Mrs Lockett and with a rather smart looking gentleman by her side.

"What a lovely photo Mrs Lockett. Your husband had a really kind face. I'm sorry to hear you lost him so early. Is that right what Steve told me about how close they were?"

With a sad expression in her eyes she said, "Yes, they all loved Peter, their father very much, but Steve, being that few years older than the others, made it his duty to step up and take his place as head of the family when he died."

He had told me that some time ago, and that he had felt the need to do this until he felt he could see they were both of an age to cope without him, and also help their mother. That was when he'd found himself free to follow his ambition to join the parachute regiment. Having now got to know his brothers, especially Jamie, it didn't surprise me in the least that he had been keen to support his Mum when she found herself widowed at quite an early age, and stepping up as a 'father figure' had given him the perfect training for his role in the army as one responsible for the training of the young men under his supervision. I was now truly beginning to get an even more accurate picture of the man than I had thought possible! With the knowledge of his family background, plus seeing the fun loving relationship banded around between the three brothers, I feel my picture of Steve was now more complete than ever before.

Having polished off the bottles of wine we'd brought back earlier, and as it was getting quite late before anyone looked at the time, Tom had rung his wife and told her he was staying over tonight and would drive back tomorrow. It was not until then that I realised that I was sleeping in what had been his room, but he said not to worry as the sofa was actually a sofa bed, so he was happy to bunk down there, and of course Jamie used his old room for the night. I could see this being because he had over-indulged on both the wine and the bottle of whisky which he 'just happened' to find in his coat pocket when he'd first arrived!

All in all I believe the whole Lockett family had felt complete for the first time in two years, and all went to bed truly content at the end of what had been a busy but enjoyable day. Although not actually part of the family I felt they were all more than happy to look on me as if I were. Mrs Lockett gave me a genuinely warm, mother-like hug and went on up, I said goodnight to Tom, checking first that he didn't want his room back. Jamie even stopped to give me a rather over enthusiastic hug at the top of the stairs, but was soon packed off to his room by the firm hand of his big brother, who then surprised me by taking over where Jamie had left off!

Why it should have done I really don't know, but for whatever reason I had not expected that. But then, who was I to argue … after all, he was obviously the boss around here (and I did enjoy it!).

Chapter Ten.

The next morning Mrs Lockett popped her head around my door with the cup of tea I'd become accustomed to. She remarked what a good thing she'd thought to give me a room with an ensuite attached otherwise I might have to join the queue. Apparently her room and mine were the only two with such a luxury, so the three 'boys' were fighting over who should go first in the main bathroom! By the time I'd had my shower and dressed it seemed Steve had given up the fight and gone jogging first, and Tom had dived in there when Jamie had to go back to his room for the towel he'd forgotten! By the time Steve returned Jamie was only just about to take his turn following Tom. Meeting me on the landing he threw me a smile and asked if I'd mind if he jumped in my shower,

'Or we'll never get breakfast at this rate. I promise I'll bring my own towel ... you can come and supervise if you don't trust me," he said with a grin.

"No thanks, think I'll pass if you don't mind," I told him.

After a walk along the river bank together, followed by a tasty lunch, we all said a fond farewell to Tom as he set off on his journey home. After last night's festivities he had decided better than to get behind the wheel too early, deciding it would be safer to wait and allow a good lunch to soak up any remaining alcohol in his system,

"After all," he said, "it wouldn't look good for a solicitor to be caught for drink driving!"

Jamie was also just off until Steve asked him to wait five minutes while we got ready, then drop us off in, or as near as possible to, Cambridge.

"We'll be ok getting back on a bus later, there are plenty coming this way."

Satisfied with that answer he agreed to do so. Though we did have a few bits left to kit out Annie, and a short list to fill from the market for Mrs Lockett, my main aim was to find my friend Sally who had been so good to me during that awful period between my running away from Steve and our reunion. Of course I had no idea where she would be at that time of day, or even if she was still studying at the college. When I'd last been here, due to family circumstances, she had been reduced to living in a shelter adjacent to the college, but after so long I genuinely had no idea even if she was still here. I decided that my best bet would be to enquire at the shelter first. Good guess, it seemed she was still staying there.

"But I don't think she'll stay to finish her course," I was told, "I think her finances are more than a bit stretched," according to the woman in the office.

Now there was a problem I could fix I thought. Dear Sally had been so good to me that I felt I owed her that at least. After all, if Jake's money couldn't do some good for someone it was not worth having. Anyway, she must only have about one term to go now. I asked if anyone knew if she was in college right now, but was told she was working at the pub, the same one I'd worked at with her last year, as she was trying to earn enough money to keep going.

"Do you remember the one you came in looking for me," I asked Steve, "When Sally told me someone fitting your description had just left I was frantic. I nearly knocked everyone's food down them in my rush to catch up with you!"

This brought a smile to his face. He told me he'd been in that same pub about three times, but decided I wasn't there, so had left.

"Come on then, it's never too early for a quick pint. Let's go and surprise her."

So that was just what we did. Sitting ourselves in that same dark corner he had sat in so long ago, we waited to see if Sally would appear, and it was not long before a voice from behind us announced,

"Sorry, you're too late for food, but I can fetch you some drinks if you'd like to ..." she stopped, staring in disbelief for a moment before throwing herself at me in an expression of sheer emotion!

The questions came thick and fast, was it really me, where had I been, how was I, and, stating the obvious, was I still with 'him'! This last question no doubt showing just a twinge of the suspicion she had shown last year when she had at first accused him of beating me up. Of course, she had been right, but I had assured her that was not the case, and that I was perfectly safe with him, especially since I'd convinced her before that Steve was my brother! I wondered what she would think if I now told her the whole story. Perhaps we should do so rather than spin any more lies, after all, it would perhaps convince her to let me help with her finances for the course.

For this purpose I suggested we collected sandwiches, crisps, amazing looking doughnuts, and drinks to wash it all down, so that we could sit by the river in a nice quiet spot as there was much to talk about. I could see Steve was not altogether comfortable with telling her the whole truth, after all I had lied to her before about the beating I'd sustained from him, but I gave him a reassuring look to let him know I'd not let on it had been him who beat me up. After all, last time they met I had introduced him as my brother, and that the beating was down to a boyfriend. I couldn't help seeing the glint in his eye as I told her the whole story, carefully talking round anything I felt would make her uncomfortable or suspicious, even making up a bad tempered boyfriend, but making it clear Steve was not him, nor was he my brother.

"Of course he wasn't, any fool could see that. Nobody looks at their brother like that, but you seemed happy to go off with him so I had to trust him," she said with a grin. I felt so much better for being honest with her, well nearly honest! And of course Steve turned on his usual charm offensive just to convince her.

She sat in some awe as I explained to her about poor Jake's murder, and, without going into too much depth, about the way Steve had finally caught the killer. When she asked where we had been since then I jumped in quickly to explain that Steve had had to return to his regiment for a while, but was now free to do his own thing.

"And what is 'your own thing' now Steve? Do you have any plans?"

"My plans now Sally are to just be free to go wherever, and do whatever I like. Certainly until I have any other plans that is!"

I'm not sure who had the broadest grin on their face at this point, but it was clear to see he had her wrapped around his little finger, as he did with most people ... well, females at least!

We spent the next couple of hours together, during which time I took the opportunity to re-acquaint myself with my old friend from the veg stall on the market. He couldn't resist whispering in my ear,

"You found your man then I see? Last time you were here you were like a headless chicken looking for him. I suggest you keep hold of him now you've found him," he chuckled.

"Oh, don't you worry. I intend to this time," and laughed as we headed off with Mrs Lockett's veg.

By the time we back to the college with Sally for her to hand in the work she'd planned on taking in earlier, I had, with great difficulty and a lot of back up from Steve, convinced her to allow me to help with the expense of her final term. After all, I told her, it would be silly to get so near and then give up. If she could just finish she would be qualified to take up a position in an accountancy or bookkeeping firm. Knowing that I'd explained to her about the money I had from the sale of Jake's house, she reluctantly agreed.

I promised to keep in touch with her this time, swapping mobile phone numbers before heading off for the bus back to the Lockett house, and I must admit to being amused by watching as Steve threw his arms around her and gave her a huge, almost big-brotherly hug, to thank her for not 'getting him beaten up' as she'd threatened last year! Yes ... no doubt about it, he'd got her well and truly under his spell!

During the time we stayed at Mrs Lockett's house we spent time improving the inside of our van. There were a couple of cupboards which we soon realised had doors which would drop off without warning for want of a couple of new hinges. One of the headlights also decided to die on us. Though we could get most of what was needed in Ely, we did have a couple more trips into Cambridge. This did give me chance to visit Sally again and properly organise the funds she needed for the college. This meant that instead of paying it in my name, which I thought might embarrass her, there was chance to open a special bank account in her own name into which she could pay the cheque I gave her. I wanted to pay for her to move from the shelter into proper digs, but she'd not hear of it, so I just made sure she had sufficient to live in reasonable comfort.

As you can imagine, during this time Steve still insisted on dragging me from my bed most mornings to go jogging along the river bank. It would have been every morning had his mother not put her foot down, a fact that I found quite amusing. There was her strapping great son, used to giving orders and having them obeyed, yet when this little, gentle lady put her foot down he never once argued with her! Um! I wondered if that was a skill I could learn from her … No, somehow I have my doubts about that.

During our time in his mother's house Steve appeared to have found an ever increasing sense of calm. It was good to see him so settled, and yet somehow the whole picture portrayed by this didn't ring entirely true, well not true in the sense of the Steve Lockett I'd got to know by now. Though he got obvious benefit from the regular, almost obsessive, exercise regime he kept up, I somehow felt there was just a little bit missing, though I couldn't put my finger on just what that was.

That was until the day before we were due to set off on our travels. We'd arranged to meet Sally and Steve's brother Jamie at a pub alongside the river. As we approached the place we could hear good lively music from inside. It soon proved to be a popular hang-out for a lot of the student popularity, and in fact as we got closer it was also clear that some were already slightly merry. We were walking toward the place from a footpath which ran by the side of the river, when we became aware of a small group of four, slightly worse for wear young men, apparently kicking something on the ground in front of them and shouting abuse at whatever or whoever it was there.

"Go on, get up and shift, you filthy old sod," shouted one.

"Er, don't touch it, the mucky old sod's soaking wet, you don't know where he's been," said the biggest, giving the object of their abuse yet another kick!

"Hey," shouted Steve as he approached, "get off him. What the hell do you think you're doing?"

They all turned to see where the voice was coming from before the big chap grinned at Steve before answering,

"It's ok, we're just clearing the streets of scum like this. Look at it … filthy, soaking wet tramp. Anyway, why do you care, it's nothing to do with you."

Well, if I thought there was a bit of the old Steve missing I was about to be proved wrong!

"Just because you're spoilt little mummy's boys that doesn't give you the right to decide what happens to anyone less fortunate. If you took the trouble to look or ask you'd find this gentleman probably has a perfect reason for being on the streets, I've been where he is, and with good reason. As for being filthy and wet, I doubt his mummy does his washing like yours does, and you may have noticed it's been bloody raining."

For a second they stood, amazed to find someone standing up for what to them was just another tramp. Then the tall chap did what I knew immediately was asking for trouble.

"You don't honestly expect us to take anything you've got to say seriously do you? Look at it … it's soaking wet and it's not raining now," and as he did so gave the poor fellow another kick!

As he went to take a second go, and backed up by the other three, all hell broke loose (just as I knew it would), and I just managed to push Sally and Jamie back out of range in time. Before any of them knew what was happening we were entertained with watching the real Steve back in action, just as I'd always known him. The tall chap found himself picked up and dumped unceremoniously in the river, two of them were grabbed, one in each hand and had their heads knocked together, and the last and smallest one took off like a frightened rabbit!

As he loosened his grip on the two he had hold of, Steve said,

"Now, first you apologise to the nice gentleman, then you fish your 'wet' mate out the river. Then get out of here and show respect for others less fortunate in future, right?"

Both nodded vigorously and, as soon as they were released, followed instructions to the letter!

In all the commotion we hadn't been aware of the audience of those sitting on the veranda of the pub watching on. But now, as Steve turned back to us they all stood up as one and cheered and clapped so loud it brought the manager out to see what was happening. Without hesitation, Steve helped the slightly bemused old man off the path and led him up onto the veranda.

"Come and sit with us sir. Here's the menu, see what you fancy."

For an awful moment I thought the manager was going to refuse to serve him, but having been appraised of what had just occurred, and looking Steve up and down, could do no more than say,

"Yes Sir. And what about a pint to be going on with while you choose?"

Well, I reckon Sally and Jamie were well impressed (though I wondered if she may have also thought from this that he'd have been well capable of the beating I'd taken last year!), and though we'd gained an extra diner in our party, we ended up not paying a penny as our fellow diners had enjoyed the entertainment so much that one after another they dropped a tip on our table rather than to the pub staff!

It seemed that the elderly man, Jack, had spent the last few years taking care of his sick wife until she died, and then had been unable to pay his rent. Being too proud to ask for financial assistance he had been living rough for the last six months. This had been the first good, hot meal he'd had in that time and it clearly was much enjoyed. Sally suggested to him that she thought she could get him into the shelter where she was staying, apparently a thing he knew nothing about. We all walked him back there after we left the pub, Steve in particular wanting to see no more harm came to him that day. Hearing the events of the day, the kind ladies at the shelter were glad to find Jack a space. They found him a small, but comfortable room to himself, presented him with a clean set of clothes while his were washed, and showed him where to go for a good hot shower.

After a chat over a cup of coffee (I got the feeling Steve needed to wait to see Jack was settled before we left), along came a totally transformed gentleman. Clean, shaved, and in all fresh clothes, even the expression on Jack was different.

"I bet that feels a treat doesn't it mate," Steve asked him, "I reckon you'll be ok here now with the ladies fussing over you! We'll leave you in their capable hands now, but if they can't find you any help, you tell young Sally here and she'll get on to us. We're going away for a while but never too far away for a mate."

Jack grabbed Steve's hand with both of his and shook it vigorously,

"Thanks lad. You don't know what it means to me, what you did. You were brilliant … army training if I'm not much mistaken eh?"

"Just a bit, why, does it show?" laughed Steve.

"I thought as much. Done a few years myself back in my youth. Got to sergeant too; but that was before I married my Elsie."

I couldn't help seeing the wistful look in the old chap's eyes as he said this. It was Steve who broke the silence and the melancholy mood by standing stiffly to attention facing Jack, saluting and saying,

"Permission to withdraw Sergeant Jack?"

Obviously impressed and touched by this, Jack also stood to attention, saluted, and said,

"Permission granted young man. Dismissed."

And before he had chance to ask about rank or regiment from Steve, I was taken by the arm and marched out of there and heading for the bus station for the last time, at least on that visit.

Chapter Eleven.

The next morning, I was pleased to say, I was allowed a last lie-in, strictly under orders from Mrs Lockett! Knowing we were off that morning she felt it only right I shouldn't be disturbed. I believe she was also putting on a brave face when I did go down for breakfast, probably wondering how long it would be this time before she saw her son again. I did my best to put her mind at rest on that score, assuring her that the idea of having the van this time meant that not only could he go off and travel, but that he could as easily travel back whenever the mood took him, and that I would make very sure that this did happen every so often. I told her that this would be the case as I had promised my parents too, so he'd not be able to avoid it from time to time. Having introduced the two Mums on WhatsApp so they can keep in touch I felt this would be a comfort to them both.

It wasn't until we'd hopped aboard Annie and driven off round the corner of the road, with both of us waving from the windows, and Steve honking the horn so loud it must have certainly disturbed anyone still in bed, that it occurred to me to ask where we were heading! All I got by way of an answer was, "anywhere you like", and a grin broad enough to force a laugh out of me in spite of trying to look serious!

"Just stick a pin in that map down there," he said, pointing to a worn out looking road atlas in the door pocket. When I said that was a pretty daft way to decide he pulled into a small layby to have a look saying, "Well, do you have any better suggestions, or somewhere you desperately want to go?"

I had to admit that, like him, I really had no particular agenda. In fact he was right, the idea of being free to go wherever the fancy took us (this time without having to avoid the police!),did have a genuine appeal. We sat thumbing through the atlas for inspiration for just a few minutes before Steve startled me by almost leaping out of his seat with an idea that seemed to excite him somewhat.

"Have you been to Wales? And what about going up Snowdon? I haven't done that for years."

I had to admit that I hadn't been there, and so it seemed that this was decided then! Even so, I did have a couple of suggestions to put forward. I asked that, if we were going cross country, was there going to be time to visit our young friend Josh, and perhaps visit my sister Jenny at some point? I hadn't done more than speak to her on the phone since my nightmare had begun last year, and then only a couple of times whilst I was safely home with Mum and Dad. It would be good to see her, though I couldn't imagine what her husband, Alan, would make of Steve! I couldn't think of two more opposite characters than those two.

"Of course we can. We can go up to Birmingham first to see young Josh, then across to Wales. When we leave there it's not such a long way to Halewood. That is where you said Jenny lives, isn't it? Anyway, there's no need to rush anywhere. If we see anywhere we fancy stopping, we can do just that."

So off we went again, heading in Birmingham direction. Josh had been a young lad we'd met last year who had found himself living rough due to problems at home. When we came across him he was sitting, looking rather sorry for himself, where he'd been trying to earn a little from busking, but unfortunately he'd rather lost heart, partly because his guitar playing wasn't up to much. Steve had taken him under his wing (being such a collector of lost causes!), and together with Steve playing and Josh singing they had quickly attracted a good crowd. At the time we had been staying in a hostel and were earning our keep working at a local pub. Steve talked the manager into taking Josh on, in fact finding him a small room in which to live, and that was when we left the area. We were both keen to see how he was getting on, and hoping he'd made the most of the opportunity he'd been given rather than go out on the streets again.

Our only worry was where to park Annie. Birmingham was not ideally designed for camper vans, or so I thought, but foregoing the old road atlas, I looked on my mobile to find there were actually quite a few sites, and of all different sizes. We chose a fairly small one not far off the road. It proved to be quiet, and had good clean facilities (always a blessing in a van with few!). We decided to have a bite to eat from the supplies his mother had packed us off with earlier, and just relax for a while, going for a 'stroll' around the nearby area. It was obviously so much quieter than Birmingham itself so gave us chance to unwind. Really this was the first proper opportunity we'd had alone since we left the rehab centre. Much as we both, so it now seemed, to love our families dearly, it was good to know we were now truly free to do as we liked without having to please everyone.

Then, completely out of the blue, I was suddenly taken by surprise by an answer he gave me to a question, even more so as it brought to mind the odd moments last year when I'd had a similar reaction to something I'd said. It was as we were just finishing our lunch that I just casually asked about a couple of photos of him in an album Mrs Lockett had briefly flicked through with me, mainly to show me Beth and her dear grandson, Sean. Without giving it a thought, and expecting a simple explanation, I enquired of Steve why there were some with him being presented with his red beret

(I believe a top honour for a paratrooper), and a couple with him in a different colour one, sort of sandy coloured. All I was doing was being curious, but I could quickly tell he didn't want me to ask about or know about this! I had just assumed he'd been in a different regiment at some point, but it was clear he didn't intend to speak about it, so I said no more on the subject. Last thing I wanted to do now he was so settled was to stir up that unpredictability again.

Anyway, later on we walked round to the nearby bus stop to catch a bus into town. We figured it would allow us to spend time with Josh and our other friends at the pub, and not worry if we had a drink or two to celebrate our new found freedom! When we arrived there we could tell it was pretty busy inside, but there were tables free in the garden, so decided to sit there. We'd barely sat down, and before Steve could ask what I wanted to drink, a somewhat taller and far smarter young man to the one we had seen last year, walked across to clear the table.

"Well, hello there young man," Steve said, patting him on the back, "so you're still here, and by the look of it, doing pretty well for yourself."

Josh looked round in surprise, spinning round to look at me across the table, before almost throwing himself first at Steve, then coming round to throw his arms around me, causing such a spectacle that all the other customers let out a cheer!

"Whoa boy, steady yourself, we've not been gone so long now, have we?"

The way Josh looked at Steve you could have been forgiven for thinking he was Christ himself! He wanted to sit down and talk but Steve sent him in for our drinks first, no doubt hoping he'd settle down a bit by the time he came back. Wrong again! Far from things quietening down, he told all the staff we were there, and they all, from the boss to the chef, came out with him when he returned. I believe we caused quite a stir all round, some enjoying watching the commotion and wondering just who this mystery man was, perhaps someone famous; meanwhile there were some who were possibly a little aggravated by the delay in their service!

Realising any hope of getting more work out of Josh while he was so distracted, the boss told us to take him out the way for a couple of hours. The three of us went off for a wander around Birmingham, keen to see all our old haunts but avoiding the rather grim hostel where we'd stayed last time! As we walked Josh was keen to fill us in on just how much his life had improved since he'd been given both a job and a home at the pub,

"I really can't thank you enough, both of you, for showing such trust in me. I honestly don't know what I'd have done if you hadn't helped me."

111

Steve turned and looked him in the eye and told him,

"Perhaps we did point you in the right direction lad, but you had to want it bad enough to make it work. Once we left there was nothing stopping you going back on the streets except your determination not to do so. I'm proud of you son."

For a split second I genuinely thought they were going to have a man hug! But instead, Steve slapped him on the back and kept walking.

"Have you got to grips with that tatty old guitar yet then? If we come in for a meal later can we expect to hear a tune or two?"

"Well," Josh grinned as he said it, "I'll do my best, but the poor old thing needs a few new strings, so I often get asked to put it down and just sing."

Having dropped him off back at the pub to help the chef with the evening's preparations, we took ourselves out to sit by the river as we'd done previously. I could tell Steve had something on his mind, so I questioned him about it.

"I was just thinking how many kids like Josh end up on the streets through no fault of their own, or because they get no proper guidance. Perhaps they should have conscription like they did years ago ... give them a sense of pride, and motivate them to do something with their lives. But then, I can't see them all getting on with military training. Even so, they could do with something to do, something to aim at. Ok, we were there at the right time and the right place to find Josh, but what would have happened to him if we hadn't? By now he'd probably have been into drink or drugs, perhaps dead in a ditch! And who would have cared? And what about the hundreds of others in his situation? It's bloody hard out there, living rough. I should know, and for me it was my choice. But for most they have no choice for whatever reason."

I listened to what he was saying and could see this was something close to his heart. This was why he'd cared so much for the young recruits he had been responsible for in the army. I suppose I'd lived a pretty cushy life until last year, but must admit that during the time we first met, Steve had genuinely taught me a self-reliance I never had before.

On our way back to the pub we made one more stop. Steve had stopped to look in the window of a music shop and, seeing a particularly fine guitar there, decided to go in to try it out. It did sound really amazing when he played it, so unsurprisingly, he bought both that and a set of strings for Josh's instrument. In fact the delay caused by this stop-off meant that, by the time we finally arrived back at the pub we could hear Josh's voice ringing out over a rather tinny sounding guitar as we approached.

With the boss and a good few of his regulars remembering how Josh and Steve had made such good music together last time we were here, they insisted on hearing their double act again. It took Steve a few minutes to tune up his new instrument, while Josh looked on admiringly. It was obvious that Josh had little idea of how to tune his properly and so Steve gave it a quick go too.

Before very long the whole place was alive with such a fantastic sound of the two of them playing and singing together, so much so that it was bringing in people off the street to listen and join in. I have to admit that they sounded so good together that people were throwing requests at them so fast that the boss had to call for a short break to allow us to eat the meal we so badly needed by then! After a hearty dinner they insisted on only playing their own choice of tunes, finishing off with the first one they had performed together, 'Stand by me'.

As we were about to leave, promising Josh we would come back to visit again one day, Steve held out his new guitar saying,

"Think you could do with a new one lad. Tell you what, I'll do you a swap. I can work on yours and see if I can improve on the tuning."

And when Josh started protesting, he said, "It's only a loan mind, so take good care of it."

Somehow I knew that was just his way of reassuring the boy that we really would be back at some point, and I don't think Steve ever meant it as anything other than a present for him. As we made our way back to the campsite I put this to him, but was told (though with a glint in his eye he thought I'd not noticed) that no, it was too good an instrument to give away, and anyway, it would be safer there than carrying around in Annie! I didn't believe a word of that, I knew him far too well by this time.

In fact I do believe that, by that time I had really got the true measure of my travelling companion. Would that be all he would ever be to me I wonder? But yes, I must always remember what he said to Paul that day … that we were like brother and sister. Oh well, as long as he feels he wants my company I'm more than happy to be there for him.

By the time we found our way back to our site, and to our van, we also found ourselves in what I thought was also our first night sleeping in Annie. Neither of us had actually discussed sleeping arrangements as such, and though I believe Steve had considered putting up the awning and sleeping in there, it had turned somewhat chilly. Neither did we feel much like struggling to actually put it up with only having done so just once before.

I put the kettle on and made a coffee each to take the chill off before suggesting the obvious solution to our predicament.

"This is silly Steve." I announced as we sat drinking this, "This table folds down and makes a double bed. So what's the problem? How many times last year did we sleep up tight next to one another in our separate sleeping bags? After all, it's not as if we're total strangers is it?"

"No, I suppose you're right there. Well, if you're happy with that it certainly doesn't bother me. It is a bit chilly to kip out there while you hog a nice warm bed!"

And so that was settled. We folded down the table, spread the cushions to make a mattress, threw both bags on top, and after throwing a shoe at him to 'persuade' him to look away while I got changed, I wriggled into my bag and pretended not to look while he did the same!

Our first day of complete freedom had come to an end, and had felt good. What was to follow I could only imagine, but whatever it was would be fine by me. I had never in my life so far felt such a feeling. It felt crazy not having any responsibility or any plans. After the year of terror I'd experienced the previous year, just to go where we wanted and do as we wished seemed somehow wrong. Yet that was just the old me talking, and I now this was the new me. Just who this new me was I was yet to learn, but as long as I had Steve with me I knew I was brave enough to find out.

Somehow I could tell that I may have signed up for a bumpy ride, but it was guaranteed to be an exhilarating one, so I'd just have to hang on and see where it leads!

Chapter Twelve.

Not being in any particular rush we made a stop or two along the way toward Wales. Our first was to go back to visit Macclesfield where we had stayed for a night in a night shelter, acting as two complete strangers. It was good to feel we could take time to have a proper look around as neither of us had been there before that time, and then we'd been having to sneak about, pretending once again, to be dirty and shabby looking homeless individuals.

I dearly wanted to pop in and say hello to the ladies who ran the shelter to thank them for their kindness, but Steve felt perhaps it would be more benefit to do something a little more practical. We pondered over just how to achieve this without making ourselves obvious. I did suggest putting some cash in an envelope and posting it through their letter box but, as Steve suggested, it could be picked up by the wrong people. Of course we couldn't do it by cheque (even if we did carry a cheque book!), as this would have our name on. Eventually we came up with a solution. We went into a nearby supermarket, collected up two big trolleys full of items, food and personal items which we knew they could use, and paid for it all in cash to be delivered, insisting it should be done without our names.

I have to say that we couldn't resist watching from a safe distance when the van delivered it. It was good to see from the expressions on their faces, just how surprised and thrilled the ladies were.

Later on, after a gentle stroll around the town, we took ourselves down to walk along beside the canal. We'd not been walking far when we came across one of the waterside pubs along the canal path. It was while we were here that we found it particularly interesting to see the assorted narrow boats passing by. The landlord was quick to point us in the direction of the marina where he told us, we can hire one of these. Of course I wasn't surprised at Steve's eagerness to try his hand at yet another challenge, so back we went to fetch our van to drive there. I must admit to getting great amusement from the chaps face as we drove in. I'm not sure if you'd describe it as dread or horror as Steve parked alongside BMW's, Mercedes etc., and I believe he would have asked us to leave immediately until Steve stepped out and walked toward him! He being all of about five foot six and a scrawny build, it didn't take much for him to stop in his tracks faced with Steve!

"We'd like to hire a boat for a couple of days please. Do you have any available, and is it ok to leave the van there?"

Poor chap was clearly at a loss to know just how to get rid of these two 'travellers', and their scruffy looking vehicle.

"Um, well there are a couple, but I'm afraid they're not cheap. Do you mind me asking how you intend to pay?"

Throwing me a quick glance over his shoulder, Steve fished in his pocket for his wallet and flashed an array of cards, picking out a gold card, and asked,

"Would that do?"

The poor man's discomfort was so obvious. I wasn't sure whether to laugh or feel sorry for him. I contented myself in the end with making a mental note to tell Steve that I really didn't think he should go flashing these cards around for his own safety, but then I thought, I'd not want to be in the shoes of anyone who tried to relieve him of them!

I don't think either of us had been used to having almost unending funds available, but now that I have the money from the sale of the house in Richmond, Steve has a good army pay out for the PTSD claim he had, plus an amount left him by his father and we both have shares in Jake's (now Andy's) business, though we have no intention of squandering any of it, at least we knew we were financially secure.

Once we'd had the controls of the boat explained to us, and a quick demonstration of how to work the locks along the canal, we went on our way. I perched myself at the back where I could watch Steve steer, manoeuvring carefully around moored boats and other obstacles, and was perfectly relaxed, dozing almost, when I was disturbed in my reverie by Steve telling me to,

"Come on girl, look lively. Grab that handle and get the lock open."

"Why me," I asked, "why can't you do it? You're the skipper after all."

He just grinned at me and informed me that, as skipper, that gave him the right to dish out jobs, and anyway, he would need to be on board to steer it in and out safely! And anyway, apparently I needed the exercise to build up my muscles! Damn cheek, I thought as he sat casually watching as I stood winding the lock gates open. Still, I suppose I should be grateful that at least he did wait for me to climb aboard when he'd driven the boat though into the canal the far side. Even so, after the first couple of locks I decided it was definitely his turn, so I refused to do the next few, giving me chance to try my hand at driving the boat.

Perhaps that was not necessarily the wisest move, so I found out as I bumped it around against the sides! How was I to know how tight a fit it was in some places? Later on we had the thrill of experiencing the Anderson Boat Lift, which carries boats either up or down, depending which direction you are travelling, and in our case, lowering the boat down to sit it down onto the River Weaver. Not too far past this we found a good place to tie up and get a meal, then settled down for our first 'nautical' night aboard! There was actually four bunk beds with curtains to pull, two on each side, so we took opposite sides for a good night's sleep. I couldn't help thinking that it did feel a little cool, being on water, but couldn't bring myself to suggest cuddling up to keep warm! Anyway, I doubt the bunks would have had room for both of us in one (even if Steve wanted to!).

Well, I have to say that this drifting peacefully down the canals, stopping now and again for refreshments or to see the surrounding countryside as we went, did have a great appeal to it. Still more often than not he seemed to think it was my job to cope with the opening and closing of the locks. And still he liked nothing better than to drag me from my bunk first thing for an early morning jog, but I was determined not to give him the satisfaction of getting the better of me!

Eventually though, we had to return our boat to the boat yard from which it came, and rescue poor Annie van from where she stood amongst the very much more upmarket vehicles in the carpark. She may look a bit downtrodden to others who saw her there, but to us she was our 'home' for as long as we wanted her to be, so to us it didn't matter how far down peoples noses they might choose to look. She was our ticket to a complete freedom neither of us had experienced for a long time.

"So where to next," I asked Steve as I saw him scanning through his phone for ideas, "or is it straight on to Snowdon next?"

"No, I've found somewhere we should go first. You'll enjoy this one I reckon, and not much more than half an hour or so from here."

When I questioned him further all he said was to wait and see. This, in my experience of his idea of enjoyment, did not bode well! Oh well, as far as I know that would be too far from the sea to mean deep sea diving, and I don't know of anywhere within half hours' drive where he could throw me out of a plane by parachute, so can't be that scary!

When we finally pulled up outside a building it was not until we went in that I actually realised what he had in mind. There in front of us was a dirty great high climbing wall! Not the sort of little one next to it where there were kids scrambling up and down … oh no; sir here had his eyes firmly fixed on a much higher one at the far end of the building.

"You're joking! You don't really think you're getting me on that do you?"

"Go on, don't be a wimp. It's not so far up is it?"

"Maybe not, but it's an awful long way down when I fall! I suppose it's not much to you, but I can't do that," Yet in the back of my mind knowing that resistance was going to be futile! I watched as he went across to speak to a chap over by the small wall. Then, seeing the fear in my eyes he said,

"You'll be fine," as he took me across to get geared up for this latest challenge, "I'll show you what to do. Seems you're stuck with me as the usual instructor Chris, is busy teaching the kids, and as he's someone I trained in the army days, so he knows I'm qualified to teach you."

"And I suppose he's allowed to let you do that?" but I knew somehow that any protest was wasted on him.

"All you have to do is look up the top and will yourself to get there. You know what they say … where there's a will there's a way.

Well, I wasn't too sure about having the will, but I have to admit that once I learnt to look up, not down, and listen to what he told me instead of panicking, somehow I did find a way. After a number of attempts with him bellowing at me to 'look up' and 'listen to instructions', I actually found myself at the top! That's when I'm ashamed to say I did what I'd been told not to do … I looked down!

"Oh my God, it's too high! It's not safe, and I don't like it. How the hell do we get back down?"

"Stop panicking and you'll do it easily. You've done the hardest bit. All we do now is abseil back down. Now just calm it and follow me. Lean back in your harness, walk your feet down and just allow yourself to slide down the rope, like this."

So saying he casually began to slide back down,

"Don't you dare go without me or I'll …I'll…"

Throwing me a grin he reached across and prised my hands from the top of the wall I was clinging to and, putting them on the rope said,

"You'll what? You'll have to catch me first!"

That was the challenge I needed. I wasn't going to be left up there looking stupid while he stood at the bottom laughing at me in front of the small group of kids who'd gathered to watch the performance. Especially as Steve's mate Chris was there with them.

As he landed alongside me on the floor, Steve patted me firmly on the back and congratulated me.

"From now on young lady I want you to use that as your mantra, where there's a will, there's a way. That way you can do anything you put your mind to!"

I couldn't help thinking that what he really meant was anything he put his mind to! Even so I was determined not to let him get the better of me whatever challenges he chose to throw at me, and it did seem he was out to make or break me. I couldn't help wondering just what else I would find myself doing as time went on, but whatever came our way I knew resistance would just make him push all the harder. It was clear who was firmly in command of this expedition! But then, why should I care? I'd never been physically challenged before, and had to admit to a feeling of satisfaction, of growing with every new achievement.

Yes, I'd achieved a degree, but all that involved was sitting at a desk surrounded with books for most of the time. Even so, being a psychology degree in some ways even this has its place in this new 'journey'. Knowing now as I do, so much of Steve's history, I feel I'm in a better position to understand this extremely complex man, and if by putting his energy into working me in a similar way to one of his recruits helps him, then perhaps we can both benefit from whatever comes our way.

Chris came across to help me out of the harness and add his congratulations, "Well done girl. I'm Chris by the way. How the devil did the Serg persuade you to tackle that? Have you done climbing before?"

I assured him I'd not done more than climb onto a bar stool until I met Steve!

"Oh no, that's mean. He should have sent you over to me with the kids to get you started. Mind you, you did well. You should have seen me first time he got me on a rope. I was a nervous wreck, so I suppose he was pretty gentle on you."

"So it's not just me he has it in for then," I asked.

"Hell no, just don't ever say no to him or he'll up the ante next time!"

Somehow I could well believe this. While Steve was returning the gear to where it came from I had quite a chat with Chris. He tried hard not to laugh when I told him of our early morning jogs, and of how Steve had sorted out those louts by the pub in Cambridge, and it was clear that, if this man was anything to go by, those under his command would follow him to hell and back!

Although it was clear there was a genuine friendship between them, it was also very clear the lasting respect this man still held for Sergeant Steve Lockett.

Chapter Thirteen.

We stayed there for a while having something to eat in the café attached to the climbing centre where I got much amusement listening to the animated chatter between the two of them. It seems they'd not met for quite a while, and I got the impression that in many ways, both men missed the camaraderie of the service life.

Over the course of the time we spent their Chris fished a photo from his wallet and showed Steve his wife and two children. I was concerned at first as to how he would react after what had happened to Beth, but all he said was that, no, he wasn't married now.

"Beth died in a car accident, same day we came home."

I so badly wanted to throw my arms around him, to comfort him, but somehow knew it would be the wrong thing to do. Poor Chris too felt really uncomfortable. I could see by his expression that he wished he hadn't said anything.

"Don't look so worried you two," Steve said (almost commanded!), "Neither of you were responsible for what happened, and I've spent months coming to terms with it now, so it's time to move on. Talking of which, anyone else like another coffee? I'm going to get one."

I didn't but Chris said yes. Poor chap looked mortified. It seemed he'd been at Steve and Beth's wedding, but knew nothing of the accident or what had happened to him since. While Steve was waiting in the queue I gave him the briefest rundown of as much as I knew.

"So dare I ask ... are you and Steve an item now Mel?"

I wanted to say 'I wish', but decided I should be honest and say,

"No, we're just good friends. He told his counsellor we're like brother and sister, it's just that we've got used to being together since he helped me out of a mess last year."

"Well, I must say I'm surprised to hear you say that. Other than Beth I've never seen him take such interest in any other woman like he seems to in you. My advice, if you want to be closer to him that is, is don't give up. Just be prepared to play the long game, and I think he might surprise you. If I'm right I reckon you'll find he's worth the wait."

As he said this he gave me a sly wink, just out of view of Steve who was heading back with the drinks. I had to glance in the opposite direction for a minute to regain my composure from this most unexpected suggestion from Chris! Luckily Steve was too busy trying not to trip over some woman's handbag to notice my slightly flushed complexion.

It was good to hear the casual way the two men got along together, but all good things come to an end eventually, and so we had to say goodbye to Chris (and that damn great wall!) and climb back aboard Annie.

"Where to next? Please don't tell me we actually have to climb Snowdon?" I asked hopefully.

"Don't be daft. You don't climb it, you just trek up it."

That was definitely not what I'd planned! As far as I remember from a trip there as a kid, there's a little train which takes people up and down. Surely, just this once, we could do something the easy way. But no, I might have known there was no chance with him! No, as soon as we got there I found myself marched into the nearest shop to equip myself with a new pair of walking boots!

"I thought you shouldn't use new boots till you've broken them in properly," was my last feeble attempt to wriggle out of what was obviously a long, hard, uphill struggle.

"No, you're right, but don't worry ... it's just far enough to break them in."

Some hours later I managed to scramble to the top with a lot of 'encouragement' and a fair amount of bullying from Steve. The view was, I suppose, worth it, but my poor feet told a different story. I wanted to take my boots off but he said that would be a silly thing to do, so we just sat eating sandwiches and enjoying the rest. Mind you, Steve showed no sign of the effort it took to get there, but then to him it was just a gentle stroll!

While we were just about to set off back down it began to rain, good, hard, steady sheets of rain coming in from the east. Of course, I had no sense of direction to speak of so had to take Steve's word for that. Just as I was thinking just how unpleasant this was going to be, trudging all the way down in those conditions, I got the shock of my life with being told we could jump on the little train which was just about to make the descent.

Grateful as I was for this small mercy, by the time I'd hobbled back the short distance to the van, to say I was annoyed was putting it mildly! Once inside away from the rain I collapsed on the seat and stretched out full length to rest.

"Well, aren't you going to take your muddy boots off? You've been moaning about them all day."

"I don't care if they are muddy, or if you care more about the floor getting muddy than you care about how I feel. There are words for how I feel, and I'm too much of a lady to use the ones that spring to mind!"

"You're what? You, a lady!" All he could do was stand there and laugh!

When I did manage to sit up long enough to take them off I could see he was still getting much amusement from watching me struggle, so as the last one was dislodged from my poor feet, I was so incensed that I threw it at him, mud and all, just missing his head! Needless to say we spent a very quiet evening, and I for one wriggled into my sleeping bag first, making very sure to take up way over my allotted space! In fact, I'm not altogether sure how he did find space to squeeze on what should have been his half, but that night neither did I care.

When I awoke the next morning he was already up and preparing some breakfast. He'd got the map out, presumably to decide our next destination. He'd made bowls of porridge, which I didn't like to admit were more than welcome. As we studied the map for anywhere we might wish to stop on our way to Jenny's, I saw something which gave me cause to hope I could possibly get my revenge on Steve, just for once!

"Ok," I told him, "It's my turn to drive, and my turn to decide what to do next. Come on, let's get ready to go."

"Are you planning on telling me where we're going? Do you think you've got something planned that I can't do?"

131

All I did was to nod my head and try not to look too smug. I was reasonably sure my idea was a good one. Not too far along the road I kept my eyes open for a place I was pretty sure was quite close, finally taking a turning which took us exactly where I'd hoped it would ... a trekking centre!

Steve's face (just for a brief second) was a picture. He certainly hadn't expected that. Trying desperately to keep a straight face, I looked round at him and said, "How about it? Do you fancy a ride? Have you done it before?"

"Not exactly, but I did ride a camel in a desert once. It can't be so much different I know. I suppose you have then by the look on your face?"

"Oh yes, I rode regularly for years as I was growing up. Come on, let's see if they have one big enough for you. Mind you, those little Welsh ponies are pretty tough, and at least you could keep your feet on the ground with one of those."

With what was quite obviously a forced show of confidence, he threw me an 'almost' smile, and reminded me of what he'd told me ... 'where there's a will...'

"Don't worry about me, I'm sure I'll soon get the hang of it."

I was really beginning to enjoy the feeling of revenge! I know it was mean of me, but after all the challenges he'd thrown at me last year, and already this, it was a good feeling. Besides, these places cater for amateurs, so I was sure he wouldn't come to much harm.

The lady in charge enquired after our experience, and did look a little dubious when Steve told her he had very little (he wouldn't own up to saying none!), and did eventually agree to us going along with the next trek. She brought out a beautiful black Welsh cob for me and was pleased to see that I knew how to mount and get myself comfortable. I looked round to the end of the yard to see how Steve was coping, just in time to see them produce what was clearly a thoroughbred. The girl near me said that this was an ex-racehorse,

"But he'll be fine as long as he sits still and keeps his legs off the horse's side."

Before I could say another word to her we were off, one behind the other, along a winding path through the woods. I held my pony back, trying to get near enough to warn Steve to sit quietly, but there were other ponies in between. I suppose it was because they could see I had more experience that they put me in front. Behind me there were assorted small children being led by someone. Poor Steve was allocated the position at the rear of the group.

I was told to follow a path which was clearly used regularly. All went well for a while. I kept looking over my shoulder to see if he was still on board and was just beginning to settle back and relax when I heard a commotion from behind.

Before I could look around I heard the woman in charge shouting,

"Grab him someone!"

Before I could look round Steve's horse shot past me, with him hanging on to anything he could! It was so sudden and he clearly had no idea how to stop it, (obviously nothing like a camel I thought!). Knowing my cob was the only one with a chance of catching him I didn't hesitate. I set off at a gallop along in the direction he'd gone, hoping he hadn't come to any harm. Revenge is one thing, but I hadn't planned on killing him in the attempt to get some!

As it happened I needn't have panicked too much. I hadn't gone too far, just a short distance and around a corner, and there he was, sitting on the path, obviously a little shaken up by his experience, while the horse stood along the verge making the most of the rich grazing there. Automatically I dismounted and went to catch it before leading both across to where poor Steve was struggling to his feet.

"Don't you worry about me. You just sort them out before you bother to see if I'm ok," he threw at me sarcastically.

Oh dear, I thought; I reckoned I'd upset him now. Even so, as I explained to him, he was clearly not going anywhere, whereas the horse may have taken off again, then we'd be responsible for anything that happened to it.

"We may have enough funds but I don't want to spend it on her vet's bills. Anyway, are you, ok I mean?"

He managed a bit of a forced grin as he got to his feet and brushed himself off, and said he was just a little bruised that was all. I couldn't help thinking I reckon the biggest bruise is to his pride! Needless to say we walked back to the yard after meeting a very concerned looking owner. She was obviously relieved to see that neither the horse nor rider were injured in any way, and thanked me for acting so quickly. In fact she went as far as to say that if I ever fancied a job there she would be pleased to take me on.

"That's so kind of you," I said, watching Steve's face from the corner of my eye, "I'll bare it in mind. Then perhaps I would be able to teach him to ride properly."

As we walked, or in his case, hobbled, back to Annie, Steve whispered in my ear, "Not bloody likely! Those things are damn dangerous."

"Now, now, you know what you told me … where there's a will there's a way."

Chapter Fourteen.

I do believe that this last adventure did, to some extent, calm Steve down a little, well at least temporarily. It seemed that now would be a good time to make the drive from there to Halewood where Jenny lives. It had been sometime since I saw her last and I was curious to see what she would make of my travelling companion. At least, as far as I knew, there was nothing too adventurous in that area so just maybe I might be allowed some rest while we're there!

It seemed that, during our antics last year, she had been questioned by the police as to whether or not she had heard from or seen me. Of course that had alerted her to what was going on in my life. As she said, when she finally let go of me, one minute she knew I was on the verge of marrying Jake, and the next she was told I was suspected of murdering him!

"So how did you prove you didn't do it, assuming of course that you didn't?"

"No, of course not, did you really think I could? As for how I proved it, that was down to Steve here. I couldn't have done it without him."

I think that until this point she'd been so pleased to see me that she'd barely noticed Steve follow me in. Alan, on the other hand, was now first to shake him warmly by the hand and say how good it was to meet him. It seemed that Steve had made his mind up to make a good impression. Phew, I thought, what a relief, knowing how good he was at winding people up if the mood took him! It struck me as quite comical watching how he put himself out to get along with my brother-in-law who had absolutely nothing in common with him. Alan worked in an office at the docks in Liverpool, and probably the most exciting thing he did was to go ten pin bowling every Friday night, or call in at the pub down the road for half a pint now and again. Somehow I couldn't imagine Steve living that sort of lifestyle.

Jenny quickly prepared a meal for us all, her being the domesticated one of the two of us. I couldn't help noticing the way she seemed to have difficulty taking her eyes off of Steve while we ate. In fact it was so obvious that on a couple of occasions I found myself kicking her gently under the table to distract her! I don't think he noticed mind you, and Alan certainly didn't. We'd barely finished eating when Steve suggested to Alan that the two of them should walk down to the pub on the corner so that he could treat him to a pint or two while, as he put it, the girls can have a catch-up.

"Sounds good to me," Alan agreed, "but a half will do me Steve."

Oh yes, like that's going to happen when you're with Steve, I thought! I was going to warn him to take it easy and remember Alan isn't like him, but they'd gone before I had chance. Anyway it was too late to worry by then, and I suppose if he gets poor Alan legless, at least I know Steve's capable of carrying him home later, even if it did mean getting us kicked out!

"Hey Sis, you're a bit of a dark horse aren't you? Where on earth did you find the likes of him? I don't mean anything against your Jake … bless him, he was lovely, but this one? He's something else altogether! I didn't know you had it in you to find yourself a man like Steve!"

"That's why you couldn't take your eyes off him at the table I suppose? Anyway, I didn't find him, he found me. And anyway we're friends, we're not an item."

She obviously didn't believe that for a minute, so I told her the whole story from finding myself in the cave, and how Steve had found me roaming about like a lost sheep. I felt I could even tell her more about the way the whole thing had come to an end back at Jakes house than I'd told our parents, even the bit about the way Steve had actually threatened to kill me in front of Morgan! Even so, her face was a picture until I reassured her it was just an act to get an admission of guilt from him. Strangely enough I did 'forget' to tell her how he nearly had to be shot to make him drop his knife! Oh, and it totally slipped my mind to add in the bit where he'd attacked me at his wife's graveside in Ely. Other than those odd little minor details I told her everything!

"Well I must say Mel, you don't sound like the same little sister I grew up with. I wouldn't have thought you capable of coping with so much, but I'm really glad to see how well you got through it all."

I couldn't help agreeing with that. I certainly knew I was nothing (or nearly nothing) like the little wimpy kid she'd grown up with and, as I told her, that was all down to Steve!

"So what are you going to do now, when you've had your holiday that is? Where are you heading for in that old camper outside?"

"Oh, that's not just any old van … that's Annie van," I could see the puzzled expression on her face. "As for where we're heading, we don't have any plans … just keep going until we find somewhere we want to visit. We don't have any plans to stay anywhere in particular."

Of course then came the question I'd been waiting for; "So how many beds, bunks or whatever do you have in that old thing?"

"I know what you're getting at, and the answer is one double," I saw the look on her face as I said that, "the table folds down and the side cushions go across. But NO, I told you we are not an item! We spent all our time last year using two SEPARATE sleeping bags, so decided to carry on doing the same now."

I know she had her doubts about this but, as I assured her that that was just how it was (even if I wished it could be different!).

"Anyway, you can sleep indoors tonight, assuming you're staying that is? Come and help me make up the spare beds, I don't suppose the men will be too late home. Alan has work quite early in the morning, and he's not much of a drinker. How about Steve? Does he drink much?"

All I could bring myself to say to this was, "In moderation." But then, moderation to Steve was possibly excess to 'normal' men! To be on the safe side of getting thrown out I made a visit to the toilet on my way upstairs, giving me chance to send a quick text threatening him not to bring Alan home too late or too drunk! All I got by way of a reply was a devil emoji with smoke coming out of its ears!!

By eleven o'clock we heard the door go, and there they were, Steve with his usual cheeky grin, and looking somewhat wobbly on his feet, poor Alan doing his level best to stay upright and keep a straight face, before collapsing on the sofa and throwing his arms around a shocked looking Jenny!

"Sorry if we're a bit late," said Steve, "we just got chatting and the time just flew by. But don't worry, we didn't forget you Jenny. We brought you a bottle of wine to thank you for your hospitality."

As he said it producing a bottle of white wine to hand to her. I wouldn't have been surprised if she'd cracked it over his head that minute, but of course, Steve being Steve threw her one of his flirtiest smiles as he held it out to her that she visibly melted under his spell!

I desperately wanted to throw something at him or smack him one, but didn't think I should do so in front of my sister. Instead I went with him to retrieve our night bags from the van, and once inside out of sight and earshot, threw at him,

"What do you think you were doing? Poor Alan isn't used to drinking. He's not like you..." and as I said this taking a swing at him to show my anger,

Catching my arm mid-swing he looked down at me and said,

"And would you like me any more if I was like him?"

He held my arm there just for a brief second or two, just looking straight down into my eyes. I expected to see that mocking grin, but it didn't come, instead the look I saw in those dark eyes of his was more one of, dare I say, affection! What could I say to him now? He really had to be the most annoying, frustrating, irritating ... yet totally irresistible man ever created, and I knew at that point that just maybe, just possibly, if I stuck by him and prayed hard enough, there was just the smallest chance that one day he may look on me as being a little more than friend or sister.

All I could do right that minute was to chuck his wash kit at him and tell him to stop being stupid and get back indoors before they go to bed and lock us out! As both Jenny and Alan had to work the next day we decided to spend a day seeing the sights of Liverpool. It wasn't until Jenny gave us a guide book of the place that we realised what a large variety of things there were to see. Obviously we knew we'd have to skip quite a few, but as Alan said, we could come back anytime we liked for another visit. If nothing else this showed that, far from being annoyed with Steve, he genuinely had enjoyed chance to escape his usual comfort zone, secure in the knowledge that his new 'bestie' was there to protect him should the need arise! Then of course Steve could do no wrong in the eyes of my dear sister.

Our first visit was to the cathedral, being as it was probably the most prominent thing as we approached the city. I for one could not believe the size of the cathedral. Apparently it boasts the highest cathedral tower in England, and no fewer than thirteen bells! With some trepidation I agreed to go up in the lift provided to look out over the vast expanse of Liverpool and beyond. Though I'm not too fond of great heights, by anchoring myself very firmly to Steve, I was really glad I did go there as the view was amazing.

Steve was keen to go on the wheel, which is very similar to the London Eye, but I said he would have to go alone as I didn't fancy too many high adventures in one day. Instead of this we chose to investigate some of the many museums and galleries on offer. I was always quite amazed at Steve's interest in such places, but then, action man or not, there was no reason to assume he'd never took an interest in more academic things too.

Having been down to walk by the waterfront we were confronted by the life-size statues of the Beatles. Though we both had obviously heard of them, and I knew they were Mum's big favourites from her younger days, it did seem strange to come face to face with them! We were going to take photos of each of us with them, but then a woman passing by asked if we'd like her to take one of us both in the line-up of the four of them.

We both took great pleasure in posting these to our Mums with a message saying, "Look who we met today!" Then we made a promise to ourselves to find and listen to as much of their music as possible as we drive around. Following this we headed back into town to eat and, would you believe, the music playing out over us while we ate, actually was theirs! Yes, we decided, perhaps our music appreciation over the years had been a little lacking.

While we were sitting listening to the music and eating, we found ourselves chatting to a local chap. He asked what we thought of the city, obviously the one he'd lived in all his life, and had we seen all the sights! We filled him in as to those we had seen, telling him we thought there was plenty to bring us back again sometime. This seemed to please him as he was obviously proud of the place.

"Have you been to the Williamson Tunnels," he asked.

When we said no and asked him about them, he was pretty vague, just saying that they were, as far as he knew, constructed by some rich tobacco merchant back in the 1800's but, though no one knew why he did this, they were now opened to visitors.

"You should have a look, bet you'll enjoy it," and then he was gone.

Ok, we thought, perhaps we could fit in just this one last thing before going back to Jenny's. After asking directions we hopped on a bus and soon found ourselves at this site. Along with a small group of other visitors, we were given a short talk as to the rather vague history of the place. It seems that no one really knows just why Williamson built these tunnels, but it seems that for many years they were inaccessible, having been pretty well back-filled. About 1995 till the present day archaeological work has been slowly ongoing to reveal the extent of the tunnels. It certainly seemed to catch the interest of all of us listening to the talk, and before long we found ourselves led down into the tunnels to see it for ourselves.

I had always been quite interested in archaeology, though I had no particular knowledge in the field, but this place was nothing I'd come across before. Usually when thinking of archaeology I always think way back in history, not the 1800's. As we followed the guide down deeper into the tunnels we were quite amazed at the thought that someone could do this, yet leave no clear explanation as to why.

All was well, following along behind the guide and taking in all he said until, as we found ourselves in a deeper section, I began to feel panicky. I took hold of Steve's hand, causing him to look down at me and smile,

"To what do I owe this pleasure," he asked.

I couldn't bring myself to answer, just to give half a smile and hold on a bit tighter! As we passed on through the next areas, the guide explained that, back in the days this was built the men would have had little light to work by. As we rounded the next corner he proved this by taking us into an area with barely any light at all.

That was it … I felt myself go into complete meltdown, and could do absolutely nothing to stop myself! I could hear myself scream at the top of my voice, my legs folded under me, and all I could do was curl up in a ball on the floor crying and screaming uncontrollably! To say I was hysterical would be to put it mildly.

I was barely aware of what the guide and other visitors did at that point, all I was aware of was Steve's arms round me as he talked quietly and soothingly before picking me up as if I was a kid, and carrying me back the way we came, back out into the daylight.

"Ssh, it's ok Mel, you're safe now. Come on, open your eyes, we're back in the sunshine."

When I did force myself to peep out I found we were sitting out on a grassy bank away from the entrance of the tunnels. I couldn't control the awful trembling which had taken over my body. We sat there quietly for a time, with Steve's arm around my shoulders, until I began to gain some sort of control of my body and my voice.

"I'm sorry. I didn't mean to do that. I just lost it and couldn't stop and ... "

Giving me a gentle squeeze he looked down at me sympathetically (not a look I've seen in him often!) and said,

"No Mel, it's me who should be sorry for taking you in there. It didn't occur to me that it would bring back your experience of that cave from last year. I promise I won't take you anywhere near anything like that again."

Yes of course, that was what had scared me. It hadn't crossed my mind, but somewhere back in my subconscious that feeling of being trapped in a dark cave had stuck firmly in my mind. We sat there together until the shaking stopped, and then I was given strict orders to sit still until he'd brought us a hot drink each. We were just about to get up when the guide who had been with us came over to see if I was alright. Steve explained to him that I was a 'little' claustrophobic, but hadn't expected it to be so dark there.

"Yes, I am so sorry for making a fuss, I should have thought of that before going along. I hope I didn't upset the other people?"

"No, don't you worry about that young lady. As long as you're alright, that's all that matters."

Well, that was certainly an unexpected end to our Liverpool visit. As we climbed back on the bus to take us back to Jenny's we vowed to return one day … but never to go into anymore caves or tunnels under any circumstances!

Once again we were given a hearty meal at Jenny and Alan's, followed by a quiet evening 'helping' them drink the bottle of wine Steve brought home for her the previous night! I was glad to sit back and relax feeling still a little shaken from the afternoon's experience (which remained unspoken to them). Alan asked where we were heading for next, but neither of us had given this much thought until then.

"Have you been up around the Lake District? It's really beautiful up around there this time of year, especially as Steve tells me you like a bit of walking."

Huh! Not so much walking as route marching, I wanted to tell him, but I managed to refrain from such snide remarks, especially as Steve had been so tender and gentle with me earlier in the afternoon. All I could do was hope the feeling would last. Anyway, I'd not seen the lakes and I had been told the scenery there was amazing. With the weather turning really unusually bright and mild for the time of year, this seemed a brilliant suggestion. And so it was decided. One last night in 'proper' beds before setting off once more on further adventures!

Chapter Fifteen.

Somehow I knew that this would never be just your average little sightseeing jaunt which most average visitors enjoy ... oh no, this was one led by Steve Lockett, action man! Though we did stop at a very pretty little café on our way to the particular place he had in mind, it soon became clear that he had other plans to fill our day. After we'd refreshed ourselves there and he'd had a chat with the owner, he marched me off further down the village to a shop which it was clear sold all sorts of hiking equipment. I was a bit concerned when he put together a collection of things such as first aid kit, map and compass, hats, gloves and waterproofs, though knowing him I was sure we could need them at some point.

That much I was prepared to tolerate; but when he led me towards a row of wetsuits hanging up at the back of the shop, I thought no ... NO WAY!!

"Not on your life are you getting me swimming in a lake."

"What's the problem? You can swim can't you," was all I got from him. "You can't go in the lake without one of these this time of year."

"I've no intention of going in the lake any time of year thank you!"

Somehow, once again, I knew the battle was lost before it began. If that was what he'd made up his mind to do, then that was what we would be doing! Reluctantly I wriggled into the suit the man said should fit, and was pleased to find 'sir', after a quick inspection, seemed happy with it.

"So where is this lake? You needn't think I'm staying in too long if it's cold."

"Well of course it'll be cold this early in the year, so that's why you need a wetsuit stupid," with a grin so wide I could have smacked him one there and then.

"Ok, just supposing I do agree to do this, will that keep you off my back the rest of the day?" I asked, hopefully.

"Well, other than a pleasant little stroll around the lake afterwards to warm us up," was all I got by way of an answer.

It was with extreme reluctance that I stood inside the van wriggling once more into that wet suit. Perhaps I may have put my foot down and refused had it not been for him pointing out another small group of brave souls already in the water. Even so, I stopped at the water's edge and hoped to find an excuse, even at this late stage, to just watch him from the shore. It was obvious that this wasn't going to happen.

"Are you sure there are no strange creatures lurking about underwater?"

I knew as soon as I said this it was just not the most logical thing to come out with, and sure enough all it did was cause a hearty laugh and an answer of,

"No silly; you are in the Lake District you know. You're thinking of Loch Ness in Scotland! Anyway, I thought you once told me you had a soft spot for the works of old William Wordsworth? You do know this was his favourite lake where he used to sit and write all those poems. I think he lived near here too."

"Yes perhaps that's so, but I bet he didn't swim in it? They didn't have wetsuits back then I know."

Even so, it was with extreme caution that I followed Steve in. As I expected, the water was drastically cold. Had I not been wearing my wetsuit I would have been back in the van watching Steve from inside. I have to admit that there was something mildly exhilarating once I'd allowed myself to relax a little, but I still think a nice warm sauna would have just as good affect as far as I was concerned.

Half an hour or so later we walked (or in my case dragged) ourselves back to the showers on offer in the car park. This was a real luxury as far as I was concerned though the water was only luke warm, and finally walked back to sit by the van for a light snack. Steve had suggested that perhaps we

151

could treat ourselves tonight to a stay in a bed and breakfast, if we could find one with space. Meanwhile, and just as I'd sat relaxing in the warm spring weather for nearly an hour after our lunch, he handed me my walking boots and suggested that 'stroll' he'd mentioned earlier.

"Perhaps we'll see old William's house on the way," he said with a grin.

Of course, once again, I was daft enough to take his description quite literally. Why did I never learn? Never mind the gentle stroll I had in mind; oh no, what he had in mind was a circular walk right around the lake of about three miles! As for the 'stroll', Steve never strolls anywhere!

By the time we finally made it back to Annie I was shattered. Once again I stretched out, complete with boots, refusing to move until he'd made me a cup of tea! Once I'd recovered sufficiently we set off in search of a comfortable place to rest our heads as a special treat. Steve seemed to have some idea where we needed to go, so I left it to him to sort out. Eventually coming to Keswick we were surprised to find there was some sort of mass invasion of the place due to an event nearby. When I suggested going on to somewhere else Steve seemed reluctant to do so, and so left me resting in the van whilst he went in search of rooms for the night.

I found myself dropping off to sleep, probably due to all the fresh air and exercise of the day, and was woken up by him tapping me on the shoulder and telling me he'd found us somewhere. Gathering up what we needed for the night we locked up the van and, leaving her there in the car park, I followed him a short distance down the road to a pretty stone cottage. On entering this we were met by a jolly little lady who introduced herself as Mrs Walsh and, as she led us upstairs, opened a door to a bedroom saying,

"This is your room Mrs Lockett. I hope you find it comfortable, but as I told your husband, we're extremely busy this week," and then, before I could open my mouth to contradict her, she was gone!

"What the hell have you told her? Did you tell her we're married?" and all I got was a nod and pushed in the door, presumably so Mrs Walsh couldn't hear the reply.

"Well, this seems to be the only room available in Keswick tonight, so it seemed logical to grab it. Besides, it means only paying for one … and after all, we did pretend we were brother and sister and husband and wife at different times last year didn't we?"

"You can sleep in the damn bath for all I care, but the bed is mine, do you hear?"

All he did was look round the door to the ensuite, then look back at me and shake his head, and grinning from ear to ear, say,

"Well I would, but there isn't one … just a shower."

"Then you'll have to stand up and sleep won't you clever clogs, but not until I've had a use of it first!"

He was clearly amused at the whole situation and, though it was more than I dared let on, so was I. He was right about the way we'd called ourselves by different names, and by different relationships, last year, normally to avoid detection by the police etc., so there was a certain thrill to the idea of doing similar again when the need arose. It had seemed that this was about the last room available in the area, so just maybe I should let him off this time.

Even so, by the time he came back from having a shower, I had put a pillow and a blanket alongside the bed on the floor, as much as anything to see what reaction I got. To my surprise, and I must admit, a feeling of disappointment, it seemed he'd taken the hint and stretched out on the floor in this make-shift bed! Damn! I had rather hoped he would choose to ignore this and climb in alongside me. I made a mental note not to do this again!!

By the time I came to the next morning he was showered, dressed and almost ready to head down for the full English breakfast he'd been looking forward to. He made no mention of last night's sleeping arrangements except to say he'd put the bed straight while I showered. I felt guilty for making him sleep on the floor, but to be honest I had sort of hoped he'd refuse as we did, after all, sleep alongside each other in the van, but then I suppose we did have our separate sleeping bags, so we didn't quite come into close contact as it were. When I asked how he found sleeping down there all he said was,

"I've slept in worse places than that. Now get a shift on or I'll go and eat all the breakfast before you get there."

The smile on his face as he said this told me that he didn't bear a grudge, so off I went to shower, just to find by the time I got back he had made the bed and gone downstairs. As I walked into the dining room Mrs Walsh was just asking him if we had slept well. Looking over her shoulder to see me come into the room he smiled sweetly and said,

"Yes thank you Mrs Walsh. My wife had the best night's sleep she's had for days," deliberately avoiding mentioning his night on the hard floor!

After breakfast and having collected our belongings, we made our way back to Annie. Thinking that just perhaps we were due a nice, gentle, relaxing day, I asked what next?

"Well, while we're here there is one ambition I've yet to fulfil. You'll like this. Have you heard of Scafell Pike?"

"Um, yes I think so, why. Isn't it supposed to be the highest mountain in England?" and then it registered in my mind, "Oh no! You're not really expecting me to follow you up there are you?"

"Well, you can follow me, or you can go in front if you like. Why do you think I bought all those supplies? On a long trek like that it's always wise to go equipped in case there's a sudden change of weather."

"Yes I can see that, but are you really expecting us to need a first aid kit and waterproofs? Look at it. The weather looks pretty good to me. And anyway, how long do you reckon it takes to get there and back?"

"Only about five, maybe six hours; depends how fit you are. You've been working up to something like this since we first met surely? You're certainly not the scrawny little thing I met up with last year!"

Well, he was certainly right on that score I suppose, but to what extent I couldn't say. All I did know was that this was obviously how the future weeks or month would progress, with Steve getting satisfaction from setting me assorted challenges, obviously expecting me to either refuse or fail, and me determined not to let him get the better of me!

At one point I did wonder if he was hoping I'd give up and that he could get rid of me. But then I remembered what Paul had said about his obsession with training those in his charge to be the best they can. Well, I suppose that must be how he looks on me, and I was most certainly not about to let him beat me! If I did I knew I would lose both his respect and, even worse, him.

Beside which I couldn't get Chris' words out of my mind, "just be prepared to play the long game and I think he might surprise you," as he put it, he reckoned, "I think you'll find he's worth the wait!"

With all these thoughts going round in my head I made up my mind that I was not about to let some little old hill defeat me! I knew just what my ultimate goal was now, and whatever he threw at me I was determined to give it my best shot.

Well, somehow I did manage to crawl behind him to the top of Scafell Pike! That really was the hardest challenge he'd thrown at me so far, and surely the hardest thing he would ask of me. Once we made it to the highest point we sat there totally exhilarated by the amazing view, but even more exhilarating to me was the feeling of Steve's arm around my shoulders as he looked me in the eye and said,

"Well done Mel. That was one hell of an effort on your part. I genuinely didn't think you'd get half way, certainly not right to the top."

I managed an exhausted but satisfied smile back as I reminded him,

"You know what you said … where there's a will, there's a way"

Chapter Sixteen.

I was completely shattered but very content as I knew I'd managed to impress Steve and achieve something which previously would have been way out of my capabilities. In fact it had impressed him so much he had suggested calling in at a rather nice, cosy pub along the way to eat before trying to find somewhere to park up for the night.

We tucked into a delicious meal, very much needed after our day's exertions, and as always, Steve was quickly taken to by the local community. In fact so much so that I was a little concerned that he could have problems driving after all the pints bought for him by them! I needn't have worried too much as the landlord said we could stay in the van in his carpark if we cared to. As he said, he would have liked to offer us a room, but the few he had were already full, but we were content to sleep in Annie anyway.

During the conversation that evening I heard one chap ask Steve if we'd been doing the 'three peak challenge'.

"What is that? Another of your mad schemes I suppose to break me!"

Both Steve and his new mate looked round at me and laughed, yet I sensed not in a critical way. He said that he had done that himself some years ago, but thought I had achieved quite enough in doing both Snowdon and Scafell Pike. He explained to me that the idea of the challenge was to do all three, Snowdon, Scafell and Ben Nevis in Scotland, all in twenty-four hours! When I asked him if he planned to drag me up that one he said emphatically no! Though I felt a little put down by his reply, he quickly explained that, though the other two were more a case of extremely hard treks, Ben Nevis entailed actually climbing, and he had no intention of being responsible if I fell and broke my neck! I was quite relieved as it happened as my only actual climbing experience had been up that wall at Chris' place, and even then Steve had had to peel me off the top of it to get me down!

That night I slept like a log, though making a point of 'inadvertently' finding my sleeping bag right up tight to Steve's. Had he commented on this I would have denied noticing or accusing him of moving into my space, but for whatever reason, nothing was said. Either he didn't notice, or just perhaps he enjoyed the closeness as much as I did.

This had happened on a few occasions since we set off on our travels, yet in my heart I knew it was just wishful thinking on my part. After all, since the visit to Chris it had left me in no doubt that Beth was, and always would be, Steve's one true love. I would never be more than a friend and travelling companion. But, what the heck … that was better than nothing.

Over the next couple of months we continued travelling where and when the mood took us. We did in fact fit Ben Nevis into the schedule at one point but, as promised, I was allowed to stay at a safe point at the base, from where I could watch with much trepidation as Steve set of for the summit with a small group of others. Once out of sight I had to settle for spending time at the visitor centre and, when I'd exhausted that, go back to the van for a read. Truthfully, I realised that since leaving home I'd barely had chance to open a book, and yet this had always been a favourite pastime of mine, but book reading was definitely not on the agenda where Steve was concerned … far too static for him!

Though I didn't actually follow him up Ben Nevis, I did find myself being 'encouraged', if that's the right word, to try my hand at just a little proper climbing whilst in Scotland, firmly attached I may add, to Steve. I must admit that, although I didn't go very high before he took me back down, I was always impressed to watch the ease with which he could do this with such little effort, but I knew somehow I wasn't cut out for great heights! No, I preferred to watch from the safety of terra firma, often using the time to ring round the two Mums, often posting photos of the places we've visited, just to stop them worrying (as Mums do!).

As we travelled about, we would usually sleep and eat in the van, but sometimes we would decide to leave it on a suitable site and book into a B&B, even on a few occasions, a couple of rather up-market hotels! We got such fun out of the latter as, going in to book rooms in our somewhat rough looking attire, they would give us extremely suspicious looks! I did suggest the first time we decided to stay at one of these that we should make an effort to smarten ourselves up somewhat, but all I got from Steve was,

"Why? Our money is as good as everyone else's. Keep them guessing," and with a wicked glint in the eye over his shoulder at me, he marched straight up to the desk and asked for two adjoining rooms, "For my sister, Lady Melanie and myself please."

Well, how I was supposed to keep a straight face after that I had no idea! 'Lady' indeed! Did that make him 'Lord Steven' then? Oh my goodness, whatever next? This man really is incorrigible, but somehow I've always known life would never be dull since the day we met!

Having seen a fair amount of the beautiful countryside of Scotland, we drifted back around the north of England, nowhere in particular, but anywhere with an interesting name, or anything else to appeal to a couple of free spirits. Steve had always called himself a free spirit from the start, and now I had truly begun to understand just what that felt like. He had lived for a good part of two years surviving on his ability to cope with anything that life threw at him, plus the survival training he'd received from his years in the army, and it was his love of this freedom that he was indoctrinating me with now. After growing up as a somewhat pampered and ordinary kid, the deeper I found myself sinking into this new, free life, the more I loved every moment. I now realised I had begun to accept the challenges he threw at me, no longer with trepidation, but with an excitement I'd not expected to feel.

During this time we came across some truly beautiful pieces of countryside, certainly unexpected to me not having been this far north before. As it also was scattered with quite a collection of camp and caravan sites, this gave us chance to park up and do a certain amount of walking. On would go our backpacks with food, drink, spare socks (and the necessary plasters for sore feet!), and now the weather was turning quite warm most days, our sleeping bags and a small, rather flimsy, tent. We didn't always use this, but on the odd occasions when we chose to, it was a pretty cosy fit! This suited me pretty well as I would never complain about the need to be as close as possible to Steve, but still this was just a matter of necessity as far as he was concerned. In fact I was somewhat surprised on one of these outings when, sitting by a small fire which he'd lit to warm a drink for us, he did actually sit, almost in a daze, talking about a time when he'd taken Beth camping! I rather got the impression that she'd not found it much to her liking, but he laughed quietly as he said this. I genuinely was lost for words … what could I say; what should I say? I found myself feeling like an intruder in their relationship, and seriously wondered at that moment if I should make my excuses and leave him to carry on without me. After all, he wouldn't be entirely alone. I knew somehow he would probably always be haunted by the ghost of his beloved Beth. Probably the only thing making him tolerate me was the knowledge that the army rehab people had insisted that he should have someone with him for at least another year, someone who knew about the demons he'd had to fight to get to this point, and it had been me who was given the task of watching in case anything threatened to make him snap again.

And if it did … if he completely flipped as he had with Morgan, the man who had killed Steve's young recruit in cold blood and my dear Jake …

what did they think I could do to stop him? Having experienced Steve at his terrifying worst, did they really believe I could do anything to stop him? Though in my heart I knew I loved this man with every bit of my being, and therefore had been happy to undertake this task, I knew I would never be able to carry it out if the need ever arose. Still, I knew I had to push such thoughts out of my mind and just enjoy every minute we spent together (no matter how wearing those minutes might be!).

On one particular expedition with our bags on our backs, we came across a rather picturesque lake surrounded by quite a thick woodland. Steve decided that this would be a good place to pitch our tent, or possibly a little further along amongst the trees in case the wind got up during the night. While he rummaged in my bag for the food supplies we'd brought, I wandered off a few yards to where there was a wooden bridge spanning a weir. I couldn't resist walking onto it to watch the, rather fast flowing, water passing through, and dropping with quite a force, into the overflow river below. Fascinated by the speed of the flow I had just half turned to Steve to call him over,

"Hey Steve, you must come and look at this, the water is really gushing through ..."

But before I could finish what I was saying I felt the wooden bridge below my feet moving! The last thing I heard before I fell was Steve shouting to get off of there now, but it was too late. I'd not noticed how weak it was and my weight on the edge had been just enough to cause it to give way completely!

I felt myself hit the water below, straight away being dragged under by the terrific force of the water dropping from above me. Desperately I struggled to get to the surface, but the water was dropping from the weir too hard for me to fight against. I tried to swim but it was impossible. I was being tossed around like clothes in a washing machine and no matter how hard I tried I knew I was just being taken deeper the more I struggled! I knew it was useless to try to shout, and anyway I felt I could fight it no longer, and then ... nothing!!

Ow! I was aware of extraordinary pressure on my chest, and as I'm rolled onto my side, a firm voice shouting at me to, "Breath Mel, breath," and a firm thump on the back encouraging me to cough and splutter up the last of the river water. Whether from shock or cold I couldn't tell but at this point all I could do lay there and shiver. Steve immediately leapt into action, sitting me up, helping me out of my soaking wet jeans and top and putting his old camouflage jacket round my shoulders.

"Oh my God Mel, I really thought I'd lost you this time. What the hell did you think you were doing on there? Surely you could see it wasn't safe?"

His words combined with the shock that was setting in from what had happened, reduced me to an explosion of sobs and unrelenting tears. Steve's reaction to this was to pull me toward him and wrap me in his warm, strong arms, holding me close, making me begin to feel safe and calm the shaking that had taken over my whole body. That is how we remained for what felt like forever. I for one, had no urge to be released from the safe haven of his arms. When he did release his grip on me Steve asked if I was feeling ok. Without thought, all I could bring myself to say was,

"Yes thanks. What would I do without you? You're always there to rescue me."

"And I reckon I'll always need to be or no telling what would happen to you. Honestly Mel, you're not safe to let loose on your own!"

As he said this he flashed that same cheeky grin I'd become accustomed to, yet this time there was clearly a deeper warmth I'd not felt before. Going to the rucksacks he pulled out our two sleeping bags. He opened them up and suggested I should take off what clothes I was still wearing, lay on mine and put his thicker one on top to get warm while he hung them all on the trees to dry off. By the time he came back to me I had done as he suggested but was still cold. Without asking he lay down alongside me, once again wrapping me in his arms. Automatically I found myself wriggle as close as I could get and, laying my head on his chest, heaved a sigh of relief before going off into a comforting sleep.

When I came to, I've no idea how long after, just for a brief second all I could think of was the swirling water over my head, and the fear of knowing I was drowning. Just for that second I began to feel the panic of that moment set back in; but Steve was still there with his arms around me, and his soft, comforting voice reassuring me that I was safe now.

"It's ok Mel, I've got you. You're safe now my love."

And before I could process those last two words, 'my love', he put his lips on mine and kissed me with such tenderness. Feeling no resistance from me, I felt his hands travel gently round my body, starting a sensation the like of which I'd never felt before. I felt a matching surge sweep over Steve, but his was a surge so powerful it was as if something had been switched on inside his head, something almost primal, almost uncontrollable!

Should I stop him? Did I want to stop him? No was the answer to both questions. After all, wasn't that what I'd fantasised about for months … and anyway, somehow I doubt at this point I could stop him if I tried.

Wow! Was that worth waiting for! Chris had said Steve was worth the wait, but I didn't really think he'd meant in that way, but then being a man he wouldn't know. I thought as we rolled apart how I'd waited and hoped for so long, but had begun to believe that could never happen. And now it had ... I looked across at Steve and wondered what was going through his mind. Regret, disappointment? Had he been wishing I was Beth? If only he could be feeling the love and contentment that was surging round my mind and body right now.

He lay there for a few minutes with his beautiful brown eyes closed. They say that the eyes are the windows to the soul, but just for an instant I felt shut out of his. After what seemed like an age to me, but was actually no more than a few seconds, he opened them and looked straight at me,

"Are you ok Mel? I mean, I didn't hurt you did I?"

Hurt me! That was the last thing on my mind. All I wanted to know was did it really mean what I'd hoped it did, or was it meant for the ghost of Beth?

"No, of course not. But did you mean to do that, or was you thinking of someone else?"

I decided to stop this now if he'd not meant it. The look on his face told me the answer, and it was the one I'd hoped for.

"Oh no my love, did you really think that's what was on my mind? No, it's you I want now ... if you'll have me that is! After all, we both have a past; you with Jake and me with Beth. But they've both gone now and we're still here. I think our time for mourning is past now and they would want us to be happy again if we can."

"So you're really sure about it then? You really want to be with me?"

Taking my face in his big hands and looking me straight in the eyes, he said, with a laugh in his voice,

"Of course silly, I told you you're not safe on your own, so it looks like I'm stuck with you. Just don't go jumping in weirs too often!"

Chapter Seventeen.

We stayed there together in each other's arms for some time. Barely another word was spoken, none were necessary. The sun was out well, and we were risking frightening the wildlife, or any passing walkers that might come our way, just lying there, naked on the mossy bank by the lake. I had suggested the idea of a quick dip in the lake, but Steve had quite sensibly suggested that perhaps I'd had enough water for one day! A while later, and with some reluctance on my part, we decided we must get dressed as our clothes were near enough dry, and anyway we had both built up a good appetite by now by just cementing our new relationship with a repeat of that first event (just to convince me it had really happened)! We sat in silence, tucking into the cheese rolls we'd packed, and drinking coffee from the flask. I can't honestly remember ever feeling the sheer contentment that was surging through every pore of my body just then.

We'd not long packed the last of our gear away in our rucksacks when we felt a few spots of rain falling on our backs.

"Come on," Steve urged, "let's get going quickly. I reckon there's a storm coming our way."

My urge was to say that we'd already had our personal storm, but found he was already packed and heading for the shelter of the trees. I found myself running after him as usual, like a child after a parent! But although he seemed the same Steve, setting off as if leading his troops into battle, I knew I would never be the same, almost childlike, girl I'd always felt, trotting along and trying to impress him. I knew that somehow I would never again feel in doubt about his feelings for me, and that gave me a whole new confidence in the knowledge that I had no need to doubt myself again.

We hadn't gone far into the wooded area when the heavens opened and we knew we were in for the second good soaking of the day. Though the trees were well covered with leaves they offered little real shelter, and so all we could do was rush on in the hope of finding something or somewhere to give more. Just as I was about to admit defeat and tell him I couldn't go on at that speed much further, Steve stopped and peered through what seemed to be a hedgerow of some sort.

"Hey look, there's some sort of house over there, a pretty big one I reckon. Perhaps they'll invite us in before we get any wetter!"

Eager at the thought that we may be able to con our way into the warmth of solid walls rather than our little canvas tent tonight, I picked up my pace to match Steve's, but as we came within clear sight of the house in front of us, it was clear to see that this was obviously an empty, and pretty dilapidated place. I couldn't help thinking though that, in its time, it would have been a particularly impressive Victorian manor, but had no doubt stood empty for some time now. But still, it would put a roof over our bedraggled heads for the night. As we came up to it I stopped in my tracks,

"Hey Steve," he obviously wasn't looking at the same window as me just then, "Did you see that? I'm sure I saw a light flash in there somewhere. Perhaps there are people in there after all."

"Oh yes, and perhaps there are ghosts," he said with a laugh in his voice.

Walking up to the window he peeped in before coming back to where I stood watching.

"I think you might be right, it looks as if they've got squatters in. Tell you what, seeing as the front door is clearly boarded up, you stay here and I'll go round to find a back entrance. Give me five minutes to find the door then tap on the window. If there's anyone in they'll probably make a bolt for the back, so I'll be able to make our introductions without you getting hurt."

"Yes, but what about you? We don't know how many there are in there."

"Stop panicking. If there's more than I can handle I'll shout for your help!"

So saying off he went, totally unperturbed as usual, leaving me at the front of the house, trying to look brave but not even fooling myself! I gave him plenty of time to do a recce at the back and then followed orders to tap on the front window.

It seems he'd been right in the assumption that anyone inside would be distracted by my knocking, so much so that they hadn't expected to be confronted by Steve strolling in from behind and greeting them with a cheery, "Hi chaps, is there room for a couple more to come in out the rain?"

He signalled for me to come round to join him, a thing I was glad to do as the rain was getting much harder now. I was surprised to find there were four men and a woman all sitting around on the floor in what would have been a particularly ornate room going by the carvings around the ceiling trusses.

As I came toward them Steve put his hand out to encourage me forward. I felt a little conspicuous, but soon relaxed as they all introduced themselves one by one, shaking my hand as they did so. It seemed that the woman amongst them, Ellen, was with a chap called Bob. The other three men were Pete, Jez (I believe short for Jeremy) and Graham. Graham was clearly the older of the bunch, around fifty I estimated. Pete was probably mid forty's, with Bob and Ellen a little younger, then there was Jez who was probably around thirty. In spite of finding themselves invaded by us in such a way, once they realised we'd not come to evict them they seemed quite happy to share their accommodation with us.

"After all," Pete pointed out with a laugh, there's more than enough room for a few more. Just a shame it couldn't be made into a shelter for us poor buggers with nowhere else to go."

"We've just made coffee if you'd like some to take the chill off," Ellen said with a smile.

We were more than glad to take her up on her offer after taking off our wet jackets and boots. She came over with our drinks as we were doing this and said with a chuckle,

"That's good of you. I'd hate to see you make a mess on the clean floor."

That certainly broke the ice, and it wasn't long before I felt quite at ease in the company there. Of course, Steve always felt at ease in any company, but having spent a couple of years living rough and moving around, I knew right away that he'd fit right in. As it got darker Pete produced a lamp, the sort I suppose used for camping. Steve pointed out that we'd still got a couple of tins of soup left in our packs if there was enough to give everyone just a little, and Ellen produced a loaf of bread to bulk it out by way of a supper.

As it began to get dusk and the lamp barely lit the one room, Graham suggested we all turned in to keep warm.

"Me, Pete and Jez normally make ourselves comfy down here, but Bob and Ellen like to use the room at the top of the stairs for some reason," he said with a wink in their direction and a voice clearly implying the same as the wink! "So why don't you and your missus find a nice cosy room to yourselves up there?" All three men obviously understood the implication of what he'd said, and so did we of course, but neither of us said anything to contradict their assumptions about our relationship, as I believe Steve was as keen as I was to spend some quality time together with a roof over our heads. Until now, any time we've actually shared a room anywhere for a night, it has been strictly on the unspoken understanding that we each have our own space. Even when we've had very little space between us, there had always been at least the thickness of a sleeping bag in between. Now, although there was clearly no furniture in the house, we still had our two sleeping bags, and we could open them right out, lay on mine (cuddled up really tight!), and use Steve's much bigger one to cover ourselves up. I wouldn't have minded a repetition of our earlier pastime, but Steve thought we really should get some good rest,

"After your accident, I don't want you getting delayed shock," he insisted, "But that doesn't mean you can't get yourself in here alongside me ... 'Mrs Lockett'!"

He obviously could see the funny side of what the others had taken for granted. Throwing him a frown, I quickly stripped off (having noticed his lack of clothing as he'd climbed under the bag), and feeling strangely embarrassed, climbed in alongside him. The feeling that swept over me as he wrapped his arms around me and pulled me close, was sheer bliss, and following a particularly tender kiss, I was asleep almost immediately.

The next morning I woke up to find myself alone under the sleeping bag. For a second or two I felt totally confused … where was I, where was Steve and, oh hell? Where were my clothes? And then it all came back to me about the house and how we'd spent our first 'proper' night together, following that amazing moment on the bank of the lake yesterday. The memory of that event, and the way Steve seemed happy to let our new friends know we were more than just travelling companions, filled me with such a feeling of contentment, but then where was he now? Surely he wouldn't change his mind and walk away now. What should I do now if he had?

Right on cue of course, there he is at the door.

"Thought you'd like some hot water to freshen up lazy bones! The room next to ours is a bathroom. Can't hot up enough for a bath, but there's a kettle waiting there for you if you care to use it. I suggest you wrap your bag round you mind you. The landings in full view of where the other chaps are!"

Had I not been already aware of the others in the house I think I may have tried to lure him back to prove to me that yesterday hadn't been a fluke, but I knew that must wait, I must be patient. As it was I did as I was bid and was quite surprised by what was at one time, a particularly lavish bathroom. Obviously somewhat dilapidated like the rest of the house, it made me feel that whoever had lived here before must have really put such love into it. It did seem so sad to think of it falling into the condition we now saw before us. Having washed, dressed, and joined everybody downstairs, I couldn't help expressing this view.

"You're quite right young lady," said Graham, "It's a crime to leave it to rot. Me and Pete have both said the same. I was a carpenter till I ended up like this, and I reckon that if I had the tools there's a lot could be done to bring the old place up to scratch. Ain't that right Pete?"

"Were you a carpenter too," I asked.

"No Mel, but I spent nearly twenty years in the building trade. Got certificates to prove it for all the good they've done when the firm gone bust and there's no work about."

Just then Bob strolled into the room with a box in his arms,

"You got that pan boiling Ellen?"

To my surprise the box was half full of eggs! Remembering how, on our adventure last year, Steve had 'acquired eggs from a farmer's coop as we passed by, I rather assumed these came from a similar source. But, on enquiring cautiously, I was told that no, they were, as Bob said, 'legit'. Apparently Bob and Ellen had built up a reasonable little smallholding not too far from the nearby town, but it had been compulsorily purchased to make room for a new road to cut through the otherwise quiet countryside! It seems that when they left they had nowhere to go where they were able to take more than, at the very least, their half a dozen hens and so after selling the rest of the livestock, they had packed these into a homemade coop on wheels made by Bob, and gone on the road, living rough in the hope of finding somewhere they might eventually be able to afford. Unfortunately this never happened and the measly amount they had been paid as compensation for their property was soon used up.

Since finding this squat they had been able to make up a pen round the back of the house to give the hens room to roam, therefore providing us all with a good hearty breakfast! As we sat around tucking eagerly into these, this allowed us chance to familiarise ourselves with the group properly. Now we knew that Graham was a skilled carpenter who had taken time off work suffering with depression when his wife died of cancer, and when he tried to return it seems that neither his previous employers nor any others would take him on. As he told us,

"They only want young chaps who will work for less … even if they don't have the skills to work with."

We'd already learnt about Bob and Ellen's background, and felt the system had driven them into living like gypsies, travelling round, dragging their chicken coop behind them! Pete's story again echoed that of Graham. Though in his case his wife had divorced him, taking his two kids with her and her new boyfriend. He had carried on slogging away even then, until the firm he worked for had combined with another, meaning half the workers were made redundant. Even though he was well qualified as a builder, so far he'd not had any luck finding employment.

I must admit that it was young Jez who rather tugged at my heartstrings. It seems he had gone less than half way through a sports science degree course not far away at Coventry University, then had suffered some sort of breakdown brought on, so I gather, partly by his parents splitting up, and partly due purely to the stress of what was expected of him. After all, I thought, we all need support, and I was living proof of that. Without the support I'd had from Steve last year there is absolutely no way I'd ever have survived what was thrown at me. As a consequence poor Jez had only managed less than half of the course before dropping out and joining the hundreds of others living rough on the streets of this country.

Having sat over breakfast learning all about the circumstances behind everybody else's demise, Bob looked across the room at us and asked outright, what had brought us to live this way? I was about to assure him that it was a bit different for us; that we could have a home if we wanted but had decided not to settle down just yet. But before I had chance to do this Steve stepped in quickly to fill in the details they were after. In his usual quick thinking way he spun them a yarn, admittedly with bits of the truth amongst it, about how he'd come out of the army (no mention of what regiment), met me, but not found anywhere we could settle yet! Well, I suppose to a point he'd told the truth. He just hadn't said we could have afforded to buy anywhere to live (possibly even this place at a push perhaps!), but that we just didn't want to be tied down just yet. He was also careful to do as they had and only use our Christian names. It seems this was the preferred way at this stage of a relationship amongst homeless folks.

I believe he felt like me that it was poor young Jez who was most lost in this sort of world. He didn't have the life experience to cope with a situation so alien to the hopes and dreams he'd had in mind. His parents seem to have turned their backs on him when he dropped out, both being too taken up with their own situations to give him the support he needed to keep going. Now it seemed he had given up any attempt to stay in touch, feeling as he did, a complete failure. As Steve said to me later when we were alone, the situation Jez was in now was just the sort which could push him right over the edge. As he said, he had seen young lads come into the army as recruits in a similar state of mind and, though most had accepted the disciplined life and training which it took to pull them out of the mire they were in, he had also seen a few who came too late to help. When I asked what had happened to them, he just shook his head and looked away. I never asked again.

Chapter Eighteen.

Over the course of the next week, Steve and I found ourselves in the thick of a true feeling of camaraderie within this little group, so much so that we decided to hang around for a bit. We mentioned to them about having old Annie van parked in a village close by, and would like to have brought her up and parked in the grounds, but being aware that we were actually all trespassing, decided not to do so.

"You must be flush to have one of those and pay to keep it parked there for long," commented Pete one evening.

Steve was quick to explain how he'd come across it on its way to a scrap yard and worked on it himself. As for the site fees, he managed to convince them he did a few jobs for the manager in return for parking in a corner away from the visibility of the paying customers! Actually, this was pretty close to the truth, as they certainly were not keen to spoil an otherwise beautiful site with our old girl. Of course, on the odd nights when we did go back to sleep in the van, we were more than happy to have a little secluded corner all to ourselves anyway. Any nights spent as we did now, up close together with Steve's bag on top for warmth, was sheer bliss to me but, thanks to my Mum's handiwork, those spent in Annie gave the added comfort of a good padded mattress rather than a hard floor. In fact I did find myself commenting to Ellen on one occasion that it was such a shame there was no furniture in the house.

"Oh, but there is. Whoever lived here had some really good stuff, but what was left behind is packed up in that old outbuilding round the back. We had a look a while ago. I'd love to get it out and bring it back where it should be before the damp or woodworm gets to it, but Bob don't reckon we should take liberties."

I went with her to look at what she'd found and was astonished at what she showed me that morning. Spread through the length of what I guessed was at one time, the stables at the back of the house, there was all manner of beautiful wooden furniture, much of it with carved decoration, most likely handmade especially for the house. As we were looking at it Graham came along.

"Beautiful ain't it? Shame to let it sit there to rot. It wouldn't take long to knock it into shape, that's if I had a descent set of tools of course."

Just then Steve came back from his usual morning jog. He'd kept that up, though not always forcing me to keep him company since my accident. Coming across the yard to see what the excitement was about, he looked in the door with sheer amazement at the sight before him.

"Hell, that looks some special stuff. I wonder why it wasn't left inside? I suppose they'll auction it off before they sell the house."

"From what we've heard they can't sell the house for a time; something about the old folks who lived here not leaving a will, bony vista, or some such thing they say," Pete said.

"Oh, you mean 'bona vacantia'? That's a law that means if the owner dies without leaving a will the property is in the hands of the crown for thirty years before it can be sold or passed on to anyone," Steve explained.

"Yes, that sounds like it. That's probably the only reason no one has kicked us out sooner, though there was a geezer came round a while ago telling us he's gonna get the place soon, then he's gonna demolish it and put blocks of flats on the site to make some cash!"

I looked round at this beautiful example of Victorian architecture we'd been sharing now for the last week. Somehow the thought of some money grabbing person coming in and bulldozing it to the ground seemed almost a criminal act. When I asked what right he'd thought he'd have to get his hands on the place, Graham said that he'd claimed to be the grandson of the family, and therefore entitled to claim it as his inheritance.

"Ah I see, but even so, if no will has been found he still has to wait till the thirty years are up the same as anyone else."

As he said that I could see Steve's mind already ticking over on some plan or other, but chose not to question him until we were alone. As soon as we'd had our usual breakfast courtesy of Bob and Ellen's hens, he told them all that we had decided to go and try our luck in Coventry. Just what he had in mind by that I had no idea, but I do know he wasn't really intending on busking, begging for charity, or anything most homeless folk would have in mind! As we made our way back to where we'd left our van, I decided that this was my chance to tackle him about it.

"Ok, I can tell you've got something going on inside that head of yours. Just what is it?"

He stopped and looked round at me, barely able to contain his words to get them over to me in a way which made much sense at first, so excited was he with what he wanted me to take in.

"Just think of this for an idea Mel; suppose we could put a bid in for the place before he got chance to demolish it?" he obviously assumed I knew what he was thinking, but all I could think of was that, as much as I liked it, I couldn't see we needed such a massive house just for us two! He stopped and turned toward me and, trying not to show impatience in his voice, went on to explain what was in his mind,

185

"Just think, if we could buy it we could help so many like those there now. For instance, take Graham, a skilled carpenter, Pete, a qualified builder, and Bob with experience in working with the land and livestock. Why are they all there? Because they're out of work; and why can't they find work?" I shrugged my shoulders and must have looked more than a little puzzled. He heaved a sigh and went on,

"Well you see Mel, the main reason most homeless folks end up living rough is because they can't get jobs. And why can't they get jobs?" he didn't wait for me to answer that question, "Because no one will employ you if you have no permanent address."

Ok, I think I was following what he had just said, but must still have had that rather bemused expression on my face at that point.

"So ... so what you're suggesting is that we should lash out a fortune to set it up as a homeless refuge? Isn't that a bit extravagant, even for you?" dodging a swift blow across the top of my head as I did so!

"Not exactly, but you've got to admit it would be a shame to flatten a place like that. I know we've only been there about a week, but somehow I already feel quite attached to the old place. No, what I had in mind was a sort of hostel cum training centre. All the time there are experienced people like those there now they could set to renovating the house and grounds. Then, as others, especially youngsters like Jez, come along, we can take them in. Graham, Pete and Bob can train them up in the basic trades. Then I reckon they could go to college once a week or whatever to get whatever qualifications they need to apply for jobs."

He waited for me to catch up with all this before continuing,

"By then, with learning on the job as it were, they will have helped convert those outbuildings into small apartments, and so will have an address which they can use when they apply for work! Well, what do you think Mel? Surely it's worth a go if it helps some of the poor buggers get their lives back on track."

I must admit that this had taken me by surprise, but at the same time I did (rather cautiously) see it just might work. After having spent most of last year living rough with Steve, although he had always made me feel safe, that whole period of not having a place of my own to go back to at nights, or a way to guarantee food the next day, certainly gave me a whole new perspective on life. But it was a risk, a big risk. If we did find a way to do this it would certainly not be cheap. Yes, we did have a pretty good income behind us both, Steve with the good army pay out plus the inheritance his father had left him, and me with the money I'd got from the sale of Jake's house. Then of course there was a regular, steady income which Jake's brother Andy was paying us as sleeping partners to the business (still hoping we just might go back and help him run it!), but my worry was, where would we be if all of Steve's plans came to nothing and we lost the lot! In spite of all this, I couldn't help feeling that one day, though we'd not talked about it, it was obvious that we might want to settle down, and where better than this beautiful house, made even better by his ideas to build up a business doing something close to his heart. After the time he's had over the last few years it was clear he would never settle to just your average humdrum, day to day existence that most are happy to settle for, he'd always need more in his life, more of a challenge. With some trepidation I asked,

"So what are we doing in Coventry then?"

"Well, the first thing we need to do is find out who the agents are who would be dealing with the sale when the time comes. They should be able to tell us how long it'll be before it can be sold. If this other chap who reckons on claiming it would still need to wait, then that gives us time to work on a plan. It sounds as if he's got no particular attachment to the place, even if he does turn out to be related to the deceased owners, so he just might sell to us anyway. Of course he might want too much for it, but might be worth a try. Once we've got all the info we could start to work on a plan."

I must have been looking more than a little worried as he looked round at me as I have to admit that I did lack his confidence at this point.

"Do you really think they'll give us permission for what we have in mind? After all, it's not exactly the usual use for such a place as that."

"Why not? After all, there's not many folks these days wanting to actually live in somewhere like that. It would need too much renovation unless it was for a hotel, conference centre or something."

And once again I could tell he'd thought of something else,

"Hey, that's another idea. When we get going and have a good part of the house and grounds sorted, we could hire it out for weddings and the like!"

Now he was getting a bit too enthusiastic for my liking,

"Now, steady on there. Just keep that brain in check for goodness sake, you're getting way ahead. We don't even know if we can get our hands on the place yet, let alone whether we can make all those ideas of yours work. You seem so sure, but suppose they don't?"

"Well Mel, stop being so negative and remember our family motto … where there's a will!"

I couldn't help picking up on the expression, 'family motto'. The very thought of him even considering us to be family in any way gave me a warm glow inside. All I could say in answer to this though was that I just hoped his will was strong enough to find a way on this occasion! I couldn't help thinking we were heading for a rough ride ahead.

We had been living for the greater part of the last week in our assorted rough clothes to fit in with the company we were living with at that point, though still managing to give a bit of a rinse out to bits from time to time. Of course this would have been made easier if there had been hot water in the property, but Ellen had found some large pans and, with Bob's help, she'd managed since their arrival to light up the big old range in the kitchen. This enabled everyone to scrub out the worst of the dirt from their 'every-day' clothes. I soon learnt from Steve that this was what, given the opportunity, homeless folk try to do, keeping a set of their better (or at least tidier) things by. As he explained,

"It's bloody hard trying to keep any semblance of dignity with no way of keeping yourself looking half descent. That's when people look down their noses at you and call you scum. When you think of it, that's just for the price of a trip to a launderette. Then of course, if they turn up to look for work in rough looking clothes, that's another reason they don't get a look in."

Of course he was right, it was obvious when he explained it to me like that, and I have to own up to a feeling of guilt for the times I have probably been guilty of looking at rough sleepers and thought they could at least attempt to smarten up a bit. Of course, in all the time I'd lived rough with Steve last year, I can't say I'd ever noticed him to be like that but, knowing him as I do now, I know I can put that down to his army training, and that he would always find a way to overcome such problems.

Even so, I was quite pleased when we got back to the van to be told we must change into our tidy clothes (the ones we kept in the van), as we needed to visit the agents first. He quite rightly suggested that we'd not make a good impression turning up at their office like a couple of tramps!

It was always a bit of a squash for both of us changing at the same time in Annie, so Steve 'kindly' said to carry on, and sat in the front seat watching me dress.

"Well ... you could go outside and give a lady a bit of privacy," I suggested, but all I got by way of an answer was, "A lady ... I can't see a lady, all I can see is you, and I rather like what I'm seeing."

I picked my old jeans up and threw them at him, in response to which he stood up and took off his T shirt coming toward me as he did so. Oh my God, I wish he wouldn't do that. He must know the effect seeing his muscly torso has on me!

"NO! We haven't got time for that. You said yourself, we need to get tidy and go to Coventry."

"We've always got time. Besides, Coventry isn't so far away so we don't need to rush. After all, it was you who started it by throwing your smelly old jeans at me, so you didn't really expect me not to react in some way or other surely?"

Oh well, I suppose I could 'force' myself if he's that determined. I'd like to say I was stronger willed than that, but I always was a soft touch; what more can I say ... yet again I gave in to his demands (or was it just a request, who cares!).

Chapter Nineteen.

By the time we arrived on the outskirts of Coventry it was well into the morning, but we quickly managed to park and enquire from a nearby café about where to find the agents, Sanderson & Co. We headed straight there, Steve full of his usual optimism, but me a little less so. I must admit to still feeling somewhat overwhelmed with his plan even though in my heart I felt it was a good one. As we entered the office a young receptionist looked up and smiled,

"Good morning Sir and Madam, can I help you?"

Steve flashed his best smile at her and replied,

"Well I do hope so young lady," I could see a blush rising uncontrollably in her cheeks, "I wonder if you can tell me who is responsible for the old derelict manor ten miles or so south of here?"

"Oh, you mean Lansdown Grange? Yes, it is Sanderson & Co. who are the agents, actually Mr Sanderson himself, but I'm afraid that nothing can be done with it for a while yet. Its previous owner died intestate and..."

Steve politely interrupted her mid-sentence,

"I know that it is in the hands of the crown until thirty years are up. Even so, could I please have just a few minutes of Mr Sanderson's valuble time?"

The poor girl quite obviously felt torn between loyalty to her employer and realising that this originally charming, yet now just a touch more demanding man standing firm in front of her desk, had no intention of leaving until he'd achieved his aim. She heaved an unmissable sigh of defeat before saying,

"I'll go and see if he has a few moments, but I know he has another client to see in a while, so it would only be very brief."

Steve thanked her with a smile on his face which would guarantee her cooperation, and pretended he didn't notice the expression on my face as he did so. It was not long before we found ourselves ushered into an office to be introduced to the short, rotund figure of Mr Sanderson. I did wonder for a brief second just what names we would be using this time, but surprisingly, Steve introduced us by our correct ones this time. On reflection I could see that this would be necessary if there was the slightest chance of achieving Steve's aim. We were invited to take seats on the far side of the desk before being asked our business.

Though he listened with interest to Steve's inquiry about any possibility of being able to put in a bid for Lansdown Grange, he did look more than a little puzzled as to what we would do with it. I must say that I quite expected Steve to make up one of his fantasy stories, but to my surprise he explained his plan with great clarity and enthusiasm, so much that Mr Sanderson was quite obviously suitably impressed. He could tell that this was a well thought out plan, not just some mad scheme plucked out of the air.

"Well Mr Lockett, I can see you've put much thought into your idea. I must applaud you for your willingness to undertake a plan like this for the benefit of quite a number of the less fortunate in these parts. There's certainly no shortage of such around our bigger cities. I really wish I could take you up on your offer, but there are a couple of problems to overcome before we could consider this."

I thought that sounded very much like a no. Even though he did seem interested I felt he was about to reel out all sorts of reasons to turn us down. But then he went on to explain,

"You see, the property is still covered by a rule which says that it can't be sold …"

"Yes, yes, I know about bona vacantia, it has to be kept for thirty years unless a will is produced?" Steve intervened a little impatiently, "so how much longer is it before the time elapses on this place?"

Mr Sanderson explained that there was just a matter of about six months, and then, if there still was no will forthcoming, it could be put on the market. Even so, he went on to tell us that if that were the case, there was also the matter of a gentleman who claims to be a descendant of the Lansdown family, but had yet to provide proof of this. It seemed that, as far as anyone knew, the only son had been banished by his parents and had no children. Steve asked if this was the same chap who was threatening to demolish the house and put up flats on the site. Though surprised Steve had heard about this he confirmed that this was so.

Steve seemed content that he had all the information he needed other than to ask for his name (totally ignoring the fact that it would need to be more my money than his!), to be registered as an interested party when the time comes, and to request to be informed via his solicitor, Mr T Lockett (brother Tom), leaving the details of his office in Royal Leamington Spa with Mr Sanderson. With a polite thank you and a handshake, Steve seemed content we could do no more at that point and so we left, thanking the secretary as we passed through the reception.

"So what next? Where do we go from here?" I asked Steve.

"I need to think about that, I'm not too sure to be honest, but let's grab a coffee and mull it over. Give us chance to take a look around while we're here too. Another thing, we should get some supplies for everyone while we're here, but mustn't make it too obvious, so need to take things out of the wrappings or get some out-of-date stuff so they don't think we're to flush."

I wouldn't have been surprised at this point to find him suggest changing back into our old gear and going begging on the streets, but even he wouldn't sink quite that low. Anyway, as he said, that would be making a mockery of those with no choice. Of course, Steve being Steve, went to order coffee while I found a seat for us, but when he came back with three coffees and three rather large, hot sausage rolls, I was somewhat surprised, but only for a moment. He put two of each on the table and disappeared outside for a minute. It didn't take me a second to realise what he was doing with the third one. Outside here I had noticed a chap sitting, looking a little forlorn, on a sleeping bag with a little dog alongside. He was obviously glad to accept what Steve offered him, and I couldn't help smiling as I saw him sharing the sausage roll with his little companion.

"There's another candidate for our scheme. He's an out of work plumber. All we'd need now would be an electrician and we'd have a pretty strong team."

"Now, now Steve, don't go getting ahead of yourself. You do realise there's a good chance you won't get the place don't you?"

Reluctantly he had to admit that there was that possibility, but I could tell this didn't dampen his enthusiasm. As we headed back, complete with supplies, to the van, I asked him what would be our next move.

"Think we should go and pay that visit to Tom and Margaret that we promised him. It would be good to see him again, and we can fill him in on developments in regard to the house. It's handy having a solicitor in the family … won't cost a fortune to get help!"

He obviously got great amusement out of that idea, but then as he said, he had done his share for both brothers as they were growing up, so it wasn't asking too much to ask a little in return!

Once back at the van we changed back into our old gear (without a repeat of the earlier hold up!), and headed back to what we now knew as Lansdown Grange where we were warmly greeted by a small, grateful, group of people, all wondering just how we'd managed to acquire such a bounty of food to stock up the supplies. Somehow they didn't seem so surprised at Steve's explanation of how he'd conned a couple of shops out of a few things coming to the end of their shelf life. Even they were beginning to catch on to Steve's many talents!

We stayed there for the night and, though not telling them anything of Steve's plans, did tell them that we would be going off to visit family for a few days, but would be back.

"That'll be good to see you both again, so don't forget where we are, will you," Graham remarked.

It seemed this view was shared by them all, in particular young Jez who, in the last few days, had been persuaded by Steve to join him (sometimes us) on his morning jogs. Of course this had really gone down well with Steve as he could tell by this that the lad had the potential to turn his life around, given the right inspiration. I couldn't help thinking I'd seen this happen before in the case of our young friend Josh who, having found himself on the streets, with a dose of encouragement from Steve had turned his life around completely.

Steve stirred up their curiosity by suggesting to them that if they stayed till we came back he might just have something of interest to tell them. Personally I had my doubts about him telling them what he was thinking, certainly as I could see there could be so many things which could go wrong with his plans, but then Steve is a bit like a moving train … when he gets an idea in his head it's almost impossible to stop him!

"Don't worry on that score," he assured them, "You won't get rid of us that easily. No, just an idea I'm working on that's all. Might come to nothing but I'll give it my best shot before I say anything."

Just as he was turning to leave he turned to Bob and Ellen, even taking me by surprise by saying,

"By the way you two, you know there's an allotment down the Coventry Road a way," Bob obviously knew where he meant, "That's where we stopped on our way back yesterday to see if anyone had any spare veg, that's where those came from we ate last night. If you go along there sometime and look out for an old chap with a beard, he says he'll give you some more in return for a bit of work on his patch."

Well, I knew he'd stopped and scrounged a few spuds and carrots, but he hadn't thought to tell me this! Once again, typical of the man! I still can't help thinking that, as close as we'd become by this time, sometimes, in some ways, he still feels that bit distant, and I think that's how he'll remain. Whether this is to do with the time he'd spent alone, in which case I just hoped he didn't feel I'd invaded his space, or whether it was to do with his service life, I'll probably not know. Yet still there seems to have been a part of that bit of his life I feel he'll keep locked away. Perhaps to do with the photo with him in a different uniform, though I could see no reason to think that. Well, who knows!

Perhaps one day we might visit Chris and I'll get chance to ask what he knows about this. Of course, I remembered at this stage that he had given me his number when we were there, in the hope I could persuade Steve to stay in touch occasionally. Maybe, I thought, one day I should have a chat with him, when Steve isn't around of course!

Before I barely had chance to say my goodbyes we were back at the van, once more changing into our best 'visiting' clothes. This time Steve seemed keen to get on the road as soon as we could, seemingly to see what information Tom might be able to offer him. I was quite happy to see Tom again having already met him at Mrs Lockett's house, but I must admit to feeling just a little anxious about meeting his wife, Margaret, for the first time. As it happened I shouldn't have worried on that score. It was her who came to the door when we arrived, and I guessed at first glance, that she was not much difference in age to me. She ushered us into the living room (a perfectly neat, clean room with well-polished furniture and expensive ornaments!), but went out of her way to make us feel at home. The children were apparently out playing with friends, but she was pleased to show me a family photo of the four of them together. The two girls did look very sweet, but I couldn't help wondering if that was just for the photo! Knowing how Jenny and I always looked so angelic on photos, yet often fought like tigers when the camera wasn't on us, I did have my doubts.

Being a Saturday Steve had known that Tom would be there, and was obviously eager to quiz him about his ideas. He explained about having found a large house which was in a rather sorry state from not being lived in for many years. He then went on to explain just what he would like to do with it.

"What on earth makes you think of doing something like that? I could understand if you'd decided to settle down there yourself, but why on earth would you want to fill it with a bunch of old tramps?"

I could see how hard Steve was trying to keep his temper under control when Tom said that! Even so, he just looked him straight in the eye and said,

"Because I was one myself until I met Mel last year. You've always had life cushy, you've no idea what it's like to live on the streets, not knowing where your next meal is coming from, or where to get in out the rain and the cold. Ok, I could cope, but many are out there through no fault of their own, and with no means of getting back to normal society."

I could see poor Tom felt well and truly put in his place by his brother. Though they'd been apart for some time it was clear to see the respect he had for Steve.

"I don't want to just use this as a hobby. I believe there are grants we could apply for to help with the costs and, as long as we can get planning permission or whatever we need, the idea is to build it up gradually and let it pay for itself as it gets going."

He told Tom about having a builder and carpenter there already, and about Bob and Ellen with the experience to set up a small market garden cum farm. Telling him about young Jez (with very little skills so far!), he explained the idea of also working with him and any who came along to build up their self-confidence by working on their fitness levels, as he had done with his army recruits. This, if nothing else, certainly drew a chuckle from Tom!

"Ok; so just what is it you want from me then? I take it there is something or you wouldn't have told me all that."

"Well you see, I know the owners died intestate. It seems there's just six months to go before anything can be done with it." Tom nodded agreement, "Well you see, Mel and I have a pretty solid lump sum in the bank (seemingly forgetting two thirds belonged to me!), and a hefty amount monthly from my army pension (which was actually not a pension, more just a claim to cover for his PTSD!) and our shares in a business."

"Ok, so what's your problem, how can I help?" Tom asked.

"There is just one problem we've found. Apparently there's a bloke hanging around, claiming to be a descendant of the family. He reckons he just wants to bulldoze the place and put up flats or something. What do you think his chances are of getting it? Or failing that, if he does, do you reckon we'd stand a chance to buy it off him?"

"Well, if you're right and there's no will. He can't do anything either until the time is up. Of course, if then he did manage to convince them he should inherit, then he could ask what he liked for it. Might be cheaper to buy a plot of land somewhere and start from scratch."

I could see the disappointment in Steve's face. Somehow, over the time we've spent there, I could see he'd formed a sort of attachment to the old place, and I believe that went for me as well. Even so, Tom said he would be happy to help in any way he could, even going so far as to offer to negotiate with this chap should the opportunity arise.

About then we were interrupted by the two girls, Sandra and Tina, rushing in through the door in a particularly boisterous way that girls have when they have disagreements! Yes, I thought, just how Jenny and I were at that age. Not the sweet, quiet, angels on the photo at all. None the less they both ground to a sudden halt finding themselves confronted with what to them must have been the rather imposing figure of their long lost uncle Steve!

"Well hello girls, do you know I could hear you coming a mile away. Think your poor Mum must get earache if that's how you treat her."

Their faces reddened slightly as they turned as one and said,

"Sorry Mum," to a poor, slightly embarrassed Margaret who had been trying to quieten them down without success.

It rather amused me a while later to see them both vying for Uncle Steve's attention, keen to show off the certificates gained for swimming. Somehow I never thought of him as being so good with children!

After lunch, and not so long before we were about to leave, Tom thought to ask a question that had not arisen before. He asked us where about this house was. When Steve told him this he was particularly intrigued to know what it was called? When he heard the name, Lansdown Grange, he said it sounded familiar, though he couldn't think just why. As he said, though not so very distant from where he lived, he had certainly never been past anywhere remotely like the place we'd described to him.

"Do you know, I reckon Mum would know even if I don't? I'm sure she told us once that our Grandfather was gardener to some posh family, and Nan worked as their housekeeper."

Steve wasn't too convinced about any connection though. As he pointed out, their mother lived a fair way off in Cambridgeshire.

"Yes, she does now. But don't you remember when we were kids Dad moved us twice because of his work?"

Tom was quick to suggest that the next time we went to visit their mother Steve should ask to get a large box from the top shelf in a cupboard in the attic. It seems he thought there were quite a few photo albums in there.

"I might just do that. Come to think of it I can't say I have ever seen a photo of either of our grandparents, and certainly had no idea where they came from," and straight away I knew what he was about to suggest!

"Perhaps it's time we went to visit Mum again, I think she'd like that."

Chapter Twenty.

As we set off heading for the Lockett household I took Steve's suggestion to phone on ahead to warn his mother we were on our way. Though we'd been keeping in touch from time to time on our travels, the thought of Steve actually coming back in person was obviously something she needed to see to believe! After his previous long absence I knew she was worried that he might do yet another disappearing act! I did tell him this, but he just laughed, so I threw him a dirty look and told him,

"Just you wait. Perhaps, if you ever get to be a father that is, you'll know what it must be like to lose a child."

Oh hell ... did I really say that? Please God don't let me bring back his awful guilt by being so careless with my choice of words! I looked at him again, trying to judge his expression, but for that moment it was a total blank. We were coming to a layby and I was more than a little unnerved as he pulled in and switched off the engine. Now what?

For a second or two he just stared out of the window. Then he turned to me, looking me straight in the eye, and took me quite by surprise with his next remark,

"What made you say that? Are you trying to tell me something?"

"No ... well I ... I didn't mean ..." the words wouldn't come, they just were not there. I'd well and truly blown it this time. I barely dared to look him in the eyes. I turned my face down toward my feet, but he put his hand under my chin and raised it up to look into those big brown eyes of his.

It was only then that I saw, not the rage I thought was building up, but a look of what I could only describe as amusement! Why? I was so sure I'd upset him with my thoughtlessness, yet all he said now was,

"Well ... are you, trying to tell me something I mean? Are you saying you're pregnant?"

Talking of things coming out of the blue! That most certainly wasn't what I thought he'd taken my remark to mean!

"Hell no! Is that really what you thought I meant? You know as well as me we've been pretty careful on that score. Now are we going to your Mum's or not?"

Apart from the worry that I'd upset him, followed by his interpretation of my words, I felt that the sooner we ended this conversation the better. Even so, as we trundled off down the road, I couldn't help churning over in my mind how he would have reacted if I had been pregnant? After what had happened to little Sean I couldn't imagine him being ready to replace him, and yet he hadn't reacted in the way I expected. Perhaps this was a sign that he was beginning to come to terms with his loss. Even so, I somehow felt it was my responsibility to ensure he wasn't put in this position, certainly if I had any hope of staying with him. To this end I must be sure to see that all necessary precautions were taken.

I had to drag my mind from my thoughts about then as we were just heading into the village where Mrs Lockett lived. I had intended offering to drive part of the way but it really hadn't seemed as far as I'd assumed it might be. As I expected, there she was, watching from the window to see us pull up on the drive, and before we could barely climb out of Annie she was at the front door to greet us. I must admit to feeling that now I had truly been accepted as one of her family, receiving almost as warm a hug as Steve! Obviously, though he was the number one son, I was credited with bringing him back to her. When I thought back to the love he received from my Mum for returning me to her safely, the irony of my careless remark to him earlier was certainly not lost. Both thought their child was lost, both owed their return to another.

Steve wasted no time in telling her how we had come across a place he had decided to convert into a place for the homeless in the area to help get them back on their feet. Somehow I could tell straight away that this, to her, sounded rather a drastic, possibly even reckless, plan. Even so, she sat quietly and listened until he finished his explanation before saying anything, probably not wanting to say anything which might upset him in any way.

When she did speak her first question was the practical one of how he planned to fund this. Once again, as he had with Tom though perhaps with a little more patience, he explained about the plan to apply for grants, and anyway we had a good enough income to cover a fair amount to get started.

"I can see you've given this a good deal of thought dear, but are you sure it's safe, taking in these people off the streets I mean? I must say I've often seen them on the streets in Cambridge and wondered why they don't look for jobs, or at the very least clean themselves up a bit."

Oh no, if this had been anyone but his Mum I know Steve would have hit the roof! I watched him as he stood up and strode across the room with his fists clenched and, after standing with his back to us for a few seconds, turned and walked back to sit alongside of her on the sofa. Taking her hands in his he explained,

"But Mum, that was me until last year. I slept anywhere I could … often in shop doorways. I tried to keep clean, but it's not easy with no facilities to do so. More often than not I barely managed to get enough food to keep the hunger off! I'm sorry to say Mum but you're just another one who doesn't really understand what forces people into that lifestyle, or what it's like to live like that with folk looking down their noses at you and assuming you've chosen to be like it. Believe me Mum, most have no choice. They're driven into it by circumstances they have no control over."

I could see Mrs Lockett was bitterly regretting her remark, but Steve was on a roll and I knew he wouldn't stop until he'd managed to explain just what he meant,

"You see Mum, the problem is that people just see with their eyes, not with their minds. It's so easy to see a dirty, scruffy down-and-out in a shop doorway and assume he's too lazy to get a job and earn a living. The fact is that the majority did have both jobs and homes. But so many find they lose their jobs, then they can't afford to pay rent for their homes. Then what's left? A sleeping bag in a shop doorway and, if they're lucky, the occasional hand-out. If not, very often, a good kicking!"

Completely taken aback by his words, Mrs Lockett took hold of Steve's big hands in her small ones, and looking at him through slightly tearful eyes said,

"Oh my God dear, that's awful. I'd never thought of it like that, and I never will again now. Is that really what you went through when you were away my love?"

211

I could tell he regretted his rant, but I knew how strongly he felt about this subject. He put his arm around her shoulders and said in a kindly manner,

"No Mum, I'm sorry. I shouldn't have upset you like that. No, you can rest assured that I never got to that stage … and anyway, you must know me well enough to know that if anyone kicked me I would have kicked them back!"

This brought a smile to her face. She obviously did know him that well. He told her about the people we were 'sharing' the house with right now, and explained the circumstances which had brought each of them to be homeless. As he told her, they all were desperate to get their lives back on track, and it had been this, added to the fact that they had all met up whilst squatting in this deserted house, that had given him the idea.

"So where exactly is this house," she asked.

Steve was eager to explain to her. Without barely stopping to take a breath he went on to say,

"Tom tells me our grandparents used to work at some big house near those parts. He said he thought there's a photo of it in an album in the attic, is that right?"

Now, he was too eager to notice the sudden and brief flash of fear on his mother's face, but I definitely did. Though I had no idea why this was, just for that instant I could most certainly pick up different vibes coming from her. She hesitated almost unperceivably before asking him,

"Did you say the house is deserted? What happened to the owners?"

"It seems the old folk who owned it have both passed away some years ago, and it's just standing there empty, badly in need of much attention. You should see it Mum, it must have been a grand place in its time, and I'd love to get it back to that again one day."

Without waiting for her to say yes or no he was away up the stairs to rummage in the attic for the albums! Before many minutes were up he came down carrying a large, rather dusty looking box full of them. Mrs Lockett was quick to get a duster to prevent dust going on the furniture, but just as soon as she had he couldn't wait to dive straight in like a kid at Christmas!

"Why on earth didn't I know you had so many albums tucked away Mum? I don't remember you ever showing us photos of our grandparents. Surely there must be some amongst this lot?"

"Oh yes dear, surely I must have shown them to you at some time? Your Grandad was a lovely man. He was so gentle, or that was until anyone upset him at least, and then … well, put it like this, I believe that's where you got your temper from if you don't mind me saying!"

Trying his best to look hurt by her last remark he replied,

"Me, a temper. What do you mean Mother? I'm as gentle as a pussy cat, aren't I Mel?"

I tried to keep a straight face, but just couldn't. I couldn't help thinking how I'd once told Paul that he was 'as gentle as a pussy cat' with my parents. Must be the effect mothers have on him; even so, his Mum clearly knew just what he could be like if pushed. Strangely, in some way, this gave me a warm feeling toward him, or should I say an even warmer feeling?

She soon picked out a photo of a rather tall, stockily built man with a beard. Not unlike Steve, I thought. Standing next to him was a neat and rather prim looking lady with her hair in a tight bun on the back of her head. There was a huge collection of assorted family photos spread over a dozen or so albums. Steve was fascinated sorting through them, and was particularly thrilled to find one showing his parents wedding and others with him as a small boy with his father. It was clear the attachment he had for Peter Lockett, though he was aware from an early age that Peter had adopted him, and was not actually his biological father. He had spoken to me last year about Peter and I could tell immediately just how close they were.

I peeped across at Mrs Lockett as he was looking at these and could see the rather wistful look in her eyes. She obviously was equally devoted to her husband, but there was more to it than just love, more like a true and deep devotion. He must have been a very special man.

As Steve lifted out the last album in that particular box he was taken by surprise when an envelope dropped on the floor in front of him. His mother went to pick it up in haste, almost as if it was top secret, but Steve just beat her to it, at first intending to save her bending for it, but then noticed it had his name on it. It was addressed to 'Steven Lockett', and in brackets underneath, 'On reaching age 18 years'.

Though I could see the worry on his mother's face I knew there was nothing to stop him reading this, whatever it turned out to be. He looked across at her enquiringly and asked why he'd not seen this before. Poor woman, I could see the discomfort she was feeling at that time and just wished I knew what to do to help her. All that sprang to mind was,

"Shall I go and put the kettle on. I'm sure we could all do with a cuppa."

"What a good idea Mel," she said, "then Steve can have a few minutes to read his letter. Sorry, I should have given it to you years ago Steve, but when you joined up I completely forgot it was in there." I heard her add very quietly as I left the room, "Please don't think bad of me dear."

She followed me out to the kitchen looking decidedly ashen faced and obviously worried sick about her son's reaction to whatever he was about to read. So much so that I took a chance and asked if it would help to talk about it. I promised that, whatever it was, it would go no further. I believe the idea of unburdening herself to another female sounded like a big relief, so much so that she decided to take up my offer.

"You see Mel, I'm pretty sure that the house you've been staying in is the one his grandparents worked at all those years ago. My mother worked in the house, and my father was gardener. I would often call in to see them if I was passing on my way home from the little shop I worked at."

She was obviously hesitant to carry on, but I felt she needed to confide in me, so I waited quietly for her to compose herself.

"Well you see, the family living there, the Stanwick family, had a son, Henry. I never did like him, he always seemed sort of sly, and was awful to his poor mother. He was about twenty eight, but I was only barely eighteen, and every time I went there, if he saw me coming he would pester me and do all he could to make me feel uncomfortable."

I believed at this point I could tell where this was going. I said she shouldn't tell me if she didn't want to, but by now she had made her mind up to get it off her chest. She took a breath, then continued,

"Well, one day I went to meet Dad but he'd been asked to help with something that needed doing inside. I could see he'd left his coat and his lunch box in the shed, so decided to sit on the bench in there and wait for him."

This was getting harder for her as she went on,

"It happened while I was in there. I heard footsteps coming and thought it was Dad, but when the door opened it turned out to be Henry. There I was, trapped, and he knew there was no way I could get passed him."

She visibly shivered and tears started to appear in her eyes,

"It was awful Mel. I couldn't stop him. I tried to scream but he put his hand over my mouth. He was like an animal, whatever I did he just carried on, I was terrified, I'd never been with a man before. Not like that. I'd been out a few time with Peter but he never made any improper moves. He was always so gentle. But Henry just wanted to prove he could get away with whatever he put his mind to and didn't care how much he hurt me."

I just had to do something and all I could do was go over and throw my arms around her, but just as I did this my place was taken by two much bigger, stronger arms than mine. Steve had been just outside the door for part of the time, but now had come in and held his mother tightly in his arms. She looked up at him, with such an apologetic look, and tried to get out the words, "I'm so sorry Steven", but he was quick to tell her there was no apology needed.

"Hush Mum, It wasn't your fault. You couldn't do anything about it. You're still my Mum."

Fighting back the tears she looked up at him and said,

"Yes, and I always will be dear, but you see ... "

"I know. Dad was not really my father, that's what you're trying to tell me. Don't let it worry you. As far as I'm concerned Peter Lockett is the man who brought me up, and a very fine job he did too might I say? That, in my eyes, makes him my Dad and the only one I ever needed. He's explained it all to me in that letter."

Looking round at me, almost for some form of help as to what to do now, he asked,

"Is that kettle boiled yet, I reckon a good old cup of tea is what's called for don't you?"

"I think that sounds just what we all need. You take your Mum and sit down while I pour it. One sugar for you Mrs Lockett isn't it?"

"Yes please dear, but do you mind if I ask you something?" I was quick to say I wouldn't mind at all, "It's just that Mrs Lockett sounds so formal. Would you care to call me May?"

I assured her that I'd be honoured to do so, in fact I had always intended to ask Steve what her name was, but wouldn't have dreamt to use it without her asking. I watched this gentle, loving son escort his poor distraught mother through to the living room, sitting alongside her and talking in such a quiet and comforting way, yet wondered just what was going on inside that unpredictably explosive mind of his! You've no doubt heard people talk about being like swans ... calm and serene on top, but paddling frantically underneath? Well, in his case it was always the reverse ... calm below, whilst the mind on top is working overtime, full of supressed temper and hurt.

"So Mum, are you saying that you think the house we've found is the same one Nan and Grandad worked at? Because if it is and it's going to upset you we can walk away. We haven't actually done anything so far, just enquired about it."

Having been calmed by his gentle voice and a cup of tea, May patted his hand, in much the way you would a child's, and said,

"No dear, that would be no reason to give up your dreams. Anyway, from what you say, if it is the same place the family are long gone, so we can't let ghosts rule our lives. That was what your father, Peter I mean," Steve quickly interrupted this by firmly adding, "Dad", she smiled up at him and finished her sentence, "what your Dad always said."

Having been assured that it was fine by her, he started working his way through the last box of albums.

"I know there are some of the house and gardens in one of them, in fact your grandparents are on a lot of them."

Sure enough it was not long before we came across one packed out with a collection of photos of Lansdown Grange. As Steve had remarked on a few occasions, it certainly looked a grand place in its day. In particular, the one Steve loved most was of his grandparents standing together in the gardens, with the house in all its grandeur in the background.

"So Mum, are you absolutely sure you would be ok with the idea of us trying to get this place? Please don't say yes if you'd rather we didn't. I'm sure there must be plenty of similar places we could find to do the same thing."

"No Steve, in fact in some ways, after all that happened there, as I see it you are owed that much from that monster," then as an afterthought, "You say the old couple are both gone; dare I ask, do you know what's happened to that son of theirs? He would be well into his sixties by now I expect. I thought someone said he died in a car crash."

Though she asked this in as casual a manner as she could muster, I could tell this was something that was playing on her mind. The thought of Steve meeting up with the man who raped his mother back then, even if he was that age, she knew as well as me the way he could react. Father or not, I couldn't see it ending well somehow.

"Don't let that worry you Mum. Obviously, if he was still alive he would have been left it in their will no doubt. It's now been empty for nearly thirty years and the only person who's shown any interest has been some odd chap who is after it as building land. He says he's related, but can't be so close or they would have left it to him, so I reckon that's just a con."

Later in the afternoon Jamie called round after he'd finished work. Though nobody enlightened him about his mother's past, she was pleased to show him the photos of the grandparents. He too commented on what a fantastic looking building this was. Steve was quick to explain that, though structurally sound, it was in drastic need of much renovation.

"So I suppose you're planning on doing that then eh?"

Obviously assuming this was a joke, he was somewhat taken aback when Steve said,

"As it happens that's just what I've got in mind."

Jamie's face was a picture. He listened with a look of shock on his face while his brother, once again, explained the whole plan to him. After a short while his concentration slipped back to the album in the bottom of the box which he lifted out and flicked through. Just as he was about to return this last one to the box he peered into it and, being curious, couldn't resist lifting out the newspaper lining it.

"Hey look Steve, this paper is as old as you! It was printed the year you were born mate!"

By this time Steve had lost interest and had been talking to his mother. In fact he didn't bother to look round until Jamie exclaimed,

"There's an envelope underneath it Mum. Did you know it was there? It looks pretty official to me."

Steve took it from Jamie to see what he'd found. It was clear that May had certainly never seen it before. She watched as Steve turned it over and read what was on the front,

"It says, 'To be presented to the solicitors dealing with the estate of the late Mrs Stanwick of Lansdown Grange'. Whatever it is it's got a wax seal on the back, so that it can't be interfered with."

It certainly came as a shock to their mother. As she'd never seen it before, she was sure her husband must have put it in there at some point, but whatever it contained had remained yet another secret from her and the whole family all these years.

Chapter Twenty-One.

May Lockett had been quite shattered by the combined events of that afternoon. Because of this Steve suggested that we should stay the night. Jamie decided to pop out to the village take-away to save anyone the problem of cooking, and then left about ten, promising to be back to visit his mother the next day to see she was ok. I wasn't sure what Steve would do about the news he'd had regarding her treatment at the hands of Henry Stanwick, but it seemed that, after having a quiet word with her in private, she agreed to allow him to bring it out in the open to both brothers. As she said, honesty was the best policy, and the way she'd always brought them all up. Why change now. Steve said that he would explain it to Tom when we visited him on our way back the next day.

Having given his mother a warm, reassuring hug, whispering in her ear as he did so, how much he loved her, we set off back in the direction we'd come from, heading for Tom's house. In fact we hadn't gone far out of the village when, to my surprise Steve pulled off the road into a layby by a small wooded area. I wondered what this was for, at first thinking, when he climbed out and marched off into the trees that he surely hadn't forgotten to use the bathroom before setting off!

I couldn't help grinning at the thought ... but then why was he so long? I decided to follow him and find out. I'd only gone just out of sight of the road when I heard what could well have been a fight! Rushing forward (as if I'd be any help!), I found Steve marching to and fro, stopping to kick and punch the surrounding trees, as if fighting an army of enemies!

"Steve, stop it! Whatever is it, please stop before you hurt yourself. Talk to me."

As he stopped to see me there I took hold of a couple of bruised and bleeding fists and looked up into a pair of brown eyes full of rage. Somewhere amongst the rage there was tears trying not to come.

"It's about him, Henry, isn't it?" he tried to turn away again but I didn't let go, "I can tell how you're feeling but hurting yourself isn't going to do any good. Come back to the van and let me clean your hands off my love, please."

Rather like a hurt child, without saying a word he followed me back to the van. Once inside he sat in silence while I cleaned the blood from his hands. When he did speak the language that poured from his lips was too much for me to repeat as I tell this story! Suffice it to say that, if Henry Stanwick wasn't already dead, he would be if Steve met him!! Now I was scared; the last time I'd seen

Steve as riled up as this was with Morgan, and this had led to him nearly having to be shot to stop him, and ending in rehab for months to recover from PTSD!

We had a small bottle of brandy in the cupboard, a drop of which I used to sterilise the wounds, and a good dose I gave him to drink. There was absolutely no way I was about to let him behind the wheel in his present state after all. By the time he'd drunk that (in one gulp!), he managed to pull himself together again. He apologised for his outburst and, though it had scared me at the time, I said I'd let him off if he promised to watch his temper in future.

As I climbed into the driver's seat and him into the passenger one, I turned to him before starting the engine and told him in as firm a voice as I could muster,

"Now, if we're going to Tom's I want you to promise not to make a scene there. Bear in mind the kids. The last thing they want is to see their Uncle Steve like that."

"Ok. I promise. Are you sure you're ok to drive there? Do you remember the way?"

As if he was capable of driving after that episode; and yes, I quickly assured him I did remember the way. So off we went. By the time we arrived at Tom's I was pleased to see Steve had calmed right down. I asked him if he felt up to going over the whole story with his brother and was assured he'd manage it. I think Tom was a little surprised to see us return so soon, but none the less made us feel really welcome. Margaret quickly had the kettle on the boil for coffee, little knowing how grateful I was that she had made this choice rather than anything alcoholic right at that point.

Once again the girls were being a little boisterous and so, sensing Steve wanted to speak in confidence to his brother, once we'd drunk our coffee, she suggested we left them to talk and took the kids to the nearby park. In some respects I would have liked to stay, which I think was my over-protective, almost motherly, instinct kicking in after his earlier outburst, but I knew I must trust him, at least with his brother. After all, Tom was most certainly the calm, sensible one in the family, so I knew somehow Steve would be fine. In fact I felt that, if anything here stirred him up it would more likely be those two excitable girls, sweet as they are.

By the time we came back it seemed Steve had explained the whole story of their mother's rape, and of course putting it plainly to Tom that this meant that he'd not actually been Peter's son, just adopted. It was clear that, once the initial shock had worn off, Tom had made it known to Steve that this made not a scrap of difference; they were, and always would be, brothers. I could see the weight this had lifted from his shoulders already.

As we arrived back Steve was just showing his brother the envelope Jamie had found. I could see immediately that this was quite clearly something Tom recognised as something of importance. Steve told him how Jamie had been tempted to open it, but Tom was obviously quite horrified at the thought.

"Didn't he see the seal? Whatever is inside would be invalidated if that had been broken. This must go to the solicitors. Do you know who they are?"

Steve said that we didn't know about solicitors, just the agents who seem to be responsible for the sale when the time came. He asked Tom if we should take the letter to the agents, but Tom was quick to say,

"No, that could be misinterpreted. If I'm going to act on your behalf it would be best if I inquire as to who is dealing with the estate. Goodness know what's in this, or why Dad had it in the first place. Whatever it is it should have been with the solicitors from the start."

And so, after a light lunch at a table with two surprisingly quiet, well-behaved girls, obviously still in awe of Steve, we said our goodbyes and set off for Lansdown Grange leaving the mystery envelope with Tom who promised to contact us when its content came to light.

Having spent getting on for two days now visiting family, being left with so much information to digest, without warning I found we were actually heading in quite the opposite direction to the one I expected! When I questioned him about this, Steve just said he thought we needed a bit of time to ourselves.

"I need to get my head together before we go back Mel. Right now it feels as if someone has stirred up my brain! I thought we could go somewhere to unwind first. Any ideas?"

I could feel for him, it had been a real roller coaster for the last two days, and a break would certainly help. Looking at the map for inspiration I soon came up with a suggestion.

"How about Stratford-on-Avon? It isn't so far from here."

"Sounds good to me," adding with a laugh, "we could be Romeo and Juliet!"

"No thank you. You do know they both ended up dead don't you?"

"Ok, perhaps not then. Shakespeare was always a mystery to me I'm afraid, but you have to admit he did make his mark on the world, you have to admire the man for that?"

"So he did," I couldn't resist adding, "and he did it all with words, not with his fists!"

He threw a cheeky grin in my direction and said, "Ok, you win. I promise to work harder on keeping my temper under control in future ... but I can't guarantee anything!"

Though he said this in a joking manner I knew he really was meaning to give it his best shot, but I also knew that it would be down to what lay ahead of us, and how hard others would push him. Try as he might, I knew so well that he had his limitations, and all good intentions would only count for so much.

Just outside Stratford we came across a particularly nice looking camp site. It seemed a good plan to park Annie there, as we'd done at other places, rather than attempt to drive straight into the town. I was fascinated by the little wooden pods spaced around in different areas of the place, most of which were unoccupied just now. It was quite early in the season yet so I assumed they would soon be fully booked. I waited in the van whilst Steve went into the office to ask where we should park, and to my surprise, when he came back he said to just put it in the carpark!

"Oh, is that the best they can offer us? Surely we could go further in?"

In answer to my question he took me by the hand, led me across to the far corner of the site, and unlocked the door to one of the wooden pods,

"Your home for the night Madam. Is this to your liking?" and as he opened the door I was surprised to see that, though fairly basic furniture wise, up the far end there was a beautifully clean, comfortable looking double bed. Ah! Pure luxury.

Leaving Annie there, we managed to find transport into town, and spent some time sightseeing around the bards town. Quite by chance we came across a place to hire bikes, this giving us chance to fit in so many other attractions.

By late afternoon we had managed to blag probably the last two tickets for that evening's performance of, by coincidence, Romeo and Juliet. Never having been to anything like this Steve sat in deep concentration, trying hard to interpret the language used in it. As we made our way back to our overnight home, complete with a bottle of wine Steve couldn't resist buying, I could sense the feeling of contentment sweep over him.

As he looked down at me, taking the moment to plant a warm and loving kiss on my lips, he said with a broad grin appearing,

"Even old Will certainly did have a way ... with words if nothing else."

The irony of his remark wasn't wasted; it did seem that this phrase was to stick to us!

When we got back to our little wooden home we were glad it had occurred to us to pick up a couple of plastic cups from Annie on our way in. I know Steve would have drunk the wine straight from the bottle, but I really didn't fancy that. I did say I would have just one drink, but somehow before we looked round, the bottle was empty, and I found the effects of the drink rather overtook any intention of mine (if I had any such intention!)

to turn my back on him and sleep. Well, how could I? I'd learnt so many things from this man over time, but resistance from his love was not one of them.

A while later I lay there, just watching him sleep, once again thinking what a strange and complex character he is, and yet, the more I'd learnt about him, the more I felt I could truly begin to understand him. Right that minute, seeing him lying there mellowed by the wine and our love, I felt a deep contentment that I knew somehow would last. Yes, I was sure there would be times when he wouldn't be as peaceful and content as he looked right now, but I felt that I was ready to be by his side no matter what.

By the next morning we both felt relaxed and ready for whatever lay ahead, though just what that was likely to be we had no idea. I must say I felt quite sorry to leave our little wood pod as it had proved to be extremely comfortable. When I commented on this to Steve he was quick to come up with the idea that, assuming we did manage to get possession of the Grange, we could always put a scattering of them in the grounds, either for those we take in, or perhaps later as a source of income by letting them as holiday accommodation.

"Perhaps, in his line of work, Graham might be able to take that on as a project, especially if we bring in more who need work. After all, it wouldn't be a bad deal in return for board and lodging."

This was a man with a one track mind, and he'd clearly set his mind on this project. It was obvious that he had no intention of letting anything stand in his way and, as much as I fully supported his ideas, I couldn't help worrying about how he'd take it if there proved no way to achieve his goal, but then the word 'defeat' didn't exist in the dictionary of Steve Lockett.

The roads were pretty quiet as we travelled back towards the village of Lansdown, which meant we arrived in time to stop at the Bull Inn for a bite to eat before returning to the Grange. For that reason we had decided to stay in our 'tidy' clothes and change later. Having parked up, we strolled off toward the pub. Realising now that we'd had no breakfast, we were feeling quite keen to have a good fill before going back to camp rations! As we approached the Bull we were taken by surprise to find Graham squatting against the wall looking quite forlorn, and obviously hoping some kind sole would take pity on him.

"Graham my friend, whatever are you doing here on a Sunday? I thought you'd all be making the most of that chaps veg he offered you? Where are the others?"

Graham looked up at us in some surprise, seemingly more bewildered by our tidy appearance than Steve's question, before saying,

"They're out looking for a new place to sleep. No time to worry about food when we've just been kicked out," then, going back to his first thoughts, "Where'd you get that flash gear? You been holding out on us and going to tell us you're a secret millionaire or something?"

This put a smile on Steve's face, but all he said in answer was, "No, not quite! Was it that same bloke you told us about who kicked you out?" When Graham confirmed it was, all Steve asked was whether or not Graham could help round up the others.

When he said he thought he could do that, Steve dashed into the pub and came out with three huge sausage rolls and a pint (half in my case). We sat together eating these before splitting up in search of the rest of our new friends, agreeing to meet up back here at six o'clock sharp.

Something told me that Steve was already having to resist the temptation to express his true feelings about the way the others had been evicted by this person, no matter who he was. As Steve pointed out, he had no right to assume he could do so until the allotted time was up, not without a will to say otherwise, and if he had that then, as Steve said, surely he would have come forward long before now!

Chapter Twenty-Two.

By six o'clock sharp we had found Jez and Pete. On reaching the Bull Inn we found Graham standing outside with Bob and Ellen. It was pretty obvious that they too were a little puzzled to see us in our better gear, but Steve didn't feel inclined to stand around outside explaining and so, to their surprise, they found themselves herded inside and sat around a large table in the corner of the room. Somehow I knew what was coming next … sure enough, when Steve went to the bar to collect menus, the publican gave him a very suspicious look before 'tactfully' suggesting that perhaps we might prefer to sit at one of the tables outside! I could see that Ellen for one was aware of the way we were being glared at across the room, but I whispered to her not to worry, Steve would deal with that.

Sure enough, just as I suspected, Steve completely floored the poor chap by fishing out his array of cards and presenting one for him to take an imprint by way of a guarantee. I know Ellen had seen this, but not knowing what to make of it, said nothing. Meanwhile the men had sat quietly whispering, wondering just what was going on.

They seemed for a moment to have forgotten my presence. As he came strolling back and handed out the menus, Bob looked up and asked suspiciously,

"Look, this is all well and good, but why? What do you want from us?"

Before he had chance to answer, Pete joined in, "You're something to do with that lot aren't you? Them who kicked us out."

Steve looked at them with in astonishment, "Would I be buying you all a meal if I was? Don't talk rubbish man. Now, if you'll just all choose what you want to eat and drink so I can get it ordered, I'll explain."

Totally floored by his attitude, they all sat in silence perusing the menu, until their orders had been taken and drinks delivered to the table. Suspicious as they were of Steve's actions, they were none the less not about to let this spoil the best meal they'd had for some time. All ate almost in silence, almost as if they felt it could be taken away at any time if they stopped to discuss the matter further. Not having had breakfast or the lunch we had promised ourselves, especially as you could say we'd worked up quite an appetite last night, we too tucked in with relish.

Once the dishes were practically licked clean, and another round of drinks brought over for those wanting one, Steve began to question them about what happened at the Grange. It seemed that this 'geezer' arrived not so long after we'd left. He had a small army of rough looking men to back him up and, he had threatened that anyone still here by midday would be beaten up and thrown in the lake! As far as they could tell it seemed none of them knew anything about Steve and me having been there.

"What right did they reckon they have to throw you out? Did they say? Did this bloke say who he was?"

"He didn't give us his name, just said he was related to the family. Wouldn't even give us time to pack our stuff up properly. All we managed to grab was our sleeping bags. Said they've got the bulldozers coming in soon. Bloody shame if you ask me," said Graham. They all nodded in agreement.

"Right, we'll see about that," Steve said to them, and went on to explain, first about how we'd come to be there in the first place (well, enough to explain something of our circumstances and why we had chosen to live this way). He went on to put to them his ideas of what he would like to do with the Grange if there was any way he could acquire it.

"I know it might be a long shot, but I wonder if, by applying for grants and the like, I could tempt him into selling it to me. It could help so many folk like you, people who have found themselves out of work, or for any other reason, homeless. And just think how much they could learn from the likes of you?"

"What do you mean, 'the likes of us'? Are you being insulting mate?" Pete chimed in with.

"Of course not. As I see it Pete, think how much you could do to help some pick up your trade as a bricky. And you Graham. I bet there's plenty would love to learn carpentry. And then there's you two," looking at Bob and Ellen, "I bet there's a lot they could learn about market gardening and livestock management from you."

"So what makes you think you know about living on the streets? You sound as if you're not short of a bob or two," Graham put to him.

"That's where you're wrong. I've just spent the last couple of years living rough since my wife and son died, so I reckon I have a little idea; and no is the answer to your next question, Mel and I are not married. You just assumed we were. We met last year and somehow managed to save one another from the messes we'd got ourselves into! "

That remark had the effect of stopping them all in their tracks. They obviously didn't expect it. It soon became clear that the whole idea was beginning to soak into their minds. Just as we thought we'd said enough to convince them it might work, and that it might help give them all a purpose in life again, one last voice popped up from the silence,

"Yes, ok, but what about me Steve, what do you think I can teach anyone?"

This was young Jez, who until now had sat quietly listening. Steve looked round at him and grinned,

"Probably nothing yet young'un, but by the time I've finished with you you'll be fit to get back to college and get that degree you wanted."

"Really? Do you really think you could help me?"

Before Steve had chance to answer him I couldn't resist chiming in with,

"Believe me, if Steve says he can, you can rest assured that's just what he'll do!"

Clearly Steve's love of keeping fit was going to be something he would be keen to thrust upon anyone able to be pushed. After all, I still found myself on the morning jogs more often than not, so why not others? I supposed that the fitter people were, the easier they would find it to be up to learning a trade of some sort.

Once again Steve did what he liked to do best. Getting up from the table to go to pay, I was aware of him holding quite a lengthy chat with the landlord. I could see the horrified expression flash across the man's face for an instant, but quickly change as Steve went to put his card back in his wallet. He called him back and I could see there were some negotiations going on before Steve turned back to us and announced,

"Right you lot; you're staying here for a couple of nights until I can sort something out. They've got three rooms empty, so I wonder if Graham could have one, Bob and Ellen another, and the third shared by Pete and Jez. Is that ok?"

The expressions on their faces said it all. They were pretty staggered by the idea of actually getting proper beds for a change and would have hugged Steve had they not been men! It was left to Ellen to do this on their behalf, and silly as this was I found myself almost wanting to warn her off! As they were all led off by the landlord (with a forced smile on his face), I turned to Steve and asked,

"Well that's sorted them, but what about us? Where do we sleep?"

I should have known the answer to this … in Annie van of course!

This time it seemed that, apart from his usual need for us to be alone, he needed to talk strategy, and this included taking a detour to pass the Grange, as he put it, to do a quick recce of the situation there.

And so that was what we did. A little reluctantly on my part, we parked a way back from the entrance and approached on foot, apparently, as Steve said, like a couple of hikers wondering what was inside those big, fancy gates. I was fine, well reasonably fine, with this plan until we came up to the gates. We'd not got within about four metres of the gates when we were stopped by two things.

Firstly the huge, ornate gates which we'd not noticed before, were closed in front of us. Then, as we approached these, two equally huge, rough looking characters appeared from what was left of one of the gatehouses at the side. My instinct was to turn tail and leave, but of course Steve took a firm grip of my arm and marched us straight up to the gate!

Doing something I'd never heard him do before, he said to them in a broad American accent,

"Howdy guys, how're doing there? Wonder if you can help a couple of lost yanks? Seems we've taken a wrong route somewhere. We hear there's a pretty big house around here? Is this the way in? We just want to get some photos before we go home."

I stood, trying my best to produce a convincing smile in the hope of looking like an innocent tourist. They looked from one to the other and grinned,

"What if it is? This is private land so you better get out of here yank."

"Whoa there ... no need to get like that pal. Surely a couple of photos wouldn't hurt? Who's your boss? Perhaps he'll let us in if you tell him we're here?"

The bigger of the two stepped toward the gate, and just for a brief second I thought he was going to let us in, but there I was, wrong again!

"Look here, don't you understand bloody English? This is not open for visitors, it's up for demolition next week, and if you don't get out of here I'll come out there and there and flatten you mate."

I would like to have seen him try, but as I was trying to fight back a smile at the image this formed in my mind, Steve wheeled me about and marched me back off the way we'd come. Instead of standing around arguing any further we headed back for another cosy night in the van. Before turning in for the night he rang Tom to update him on the situation here, and Tom promised to speak to the solicitor first thing tomorrow.

What would be the outcome of all this I couldn't help wondering, but whatever happened I could see it was going to be quite a long slog. Yet for all these thoughts in my head, Steve seemed completely unperturbed. Typical of the man, when he got an idea in his head it was a certainty that there was nothing anyone could say to change his mind. I knew it was pointless arguing with him, and so we walked back to the van in relative silence. Obviously, though he barely spoke, there was much buzzing around in his mind, and I was sure he'd talk to me when he was ready. I was right on that score; when we reached the van he finally did speak but only to suggest that we should move the van from the layby where we'd left it and move it to a quieter spot. I was a little puzzled at this as the place we'd parked was pretty quiet anyway, but I just climbed in and left him to decide.

We spent the night parked in the little clearing by the lake, within a stone's throw of the spot he'd had to rescue me from drowning in the weir! Somehow this did seem appropriate. We sat outside for a while with me in my favourite place, wrapped in his arms, as we watched a particularly beautiful night sky. There was not a cloud to be seen, just an almost full moon surrounded by stars twinkling as if they'd been thrown up into the sky purely for our benefit. Barely a word was spoken ... I certainly had no urge to break the perfect peace I was feeling at that moment. When eventually Steve spoke it was to suggest turning in. Perhaps surprisingly, that night neither of us felt the urge to do more than lay cuddled up together with his arms wrapped round me like a human blanket.

As I drifted off to sleep I could still see the glittering stars through the little window in the roof of the van, and it was not too long before I drifted off into a deep and peaceful night's sleep.

Chapter Twenty-Three.

The next morning I awoke to the smell of fried bacon sizzling in the pan. Rather bleary eyed, I climbed out of bed and, with the blanket wrapped round my shoulders, peeped out the door to investigate. Steve had already gathered wood, lit a small fire, and was sizzling our breakfast before my eyes!

"Don't you ever want to lie in," I challenged him.

"Not on a lovely morning like this, and besides, we've got things to be doing. Can't lay around half the morning."

I looked at my watch to see just how far into this 'lovely morning' we were, just to find it was still only just turned seven! I soon learnt that I had indeed got off light; he had already been for a short jog. When I asked where to, somehow I wasn't in the least surprised to hear that he had been back to the Grange. He quickly assured me not to panic, he'd apparently just done a tour around the perimeter fence to see if the two men we'd seen were alone, or had others there with them. As far as he could tell there were a handful of others, mainly guarding the house itself. In all he'd counted about eight.

"So no real problem then," he said with a grin.

"Look Steve, I don't know what you've got in mind, but if you've got it in mind to storm the place and get rid of them, just remember that I don't reckon Graham, Pete and the others could make up an army to back you up, even if they wanted to. As for me and Ellen, you've said yourself I can't look after myself, and I doubt she could either."

Stroking his beard and looking me up and down, he said,

"Umm, I reckon you're right about that. I think it's time we did something about it."

When I asked him what he meant by that he just nodded and said,

"Yes, I think you need to learn a little self-defence to keep you out of trouble. Just in case I'm not about to do it for you one day."

Feeling a little riled by the implication that I was helpless, I found myself turning on him with,

"I'm not as damn useless as you're making out you know!"

"Come on then," he challenged, "attack me."

I felt myself bristling with indignation, so much so that I found myself rushing forward, intent on doing … well doing something … but, before I barely came within touching distance of him, I found myself put (fairly delicately I must say), down on the ground at his feet!

You just wait, I thought as I got up onto my feet again, you won't do that again so easily.

I made a grab at him, intending to try different tactics (though still not sure what these would be!) but this time found myself in some sort of strangle hold!

"Ok, ok, I give in. But how do you expect the likes of me to tackle someone like you? It's hardly a fair match when you've had all your training, and besides, you're so much bigger than me."

"I hear what you say Mel, but size, as they say, isn't everything. And as for the training, if you knew how to handle yourself you'd have the advantage of surprise. Men wouldn't expect a girl like you to be able to defend herself after all."

I had to admit I could see what he was getting at, but just at that point I honestly couldn't imagine me as a sort of female ninja! Even so, he seemed determined to work with Ellen and myself, plus any of the others who fancied it, just to give us more confidence if the need arose.

Within the hour we had eaten breakfast, packed up and gone back to the village to meet the others. Steve had taken the opportunity while I'd packed away the breakfast things to speak to Tom, just to update him on the 'take-over' of the Grange, and Tom had promised to make this his priority to speak to the agents first, and then to track down and contact the solicitors. Now we just needed to bide our time with what little patience Steve could, till we could do anything.

Having told them all of our expedition to the Grange last night, Steve said he had decided to take a trip into Coventry again. This time he took Graham, Pete and Bob with him, leaving me with Ellen and Jez. I don't think he had a particular reason to go, just a case of not being able to sit still too long! I warned him not to go getting too keen and spending money yet, not until we knew whether or not there was the slightest chance of getting our hands on the place, and he said that he was only going to price up tools and things, perhaps get a few food supplies. Somehow I didn't quite believe him!

With Pete and Bob squatting down on the floor of the van so that they couldn't be spotted (as there were only seat belts on the front two seats), off they went. Jez, Ellen and I took ourselves out, once again heading for the lake. It was a beautiful, sunny morning and, as much as I loved him, it was rather pleasant and relaxing just hanging around watching the ripples blowing across the surface of the water. Having felt that now I could truly say Ellen and I had become close, when she commented on what a lovely spot this was, I almost felt like sharing with her just why this place was so special for me, but of course I couldn't do that with young Jez there I suppose. I'd hate to embarrass the poor lad. Anyway, that was an experience personal to Steve and myself.

As we took ourselves off for a stroll by the lakeside, we had quite a chat. Though she had put on a very brave, almost carefree, attitude in front of the men, she now opened up so much more, and I couldn't help feeling so sympathetic towards her as she explained the struggle they'd had to get their place established in the first place. Apparently they hadn't been married so long before this rather run down small holding had come available, and they had taken nearly four years to get it to the point of paying for itself. It was then that it had been taken away from them for less than they had originally paid for it. The truly upsetting thing I felt was that she confided in me, out of earshot of Jez, that they had just decided that they were ready to try for a baby. Now that was out of the question.

We walked across to where Jez was skimming stones across the surface of the lake. Just for a few minutes we both joined in with him, certainly a thing he hadn't expected! At one point, in his eagerness to get the best skim, his foot slipped on the wet edge of the grass. Ellen and I both made a grab for him, catching him just in time to prevent him sliding into the water, but leaving all three of us stretched out on the grass. All we could do was lie there and laugh.

As we got to our feet and walked on I couldn't help feeling that it seemed the whole incident somehow had the effect of bringing Jez out of his protective shell, the imaginary one he'd obviously been hiding in to avoid getting hurt more than he already had. It was pretty clear to me that he'd never had anyone in his life to trust or relax with. Hopefully we could turn this around for him if Steve's plan came to fruition.

We'd taken a pack of sandwiches and a drink each which we eventually sat eating. As we were doing this Jez turned to me with a slightly worried expression and asked,

"Do you really think Steve means it when he says he can help me? I mean, do you know what he can do … or, come to that, why he would want to?"

Trying not to look too amused at his words 'can' and 'want to', I looked him straight in the face and explained to him that Steve's previous occupation had been in the army, in particular being responsible for bringing recruits up to required fitness levels, and if he said he would, believe me he won't stop until he achieves his goal! As I told Jez, since I first met him he's never let up on me, even though he thinks I'm a lost cause!

I then went on to warn Ellen and Jez about Steve's latest idea that we should also learn some sort of self-defence, an idea that Jez took to with enthusiasm, though I believe Ellen was a little more reserved. Even so she did agree that there had been quite a few times when she had felt intimidated by people, especially with them looking down their noses at her as being just another 'tramp', so she could see that it could help to have the confidence of knowing she could defend herself if the necessity arose. After all my experiences from last year I knew she was right, though of course I had always had Steve there in the background to come to my rescue when I needed him.

She asked me how I'd got to know Steve in the first place, a question I knew would come up at some point, if not from the men, it was the obvious question from another woman. At first I did wonder if I should explain the whole story to her, whether it would bother Steve if I did this, but as it was clear by now that he was determined to keep this group together, hopefully finding ways to get them back on their feet, I decided that perhaps honesty would be the best policy.

Both Ellen and Jez sat in shocked silence as I recounted the whole story, from finding myself in the cave, meeting up with Steve (who was living rough), and how we'd travelled the country in order to track down Jakes killer without getting arrested for committing this crime myself. However, as before on a couple of occasions, I somehow missed out the bit about him attacking me at Ely, in the same way as I explained that it was him who caught Morgan, but also managed to gloss over the full description of that day's events!

Both seemed visibly shaken by the whole saga. After a brief moment of contemplation Ellen said that she could now understand where he was coming from, why he wanted to do what he was suggesting. Jez was left positively in awe of the man who he now saw as some sort of super hero. I just hoped that Steve wouldn't mind me having told them so much, but then I decided it might show them that he had no hidden agenda and could safely put their trust in him in the same way I have.

Eventually we were about to stroll back toward the village when I saw the van coming towards us up the lane. As he drew level with us Steve opened the window and said to go back to our parking spot by the lake and he was cooking dinner tonight. By the time the three of us walked back he had parked up in the same spot as last night and lit a useful looking little camping stove.

"Burgers all round?" he asked opening a pack and fishing out a pack of burger buns, "Just the right number, eight in a pack."

"But there's only seven of us, so who's having the eighth one?" I asked him.

"Oh sorry Mel; I haven't introduced you to Dave. Dave's a plumber you know,"

As I threw a dirty look at Steve behind everyone's backs, I then looked round, forced a smile, and said to this scruffy, dirty looking character coming up to shake my hand,

"Hi, I'm Mel. So you're coming to join our gang then? Pleased to meet you. Haven't we met before?"

He did look a bit familiar, but from where I couldn't say.

"Sort of. Your man Steve here bought me a cuppa and a sausage roll last week in Coventry."

So there we were, increasing our numbers, just what I'd warned him not to do, just in case things didn't work out. I might as well have not bothered saying anything, if he wants to do a thing he always does it regardless of anything I say!

Leaving Ellen in charge of the burgers he said to come and see what he'd got the van. For a minute my heart sank at the many possibilities this could cover. As we walked away from the others I couldn't help asking him just what he was planning on doing with Dave tonight,

"After all, the others only have tonight at the Inn before they're out on the streets again. Perhaps you want to share Annie with Dave and I'll share with Graham tonight, is that your plan?"

Flashing a particularly cheeky grin at me he said,

"Now there's a thought. Didn't know you fancied Graham, but don't let me come between you."

Dodging a swift swing of my arm, he opened the door to reveal a pile of bags and boxes filling a large part of the space inside. I did wonder how he'd managed to fit his passengers in as well, but decided not to bother asking.

"This should answer your question. These are all full of good, warm sleeping bags, cooking equipment and tents, enough to go round until we get back in the Grange,"

"What you mean is, if we get back in the Grange?"

Clearly he had no intention of seeing anyone sleeping out in the open, or going without food for want of means to cook it, any more than he had any intention of giving up on the Grange.

I must say that, in spite of all being homeless, we did make a pretty jolly group. It seemed that as we sat around tucking into our burgers and chatting, somehow they had all began to gel together, almost as a family, and had automatically accepted Steve as being in charge of what fate had in store for them all.

By the time the majority had gone off for their second night's luxury at the pub, Steve had helped Dave erect his tent and supplied him with a nice new, clean, sleeping bag, and I'd cleared up the cooking things, I think we were both more than ready to turn in for yet another night in Annie. As we climbed into bed that night, Steve put a warm arm around me and whispered quietly in my ear,

"It's all coming together Mel. I know it is."

For his sake, if not anyone else, I did so hope he was right.

Chapter Twenty-Four.

As I came to the next morning I stretched, yawned, and rolled over, expecting to find Steve there alongside of me, but he wasn't! I suppose I wasn't so surprised really. I knew him well enough by now to know where he'd gone! He'd left me half a kettle of warm water by our little sink, so I made use of it to freshen up. I couldn't help thinking how ironic it was that those he had booked rooms for at the pub had the luxury of a proper shower, whilst we, who could afford a comfortable home, are sharing a kettle of water in a tiny sink in a clapped out old camper van! By the time I took myself outside, I found Dave sitting outside his new tent, looking pretty content to be there. Giving me a nod of recognition and a smile, he remarked,

"He's a bit keen, that bloke of yours, isn't he? I'd barely surfaced when I heard him outside. When I looked he was doing press-ups and the like! Just said hi, then took off jogging through the woods. Hope he don't expect me to join in?"

"Oh, you wait; he's got me at it most days, and I think his plans will be to get everyone as fit as they need to be to get back to work when the time comes."

Shaking his head a bit half-heartedly he admitted that he was quite a way from being as fit as he should be, "So I suppose he does have a point. He'll have to take it easy mind. How come he's so fit then?"

Knowing that, by now, Ellen and Jez may not have passed on the information about Steve which I'd given them yesterday, I thought it only right to repeat it to Dave so that he too would have faith in what Steve was trying to achieve. It seemed he wasn't in the least surprised, and felt it gave him a greater respect by knowing where Steve's ideas were coming from.

By the time he came back I was ready to start on a filling breakfast of bacon and eggs. You may wonder where the eggs were coming from, since the eviction from the Grange, but it seemed that the only thing Bob managed to rescue while the others were trying to stall the process, was his chicken coop on wheels! Once again, he'd saved their beloved hens, all that had stood between them and sheer desolation before.

He'd set them up in a small clearing away from view, and it seemed they had continued laying. Knowing Steve had insisted the others got a good breakfast before leaving the pub, I felt sure they wouldn't mind us having eggs with our bacon this morning.

"So what next," I asked him after we'd eaten.

"That's the frustrating thing. We can't do a thing until Tom has spoken to the agents. Even then he'll still need to see the solicitors. Hopefully one of them can throw a light on just who this character is who says he's a descendant of the Stanwick family. If he really is then it could make it almost impossible to persuade him to sell. Then of course, we don't know if he'd accept an offer. All we can do is wait and hope now until we hear from Tom."

As Dave had gone for a walk down to the village we felt free to talk openly. I took a chance to voice a thought which had come to mind last night, and just hoped that what I said wouldn't upset him too much.

"Steve, I've been thinking," he looked round at me and waited for me to continue, "Well, it's just that, after what happened to your Mum," dare I go on? Yes, I must, "Well has it occurred to you that this chap could be related to you in some way?"

"Well I suppose so. I must admit I've not given it much thought. He can't be so close to the family though or they would have left it to him in their will; and it certainly can't be that bastard, Henry. Mum was pretty sure he died a few years later in a car crash," and then, as an afterthought, under his breath I heard him say as he walked away from me, "If he isn't now he bloody well will be if I catch up with him."

That much I knew without hearing him put it into words.

The rest of the morning he was particularly restless, desperately waiting for Tom to call. I felt the need to do something to take his mind from this, and so, with Ellen and Jez as backup, persuaded him it was a good time to start teaching us a few of these self-defence moves he'd mentioned. At first it was difficult to talk him into it, but we persevered, and finally talked him round. Obviously the other two had no idea why it seemed so important to me to talk him round, but none the less, both were happy to try their hand at something to pass the time. When we started this the rest of the men were inclined to sit around and make rude comments, but when Steve told them to take themselves off or he'd get them joining in, they suddenly remembered they were planning a stroll, and perhaps a spot of fishing. It seemed that the first thing we had to learn was how to fall without being hurt. Sounded like a good idea to me, but turned out not to be as easy as he made it sound! I reckoned that by the time we'd finished I'd be black and blue with bruises, but he wouldn't let up on us until he was happy with our progress. I did begin to wonder if this was such a good idea after all, but I had no intention of saying anything as I could see that at least, having this to do was keeping him occupied for a while.

It was not until around midday that his mobile rang. As he answered it I kept my fingers tightly crossed behind my back, praying it would be Tom with some news, hopefully some promising news at that. All I heard was enough to know that it actually was Tom, but aggravatingly, he took it across into the van, obviously wanting to keep it private. All I could do was wait and hope. After what felt like an age he stuck his head out the door and beckoned me over. It was difficult to judge from his expression, just how he was feeling about what had been discussed, so I sat quietly (hopefully!) and listened as he went over the conversation he'd had with his brother.

Tom, acting on Steve's behalf, had paid a visit to the agents. It seems that, though Mr Sanderson had at first been a little dubious of Tom, acting as he was on behalf of his brother, once he had checked his credentials, he did agree to pass on the details of the appropriate solicitors. This had enabled Tom to pay them a visit whilst he was still in Coventry. As he said, it was convenient to find that they too were based in the same area.

He had taken a chance and headed straight round to Dean & son, solicitors, and had been just lucky enough to catch the 'son' John, before he left for his lunch break! Steve reckoned that Tom had smooth talked him over lunch and a couple of drinks, to give up a bit of his valuable time to discuss a little business in the office afterwards!

It seems that the first subject up for discussion had been the possibility of Steve being able to acquire the place at the end of the few months left under the bona vacantia rules. Though I believe Steve was not at all happy about it, Tom had taken a chance on showing him the letter from Peter Lockett, in a hope that this might hold some sway by perhaps making it clear that he considered this did in some small way, prove a distant, though possibly dubious, link to the family.

Apparently Mr Dean had appeared quite shocked by this news, but not being old enough to have known the Stanwick family, couldn't say if this would hold sway in a court of law. What he could confirm, with some reluctance, was that he did know that Henry Stanwick had died in an accident, but more than that he either could not or would not say. It had been his father, Mr Dean snr, who was actually handling the estate and he was at present in court that day, Tom was asked if he could leave the sealed envelope there with his son, and he would be hearing from them as soon as Mr Dean snr was able to attend to the matter.

I could tell by Steve's expression that he was rather disappointed by the delay. He quizzed his brother as to what chances Tom thought he would have, but apparently Tom had been very non-committal at this stage, just telling him that he must be patient! And there was me thinking he knew Steve!

"At least Tom has started things moving. These things can't be rushed you know I'm sure he'll let you know as soon as he hears anything."

The rest of the day was spent either setting up our camp amongst the trees where they were out of view of anyone passing along the nearby footpaths. It seemed sensible to keep much of the equipment in the van, just getting it out when some of us are around to keep it safe.

Later in the afternoon Steve took them all by surprise by suggesting a 'brisk walk' along the side of the lake and back! Though Graham was quick to point out that, as the eldest, he wasn't sure all this energetic stuff was for him, Steve, with a little help from the rest, goaded him into giving it a go.

"After all, I'm not asking you to jog mate, just a little stroll."

I couldn't help thinking that this might be all he meant now, but for how long?

Leaving Ellen and I to walk at a reasonable pace with Graham, away he went with the rest on what was to become quite a regular feature of most of our days. Even so, we were all suitably rewarded in the evening when he suggested all paying another visit to the Bull Inn for a good meal, much to the dismay of the poor landlord! Mind you, as the majority had made good use of his showers that morning, he must have noticed a vast difference in their appearance, and the fact that he was being paid for eight more meals than he would otherwise have done, all brought over with a somewhat forced smile on his face!

Later on all eight of us strolled contentedly back to settle down for the night, suitably full, and I noticed a feeling of contentment wafting through us all.

Without Steve knowing, I had whispered in the ears of Ellen, Bob and Jez, suggesting the idea of some of us surprising him by joining him for his morning jog. I'd not held out much hope, but left it for them to consider. To my great surprise, though he obviously noticed me getting up and ready, as we came out of Annie the other three were lined up outside waiting for us to appear!

"Where are you lot going this time of morning," he asked.

"You tell us, wherever you are," answered Bob with a grin. "Thought you'd like the company."

The look on his face was priceless. It was clear he thought he stood little chance of getting this bunch to embrace his need to get them fit ... get them fit to work and find homes, but not 'fit' in the way he was. Well maybe they'd never get to his level, but it soon became evident that they had elected him as their leader, and as such they would do all they could to impress him.

As we set off behind him, as I'd done so often, I couldn't help wondering just what is it that makes people follow this man the way they do!

By the time we came back, those left behind were cooking breakfast. Eggs again thanks to Bob's hens, and more bacon which we'd bought in the village yesterday. We'd barely finished it when Steve heard his phone ringing from the van. Being nearest I rushed over and answered it to find Tom on the other end.

"Hi Mel, is Steve about? It's something quite urgent."

I called to Steve to come, telling him Tom needed an urgent chat. Whatever this was I couldn't tell, just that he had a rather puzzled expression on his face. I waited until he put the phone down and sat down.

"What is it Steve? You're worrying me now. Is it bad news?"

For a second or two he just sat, obviously thinking something over, and then he turned to me and said,

"We've got to go to Mum's."

"What, do you mean now … today? Why?"

"I don't know exactly, but Tom has had a call from Dean's, and the old man wants me to go there tomorrow, and to take all sorts of paperwork. I've got to get my birth certificate, Mum and Dad's marriage certificate, my adoption papers and some sort of i.d, probably my army papers."

"Did he give you any idea what this was about? It sounds quite urgent," I queried.

Still looking somewhere between shocked and just plain bewildered, he said he didn't have a clue,

"But you never know, perhaps the old girl saw fit to leave me a couple of quid to compensate for what that damn son of hers did."

I just stopped myself in time from reminding him that the 'damn son' he spoke of was actually his biological father! I really didn't see Steve taking kindly to being reminded of that.

Leaving the others to clear up the breakfast things and organise their own day, we jumped in Annie and shot off, leaving them all somewhat bewildered over our sudden departure, and headed off once more for the Cambridgeshire countryside. Steve had decided it best not to say more than was necessary to them … what could he say; he genuinely had no idea himself just what to expect next!

By now it seemed that his Mum had accepted that he was not about to disappear again, but was none the less, surprised to see us again quite so soon. Though she questioned him as to why he needed these paper, she had to accept that he knew no more than her. All he could say was that it was something to do with the sealed envelope. She thought, as he'd suggested, that old Mrs Stanwick (who she said was always so kind to her family), had perhaps chosen to make some reparation for her sons behaviour.

"If there's any chance of getting hold of the place every little contribution would be welcome, so keep your fingers crossed Mum."

While Steve sorted out the necessary paperwork from yet another box kept in the attic, I helped May prepare a spot of lunch for us. She did confide in me whilst we were doing this that she couldn't help worrying a little about Steve.

"He's so determined to do this dear. What will happen if he finds it's beyond him? It's not going to be cheap, and even if he can raise the money, will it make him happy do you think Mel?"

All I could do was be honest with her about the cost, though it was going to depend on whoever this other chap was who thinks it should go to him. Hopefully, if all he wants is to demolish it, perhaps he'll agree to sell it.

As for making Steve happy, I felt I could confidently say that, having a project like this, one that he truly believes in as he does with this, one that would allow him to put to use all his energy and abilities, would be exactly what he needs. He was never going to be just another nine to five worker, doing a monotonous job like most men after all!

Not so long after lunch we headed back to our little campsite, as Steve said, so that we were nearer to Coventry where he was to meet Tom the next morning.

Before we left May had packed up some containers full of frozen casserole, plenty for our growing family! It seemed she had now accepted the reasoning behind the fate of those we were living with, and had been prepared to make reparation for her previous misinterpretation. By the time we were all in need of food that evening this had defrosted well and was a beautifully quick, filling and easy meal.

Before turning in that night Steve and I sat looking through the papers he'd collected from his mother's. His parents' marriage certificate was pretty much as normal, showing a Peter Lockett marrying May Louise Burgess. His birth certificate dated six months later showed Steven Lockett, mother's maiden name Burgess but was unusual in that it showed no father's name, though under the circumstances that was to be expected. Dated just after Steve's birth he showed me the adoption papers, naming Peter as his new, adoptive father. Nowhere on anything did we find mention of Henry Stanwick's involvement. The one set of papers he was genuinely pleased to go over though were his army recruitment and i.d. These he looked at with great pride, and I couldn't help seeing a wistful, possibly a longing look flash across his face just briefly. I suppose this shouldn't have surprised me, after all, the army had been his life since he was eighteen (before that, according to his mother, the army cadets).Now all he needed to do was to replace it with something, anything, he could throw himself into with anywhere near the amount of enthusiasm he'd had for that.

I prayed that night that the things he was so keen to use as that replacement would actually become reality. I doubted he would find defeat an easy pill to swallow.

Chapter Twenty-Five.

As you can imagine, the next morning Steve was up early, still ready for the morning jog, but making it that bit tougher on us trying to keep up with him! In fact even Jez commented that, if this was the speed we were going to be expected to go from now on, he would have to admit defeat. I assured them as best as I could that it was just that he had something on his mind distracting him, and that I promised to have a word on their behalf before tomorrow.

Once again he said nothing to them as to why we needed to go into town that morning, but promised to bring food back with us later. We made an effort to tidy ourselves up as much as possible, determined not to give the appearance of a couple of gypsies. Steve even went to the lengths at last of trimming his, normally short and neat, beard back into shape.

We had agreed to meet Tom outside Dean's office at 9.45 for the ten o'clock appointment he'd made. As it turned out, we were standing there, waiting for him by 9.20 sharp! When he did arrive he had brought along a colleague of his. As he explained, He was concerned that Mr Dean may be a little suspicious of Steve having his brother to represent him. We sat quietly in the reception until the young lady we'd seen before invited us to go through. When she implied that I should wait outside, Steve would have none of it. As he said, we had no secrets between us, and whatever this was about he wanted me to be there to hear it. Seeing she was in no position to argue, she quickly backed down and sent us all in.

Mr Dean snr was a tall, distinguished looking man. Having shook hands with us all he invited us to sit down. Looking across the desk at Steve, he asked if he had brought the documents he'd wanted to see. Steve handed them across to him, and we all sat watching while he browsed slowly through each one, appearing on occasions to compare their content to another document already on his desk.

"So, can you please confirm your full name and date of birth please?" he asked Steve.

"Sgt Steven Peter Lockett, 9th April 1985" (Damn, I thought. I've missed his birthday!)

He asked what Steve knew of a man by the name of Henry Stanwick. I saw Steve's expression harden, and his fists clench in his lap, before he looked across at Mr Dean and told him that this was the (I hoped he'd watch his language) man who raped his mother. There was absolutely no way he was going to actually say the words, 'biological father'.

By way of an address he was quick to give his mother's. Phew, I thought! Saying 'no fixed abode' wouldn't have gone down too well!

After a couple more questions, obviously for identification purposes, he stopped for a second before looking across at Steve.

"Then Mr Lockett, having first read the letter written to you by your adoptive father, Mr Peter Lockett, and verified that you are actually the person mentioned in the documents I now have in my possession, I can tell you that I have here the document your solicitor delivered here in the sealed envelope. As solicitor acting for the estate of the late Mrs Stanwick, I have verified the signatures on this as genuine, and can now reveal to you the full contents.

We sat in suspense listening as he began to read all the usual jargon always written at the beginning of a will. It wasn't until he got to the bit about 'I hereby bequeath' that we both found ourselves sitting up, listening with shocked disbelief!

'I wish that the whole of my estate, including Lansdown Grange, all grounds

and possessions included, any monies, shares, and other investments, to pass

to one Steven Peter Lockett, illegitimate son of Henry Stanwick and May Lockett

nee Burgess.

No part of my estate is to pass to Henry Stanwick or any other descendant of his.

Whilst Mr Dean carried on reading the rest of the legal spiel, all Steve and I could do was sit, speechless, looking at one another, unable to take in what we'd just heard! I've never seen Steve at a loss for words, but this had left him completely dumbfounded, and with a face as white as a sheet. I looked across at Tom, who was obviously as shocked as his brother. He quickly pulled himself together to ask,

"Do we understand that correctly Mr Dean? Lansdown Grange and all Mrs Stanwick's estate is now to go to my brother?"

"Yes, most certainly. I must say that finding the will at this time was a good thing. I have had another descendant of the family waiting to claim it, and had this document not been forthcoming in the next couple of months, he would have had a good case."

Steve had by now pulled himself together sufficiently to ask,

"Can you tell me who this is who is so keen to get hold of the Grange?"

Mr Dean glanced at yet another piece of paper before answering,

"That would be a Mr Luke Stanwick, son of Henry Stanwick. It is because of the family connection that we assumed he could possibly be the only one with a claim on the estate. But now, reading Mrs Stanwick's wishes that no descendant of her son Henry, should have any right to claim it,

I am just glad the will turned up when it did," and then, standing up and holding out his hand, "May I be the first to congratulate you Mr Lockett."

Steve stood and shook the waiting hand gladly. There was obviously so many questions to ask, so much to take in and digest, where to start he obviously had no idea. Just for once someone had got the upper hand of him, leaving him completely shaken and with no idea what to do next.

Before leaving the office Mr Dean said that, if we would care to return later in the day he would have a document drawn up to prove ownership as Steve had expressed his concern about what he assumed was this Luke's men having taken possession of the Grange, and were planning on bringing in bulldozers at the weekend. (He somehow forgot to mention that we, along with a few others, had been squatting in there before!).

When we left the solicitors office that morning, Steve had a grin on his face so broad that I expected him to burst into song any minute. He persuaded Tom and his colleague to come with us to a nearby pub for an early lunch, though neither felt they could help him celebrate with anything alcoholic as they had to go back to work fairly soon. Even so, Tom was obviously so excited about his brothers inheritance. And so it was left for Steve to have a couple of whiskeys to celebrate, while we bought both Tom and his friend a bottle of something to take home for after work!

271

"Do you need us anymore today Steve? If not we'll get back to the office now we've eaten. I can't believe what's happened today. Always did say you were a jammy bugger!" Tom laughed, "But seriously, I'm so pleased for you Steve. You deserve it. Just don't forget your poor relations will you?"

Steve gave a hearty laugh, embraced his brother, thanked him for his help, then told him to, "Clear off back to work ... and thanks."

Not feeling ready to rush back to our encampment straight away, Steve obviously had the need to come to terms with what had happened that morning. We saw a sign for Allesley Park and, not having been there before, chose to head for this as a place to unwind and come to terms with all that he had buzzing around inside his head. It proved to be a good choice as there was plenty of empty space, and hardly any people about just at that time. For some time we just walked, hand in hand, in complete silence. When he did stop walking, he just turned to me, looked me in the eyes with such passion pouring from him that I wouldn't have been surprised if he'd thrown me on the ground and made love to me there and then!

As I could see a group of children playing a little way off I was rather relieved when he said, "Let's go back to the van Mel."

The expression on his face as we walked was a picture. At one point along the way he stopped, turned to me, and said,

"You see Mel; haven't I always said, where there's a will there's a way? This time there actually is a proper will!"

It wasn't until about an hour and a half later that we realised we'd not got the shopping we'd promised the others. But then, as he said, a bit of do-it-yourself food (as he put it), wouldn't do tonight. We would take them down to the Bull Inn again for a real celebration meal (and no doubt more than a few drinks to wash it down!) And so the only stop on our way back to them was to collect some paperwork from Deans as we passed by. Mr Dean explained that he would need to complete such things as probate and the like, but what he'd given us was proof to show anyone that the property was now Steve's.

Needless to say, I drove back that day! There was no way Steve was in a fit state to do so. I did wonder how the news about the Grange would be taken by the others, but of course, when we gathered them round in a circle around the fire they were about to cook over, they all sat there in shocked silence, not knowing at first whether to believe him or whether he was just kidding until I backed up his story.

"So all your ideas of us getting back in there, and your plans to make a business of it … you really mean to do it?" Graham asked.

Steve patted him on the back and replied,

"There's nothing stopping us now, and you lot will be taking up important positions in it, so I hope you're ready for some hard graft."

Once again all eight of us invaded the pub, spending even more this time due to Steve ordering a couple of bottles of bubbly for those who wanted it, and anything else anyone preferred for those who didn't! I really believe the locals and the landlord were used to us by now, and had even begun to accept us as part of their community.

By closing time it was clear that there were those amongst us, and one in particular, who were extremely merry! In fact it took me all my time to persuade Steve to give in and come to bed that night. He wouldn't stop singing all the way back (by the sound of them, these must have been songs from his army days!). Then, when we did get him back to camp, he was determined to strip off and dive into the lake for a swim before bed! It took Pete, Bob and myself all our effort to persuade him this was not a good idea, while Ellen, Graham and Jez watched with obvious amusement!

When we did get him into the van I told the other two I could handle him, somehow wondering if I'd get allowed to sleep that night! As it happened I needn't have worried on that score.

Though he was already half undressed from his swimming plan, when he collapsed on the bed all I could do was to remove his shoes, somehow heave him out of his jeans, and cover him up. I just managed to squeeze into a small edge of the bed alongside him. He was out cold and remained so until quite late into the next morning!

I really don't think there was anyone in the group fit for morning exercise the next day as it happens. In fact, even the thought of bacon and eggs was not as appealing as usual for some reason. There did seem the need for plenty of black coffee on the other hand. Though everyone else managed to creep out of their tents one at a time, with the exception of myself and Ellen as the bubbly we'd been drinking hadn't had quite the same effects as the stronger drinks the men had followed it down with, 'Lord Lansdown' as he'd been named by the others, didn't actually surface until nearly ten thirty that morning. I bet that was the latest he'd slept in till since he was a kid!

After enough coffee and a couple of slices of toast to soak up the remnants of last night, he announced that he thought we should pay a visit to the Grange in order to start the eviction process and get our home back. All seemed in agreement, though a bit dubious as to how this was to be done, and so that was settled. I did have my doubts, but then I knew that, if that was what he'd set his mind to, there was little that would stand in his way.

When we arrived within sight of the place Steve stopped and looked to see if there were any guards on the gates this time. Of course there was still the same two hulks we'd seen before.

"Now what, we'll never get past them," Pete said.

"Don't be too sure of that, you ask Mel; our motto is where there's a will there's a way, isn't that right Mel?"

This brought a smile to my face since he'd not reminded me of this for a while now. I was quick to assure Pete that Steve did have a knack for finding ways that others wouldn't think of. Mind you, taking this second look at these two inside the gate, I did wonder just what 'way' he had in mind this time.

For a second or two he stood deep in thought before turning to us all and giving his orders,

"Right, what I want you to do is to give me about five minutes or so, and then go up to the gate and distract them. Talk to them, shout at them, even throw stuff at them, but don't take any chances. Your job is Just to keep them occupied, but I don't want anyone to get hurt, so just be careful! If they open the gates get out of there fast. Do you understand?"

I took hold of his arm as he was about to leave us,

"Steve, what are you planning? Can't I come with you? I know what you're like and whatever you've got in mind it probably isn't a good idea."

All he would say was not to worry, that he was only planning on seeing who else is in 'our' house! He was sure that, whoever was there would be quite happy to leave once he introduced himself!

I turned back just for an instant to see the others gathering together, but in that split second, I looked round but he was gone. How did he always manage to do that? He seemed to have a knack of vanishing without a sound, and without a trace. He really could be so annoying at times, but that was probably what attracted me to him. I reckon that, after Steve, any lesser man would hold no appeal to me now, so I could see by this time that for me it was him or no one.

We followed orders and waited, just out of sight of the gates at first. When we thought our five minutes were up we cautiously approached them and called out to the men inside. One of them came over to see what was going on, and didn't take long to come to the conclusion that these were the same bunch of squatters they had thrown out not so long ago.

"What do you lot of tramps want, there's nothing for you here?" and then, as I stepped forward, added, "And what's that yank doing with you?"

"I'm no 'yank', as you put it, and what we want is to come in."

The other one had come to see what was going on. He had obviously heard what was said, and was quick to notice something his mate had missed.

"Yank or not, where's your mate; the fella with the attitude? He's a yank for sure ain't he?"

I carried on the conversation with them as long as I could and, with help from the others chiming in as well, we managed to keep them busy for some time. Before too long I was aware of Steve creeping up behind them, and before they had chance to see him coming he had one of them in some sort of headlock.

"Right, now perhaps you'll be kind enough to tell me where your boss is."

"Huh, who do you think you are? You don't really think you can keep me from breaking your neck do you?"

"Well I wouldn't bet on that. Besides I reckon you'd need to get out of this first," and as he said this he tightened his grip.

The second one made a move toward him, but Steve spun his captive round to face him saying,

"I wouldn't if I were you. Not if you don't want your mates neck to be broken. Now I suggest you go and get your boss out here before I lose my patience and do it anyway."

For just a brief second he seemed unsure just what to do, but Steve once again tightened his grip, causing his victim to choke briefly. This was just sufficient to send his mate scurrying off toward the house as if pursued by a pack of hounds!

While he was gone Steve directed his prisoner toward the gate and held him against it, telling Dave, who was nearest at the time, to feel in his pockets for keys. He proved to be right, they were in there. As Steve moved away from them, he told Dave to unlock and open them wide, and to come in to 'his' home!

I must admit to just a very, very tiny feeling of sympathy for the poor chap Steve still had a tight grip. Big as he was he had stopped struggling and admitted defeat to this unknown man threatening to break his neck! All he could do now was wait in the hope his boss would do something to help, but then he also knew that, having failed to do his job satisfactorily, he would probably be out of a job anyway. Even so, surely he must be thinking, better no job than no neck!

It was barely more than a few minutes before we saw someone approach from the direction of the house. Obviously more than a little annoyed he marched straight up to Steve and demanded to know just what he thought he was doing on his property, and why had he got hold of his man this way?

Looking from where I was standing just then I couldn't help but notice just the very minutest glimpse of familiarity in his features, but tough as he might be, Steve always had an air of control and one of kindness. This face bore what could only be described as a scowl, not so much as a glimmer of kindness behind those eyes!

Steve looked him in the eye for a second before speaking,

"So tell me; who am I speaking to? And anyway, I believe if you read this, you'll find it's you who's on my property, not the other way around."

Somehow I knew who this was. It had to be Henry Stanwick's son, Luke. It was obvious to me that Steve also knew this. What would happen now I had no idea, but could only stand back and wait. Luke was quick to say he was Luke Stanwick, and had inherited the property from his grandparents. Steve's face just at that moment was totally expressionless. He stared at this unfriendly, not particularly good looking and much shorter man, before answering,

"I think you need to read this before assuming that. I think you'll find it names me as the heir to the estate."

He handed the paper to Luke who read it with a look of incredulity spreading across his face before asking,

"So what claim do you think you have?"

"Apart from the will which is now in the hands of the solicitors you mean? I suppose you could say that I too am Mrs Stanwick's grandson. My name is Steven Lockett. You could say we shared the same father, though I'd rather not be reminded of that fact."

"Oh, I get it now. You're the bastard from that slapper father told me about eh?"

Well, I had thought it was going too well! I'd just thought he was keeping his temper so well, but as soon as I heard Luke badmouthing Steve's mother I knew all hope was lost!

Before anyone could stop him, Steve punched Luke right in the face, threw him on the ground, and put his foot on his neck! To my great surprise though, just as I expected something far worse to follow, he took his foot off, grabbed Luke by the collar of his coat, and physically threw him outside the gate. The other two men didn't wait to be evicted, they just disappeared up the path the way we'd come. Muttering some particularly choice words, Steve just turned away, leaving Dave to lock the gates behind them, and walked off in the direction of the house!

Chapter Twenty-Six.

I followed him inside and found him upstairs in the room we'd used before. The door was closed, but I went in anyway; I was feeling particularly worried about his state of mind. I believe I was right to be concerned just for a while. He was just sitting on a box in the corner, one we had used as a seat by the window when we'd slept in here before. I said nothing at first, just went across and sat down with him. His fists were clenched tightly and his face was still so obviously fighting the fury coming from inside his mind.

"You know you don't have to do this Steve; I mean we can just walk away from here and forget we ever saw the place. We were happy before we came here, and we can be happy again somewhere else. That's all I care about, just for us to be together and be happy."

For another minute or two he still didn't speak or move, but then he turned to me and said, "You're right Mel, we don't have to do this, or stay here come to that," he hesitated before walking across, looking out of the window and saying, "But just look out there. Look at this place. It's all mine Mel; why shouldn't we do what we wanted to?

Why should I let the likes of that piece of scum get in my way? After what happened to poor Mum, I reckon they owed me something, and I'm damned well not letting that piece of dirt stop me."

(Actually the word 'dirt' was not exactly the one he used!)

"Are you sure about that, take your time to think about it first," but by this time he'd sprang back to life and was ready for action.

When we went back downstairs we found the rest of the group in the main hall, looking rather shaken by the experience, and clearly concerned for just what was to happen next. Having pulled himself together sufficiently, Steve immediately began allotting jobs to us all. He said that some of us should go back to collect up everything from our campsite. I said I would go for the van and we could pack as much equipment inside to save carrying it, but he insisted on going himself, just in case Luke and his men were out there anywhere.

As a consequence Ellen, Jez, Graham and I were to stay here, while Dave, Bob and Pete were to go with him. I asked if he thought he'd be able to get everything in the van, but he said that, if not he'd make a second trip. I must admit to feeling just a little concerned at just the four of us being left here without his protection, but then, isn't that just the sort of situation he had in mind when he'd suggested teaching us self-defence? Problem was that we'd only just started, so decided to keep the gates and doors firmly locked until he returned!

About an hour later we heard a vehicle approaching and were relieved to see it was Steve driving the van. Alongside him sat Dave. As they pulled up outside we went out to meet them and found Bob and Pete sitting inside on top of all the hastily packed tents and equipment. And then, Ellen burst into fits of laughter! When I looked behind Annie to see what was so funny, there was Bob's chicken coop, roughly tied on behind!

"Well we could hardly leave the girls behind now they've got a home to go to, could we?" he told her.

For the next few hours we spent some time looking through the content of the assorted outbuildings. Those nearest the back of the house appeared to be what was once a rather impressive stable block. These contained an array of most beautifully carved furniture. Though old and dusty, Graham was quick to say that it would be worth a fortune in the antique market, but Steve said he felt it should be brought back into the house where it belonged. Amongst this there were beds, chairs, and a table which would easily seat ten or twelve people! Temporarily all we could do was to brush it all off as best we could, but Graham said that the next time he went into the village he knew just the place to buy the polish he needed to bring it back to something like it should look.

Having made a list of necessary items to buy that afternoon, Ellen, Graham and I were about to set off for the village when we met a police car coming up to the gates. I immediately knew this meant trouble as he had Luke Stanwick and his two men with him. It turned out I was right as he asked to speak to Mr Lockett. I escorted him back to the house and took him in to the hall where Steve and the others were busy arranging the furniture we'd found.

"Someone to speak to you Steve,"

He looked up from what he was doing in surprise,

"Yes constable, can I help you?" he asked, as calmly as if this morning had never happened.

"Yes sir. It's about an assault on this gentleman earlier.

Steve turned to look at Luke, then back to the constable, "Yes constable, I can see the poor chap has a nasty bruise on his face. How did that happen?"

Well, I just had to turn away for a second to regain my composure!

"Mr Stanwick here tells me that, not only did you attack him, but you also evicted him from his own property, namely Lansdown Grange. Is that correct sir?"

Still Steve kept a totally inscrutable expression. Luke turned, red faced to the constable telling him,

"It was him constable. My family, the Stanwick's, have lived here for generations, he has no claim on it. As for the assault, he came here with that gang of his and beat me up. You ask my men here?"

Steve reached in his pocket and handed the constable his paper from Deans. To settle this matter the constable reached for his phone and rang Mr Dean. Two minutes later he was able to confirm that it was a genuine claim, Steve was actually the owner.

"But what about the assault constable? You're not going to let them get away with it are you?"

Steve looked at our group and grinned, before turning back to the constable and saying,

"I'm sorry you've had a wasted journey constable. It seems Mr Stanwick has quite an imagination. You see we are about to set up a home for the homeless and training centre. These are the first folks I've met locally who have been living rough for some time. I mean … just look at them, they couldn't throw a dish cloth in a sink, let alone a punch!"

"What about you sir? You look well able to do so if you don't mind me saying."

"I am sorry you've had your time wasted, but to be honest I wouldn't dirty my hands," then looking at the man he'd had in his grasp earlier, "Did you see me do this?"

His eyes stared, unblinkingly at the poor man, just briefly but that was enough to cause the poor chap to visibly (well, to me anyway), shudder, before saying,

"No sir, I didn't see anything."

What more could the constable do but assume Steve was correct in telling him that Luke was just using this as a means to get the property back? Having apologised to Steve for the disruption, and accused Luke of wasting police time, he was just turning to leave when he stopped and came back.

"So, do I understand you to mean sir that you plan to turn this into a homeless shelter?"

Steve had just been turning away to come back in, but stopped to explain that it was in some ways, but as he went on to explain, not for those who just wanted to lay around drinking and smoking drugs. For a second or two I quite expected the poor chap to risk a good talking to by asking if there were any other sort, but Steve gave him no time to do so before continuing,

"My plan, or should I say our plan, is to take those who are living on the streets through no fault of their own."

When he saw the slightly puzzled expression on the constables' face he called some of the others over.

"You see, Bob and his wife had a perfectly good smallholding until it was taken from them on the cheap for the new road to go through. Graham lost his wife and was later made redundant, and couldn't afford his rent, Pete worked for a business that went bust, so the same situation hit him. You see, all these people have a reason for their misfortune, and all need help of some sort, not to scrounge off, but to get back on their feet and, even more importantly, to get back some self-pride!"

"Ah, now I see. Well I for one think you've got a brilliant idea, and it's good of you to even try to understand their situation, not many would."

"That's because most people have never tried living rough, I did for a good two years."

The constable stopped and stared at Steve with a puzzled expression before saying,

"But now you own this massive place, and you're happy to fill it with these much less fortunate people? I'd take my hat off to you if I hadn't got it my hand already! So, if I come across anyone out there, should I send them to you?"

"By all means. It's a long way from perfect yet. Needs a lot of work to bring it up to scratch after so long, but if they are prepared to work for their board and lodging, hopefully learn a trade to support themselves, we'll take in as many as possible. The plan is to give them an address to use when they look for work, and perhaps help some find places in college to get qualifications, perhaps the odd apprenticeship."

The constable went off suitably impressed with Steve and his plans, so much so that he knew he was right in believing Steve over Luke earlier! Besides, he could see what Steve had meant when he said that none of us would be capable of delivering such a blow as someone quite obviously had on this Stanwick chap.

Dave followed him down to the gate and locked it behind him and, as we watched the police car disappear around the corner out of sight, the whole group let out such a cheer for Steve that I wouldn't have been surprised to see him come back to find out what the noise was about.

After all gathering around to talk about what had happened, all except me quite amazed at the cool and collected way Steve had handled it, Graham reminded us that we were supposed to be going shopping. This time we did actually manage to do just that, this time with Ellen taking a turn at hiding from view in the back. I made my mind up to suggest to Steve that, if we were possibly going to be needing transport for more than just the two of us, we might need a more suitable vehicle. After all, it seemed we had got off to a good start with the local constabulary, so we must at least try to stick to regulations!

By the time we returned with supplies and equipment, brooms, buckets cleaning fluids and a selection of basic tools, and obviously a good supply of food to sustain the workers, it was agreed that we'd done enough for one day. Not having electricity, and therefore no means of freezing food, we had taken the decision to stick to BBQ food for today. While we were getting this going I discussed with Steve the need to get the electricity in the house sorted as soon as possible. As I told him, this would make it possible to buy a decent sized freezer, and perhaps replace the old solid fuel Aga with a more reliable electric version.

In fact we could see that there really was so much to do that, just for a very brief moment, we did begin to wonder just where to begin, but everyone in all our brilliant new family were so full of enthusiasm, it was almost impossible to allow our doubts to take over. In fact I really can't remember anyone having a word of doubt to express, least of all Steve.

Though we were all still in the same state as we were before being thrown out, it seemed all were more than happy to spend what would be the first of many more nights, in sleeping bags on the floor! Even so, Steve made them a promise that, as soon as it was possible to do so, all would be provided with proper, comfortable beds! Though I, as much as any, was pretty eager to have the feel of a good, soft mattress under me at last, I had make the suggestion that perhaps the priority here would be, as I'd already said, to get the electricity sorted first. It was clear that all were in agreement.

"Ok, first thing tomorrow we'll head out in search of a firm who can take on such a big job. After all, they'll find it well worth their while, especially as we'll need the outbuildings done next."

And so that was the next day planned ... not bad going, all in one day!

Chapter Twenty-Seven.

On our first full day in our new home Steve decided to head off to Birmingham in search of a reliable firm of electricians. Knowing that this would be a good opportunity to also do some tool shopping, he thought he should take Pete along. Graham was keeping busy now in his attempt to bring some of the woodwork back into shape, and Dave said he thought he needed to do a more thorough survey of the facilities there before deciding just what he needed. Anyway, as he said, it would be good to get the power on first and meanwhile there was nothing to stop him hunting for the stop-cock to see what happened when he turned the water on! As he said, there was always the chance we'd all get a cold shower if the pipes were dodgy.

Meanwhile the rest of us carried on with the general clean-up operations until we saw Steve heading back up the drive. It was pretty clear that he'd had quite a successful day. He soon filled us in with the news that he had managed to coax a firm with a particularly good reputation that it would be well worth sending in a crew of electricians to rewire the whole place. Pete reckoned that the expression on the boss's face when Steve told him the size of the place was incredible,

"When he saw us out he all but bowed to 'Lord Lansdown' here," a remark that sent us all into hysterics.

In fact it was the very next morning that a van arrived with four men in it to survey the job and make lists of materials and equipment they might need. Their boss came along with them, probably to check out if this Lockett bloke was for real. I must admit though that when he saw the rest of us, especially as we were all in our tattiest clothes for work purposes. Steve obviously decided it was best to explain what he was doing with the place and, though the chap did look somewhat bewildered, he had no intention of turning down the best job his firm had had for some time.

Knowing Steve had stressed the importance of getting the place safe and the power installed, the following day we could barely move without falling over an electrician! In fact it was too crowded to do much at all inside, so Bob suggested setting to and giving him and Ellen a hand to start on an epic garden tidy! It really wasn't until we started this that we realised just what effort would need go into it to bring it back to any decent state. Mind you, it was a beautiful day, far too good to spend indoors, so I believe the idea was a good one.

By the end of another long, tiring day, Ellen came to the village with me to find food. None of us could find the energy to fiddle about with the BBQ, and it would be a few more days before we could even consider acquiring a cooker of any sort, so had decided to go to a take-away. I wasn't sure how the villagers would take to having to wait in a queue while we ordered eight portions of everything, but to my surprise, it seemed that the village constable, the one who Steve had spoken to before, had spread the news about 'the new folks at the Grange' and, though we were concerned they might not approve, to our surprise, we found ourselves inundated with their welcomes and good wishes!

This feeling was gradually extended, especially after we apologised on more than that one occasion for the hold-up at the take-away, but explained that we had no means of cooking just yet.

To our great surprise a few days later, we were just about to drive off to the village when we saw a car pull up outside. Giving it what must have been a rather suspicious look, I went across to see who this was. You can imagine my surprise when I was met by a couple of the ladies we'd spoken to in the queue at the take-away on a couple of occasions!

"Hello there," one of them said as the other walked round to the boot of the car, "I do hope you don't mind, but since you explained what you're doing here, we wonder if this may be of use to you?"

As she did so lifted out a box containing four large food flasks,

"It's just some stew us W.I. ladies made up for you. We remembered you saying you have no cooking facilities yet, and many of us have masses of fresh vegetables in our gardens. Oh, by the way, we hope you all like beef? The butcher in the High Street supplied that."

We really couldn't believe our luck. I mean, BBQ food is ok, but you really do need a change from time to time. I took them in to introduce them to Steve and the rest of the gang. Of course, as I expected, Steve put on his most charming character and, although everyone was somewhat scruffy from the hard work of cleaning the place up, all were on their best behaviour. It seemed that both ladies had lived in the village all their lives, and expressed their pleasure to think the Grange was at last to be put to use.

"Would you like a look around ladies?" Steve asked.

I could see they were both hoping he might say that! We both took them round, and as we went from room to room we explained exactly what our plans were. I must admit to being pleasantly surprised to find that they were greatly impressed to hear that someone owning such a place would be keen to help those so much less fortunate. They even suggested that they could perhaps help with any curtains from their members, as they said, quite a few do have a habit of changing them just because they go off the colours, or perhaps redecorate. With so many windows to cover I said this would be a god-send.

That being the case I later suggested to the team that perhaps we should at the very least, give as many rooms as possible a coat of emulsion before hanging curtains. Consequently it was down to Ellen and myself to go off in search of quite a few cans of emulsion, mostly magnolia in colour to go with whatever curtains were forthcoming. As our new home was fairly evenly distanced between Coventry and Birmingham we had the choice of destination, but I suggested Birmingham as I was keen to pay a visit to Josh. Steve suggested that perhaps, while we were there we should check out the cookers and other essential equipment.

As it happened it proved to be a good choice of destination. We parked in the same place we had done before, going into the centre from the park and ride. As this meant passing the pub where Josh worked, I suggested stopping off on our way in to say hello, and just caught him on his way out. It turned out that he wasn't actually on shift until the evening. When I explained what we were doing there, and of course about Steve's inheritance, he was completely lost for words. I could see he wanted to ask so many questions, but was trying not to pry too deeply into anything that might cause offence. It was so obvious that he still very much hero worshipped Steve!

Hearing about our mission to find a cooker and assorted kitchen equipment for our project, he was quick to offer his services. Since we first introduced him to the landlord of the pub, it seems that he'd gone from clearing tables and filling the dishwasher, to actually doing a good proportion of the catering. It would appear that he was now blossoming into a pretty capable cook. In fact he even told me that he had been doing the necessary training and qualifications part-time to become a proper chef, whilst working in the kitchen of the pub.

After listening to my description of the Grange and the way Steve had inherited it, he suddenly surprised me by coming out with a brilliant suggestion.

"If the place has big gardens like you say, have you thought about the idea of hosting weddings there? You could do them in a big marquee in the good weather, and get caterers in. I made a mental note to mention this idea to Steve as soon as we went home.

With Josh along to advise us (though, unlike me, Ellen was a pretty good cook, I was very much less so!), we found ourselves returning with a van full of food mixers, pots and pans, cutlery for both cooking and eating with, and an array of casserole dishes, china etc. Most importantly, and this being where Josh really came into his own, we had ordered a pretty big electric Aga, a large fridge freezer, plus a washing machine and tumble dryer! Josh had taken us to an electrical wholesalers, and the look on the salesman's face as we watched him enter all this onto his computer was priceless! I had all I could do to keep a straight face as I handed over my credit card. I truly think that, if Josh, who he already knew, hadn't vouched for me, he would have been much less keen to accept this.

With a slightly reluctant look on his face though, he did accept it, promising to have it all delivered as soon as possible. I believe that the address of Lansdown Grange did help to convince him in the end. By the time we walked out of there and out of earshot of the poor man, we all three absolutely curled up laughing!

"I'm sure the poor fella didn't believe you could afford all that stuff," Josh said, when he could pull himself together enough to speak.

"I suppose you can't blame him, after all, I can hardly believe it myself. As we told you last time we saw you, I did get quite a chunk from the house I sold in Surrey and had planned on needing that to buy the Grange, but when Steve found it had been left to him anyway that meant we were better off than we'd expected.

We stayed and sampled some of Josh's cooking for our lunch before heading back, but made sure he knew where to find us anytime he had a day off and wanted to come for a look round.

"Though I can't promise you won't find yourself with a paintbrush in your hand," Ellen told him.

"Oh, knowing Steve like I do I'm sure you're right,"

On our drive back Ellen remarked what a nice young man he was, and asked how we knew him. It didn't really come as such a surprise to her, not until I told her that Steve had picked him up off the street whilst we were still 'on the run' from the police ourselves.

"Why on earth … why would he care about someone like that at a time like that?"

This brought a smile to my face. As I said to her, that's just the nature of the man. After all, when he took me on I couldn't even remember who I was, and even worse, by the time we found that out, we also found I could have been a murderer! But then, as I explained, he was living rough too at the time.

By the time we arrived back home (that word 'home' sounded good), we passed a van load of electricians going away for the night! Steve had obviously stressed the importance of getting the work done as quickly as possible, and I must admit they all looked pretty shattered. Even so, Bob told us that they'd promised to be back first thing the next day to carry on. It seemed that, while they had been busy working on the wiring, Dave had set to and, with a little help from Pete, had achieved great things in the plumbing department! Though it was only cold, we could at least now get running water in the house.

During the next few months everybody put their very best efforts into the huge amount of work, some planned, and quite a lot completely unexpected, and it was rewarding to us all to see our hard work paying off in leaps and bounds. The electricians did a marvellous job on their part, meaning that it was earlier than expected that we were able to get them connecting up the new cooker and fridge freezer. Meanwhile, our friends from the W.I. had made us their favourite charity by turning up fairly regularly with hot food. As soon as they saw our freezer was in working order in the kitchen, they turned their attention to bringing us frozen vegetables from their own gardens to fill it! They also turned up in force one day, armed with a huge heap of assorted curtains, all of which they stayed and helped us hang. Though I had never seen myself as a W.I. type, I believe that they came pretty close to converting me!

It proved a good thing that we'd bought plenty of paint, and had remembered a good number of brushes, as practically everyone turned their hands to that job on the odd occasion when it was wet. The dry days were often monopolised by Bob and Ellen press ganging anyone they found jobless to help in the big garden tidy! Mind you, it was clear to see just how impressive these must have been once. Steve stood upstairs one day looking out at the front garden with such a thoughtful expression that I had to ask what was in his mind.

"Oh well, I was just thinking how hard my grandfather must have worked to do this all alone. But perhaps, once he'd got it round, it would have been easier. Do you reckon he'd approve of this Mel? I don't mean just the garden, I mean me having the place, and what we're doing here?"

"Do you know Steve, I'm absolutely sure he'd be thrilled to see someone bring it all back to life, and even more so his grandson. I know what you're thinking, you're thinking he might resent you for what Henry did, but I bet he would be more concerned with his daughter and the son she produced. Did he ever see you, do you know?"

"No, Mum always said he died just before I was born. He was at her wedding though, so he knew Peter would never let anyone hurt her again," and then added thoughtfully, "and then I go and do just that. But never again, I swear to that!"

Right from those early days while we were getting into our stride, Steve set his basic plans into action by pushing everyone able to do so to turn out each morning for an exercise session on the lawn, followed by a jog, slow at first, but gradually turning pretty brisk! He also kept up his self-defence class for those wanting to join in. With these though, he made it clear that he was not teaching us to attack anyone, in fact the idea was to defend ourselves with as little effort as possible. Using martial arts type techniques of catching the other person off balance, we soon began to understand the principal … putting it into practice was another matter!

As I'd predicted, Josh did turn up one week, unfortunately too late to muck in with the painting! He was genuinely amazed by the sheer scale of the place and what we were setting out to achieve.

"So what are you doing to fund raise? With a place like this there's no end to the possibilities!"

While we'd been so busy with the renovations we'd not truly thought past applying for a grant as a charity. It had been obvious that we'd need to get some sort of income if we wanted to make it work, but hadn't thought seriously about much else yet.

And here was Josh, the down and out street lad, the one who had no hopes or ambitions until Steve helped him, here he was telling Steve what he needed to do!

"During the winter you could hold conferences here. It's near both major cities so there are always plenty of them, and no real for accommodation needed when there are hotels all around. Then I expect there'll be a lot of groups and the like wanting somewhere to host Christmas parties and dances."

Steve looked thoughtful for a second, but that was a second too long for the lads' enthusiasm,

"Come on man, you need to get your name out there before they find other venues."

This brought a smile to Steve's face. Patting Josh on the back, he said that he was probably right,

"And can you recommend a young, energetic chef to do the catering for all this by any chance?"

Obviously that was just the opening Josh was waiting for. He also pointed out that he could find others amongst his mates from catering college who would be pleased for the opportunity to practice their culinary skills this way.

Chapter Twenty-Eight.

Now, when reading this, you may be thinking that it seemed strange that Luke Stanwick was so easy to fob off finding, as he did, what he'd been so convinced should have been his inheritance? Well, I'm sorry to report that this was certainly not the case. While we were putting all our efforts into building, not just a strong team and a well organised business under Steve's leadership, what we didn't realise for some time was that he had been working hard to contest the will, using Steve's illegitimacy as his reasoning to do so.

As soon as we were made aware of this, Steve instructed Mr Dean to act on his behalf in the matter. This meant, as he did have the will firmly in his possession, that there was not a thing Luke could do to persuade the courts to overthrow that. This therefore barely concerned us at all.

By this time we received the good news that Lansdown Grange Homeless Shelter and Training Centre was to receive a sizeable grant to help with our sizeable costs. This was particularly well timed as each visit Steve or myself made into Birmingham, Coventry or even Leamington, we seemed to attract more street folk, most but not all, desperate for help, and more than pleased to accept the help we could offer. Before us actually accepting them though, they had to be made aware of the strict rules as laid down by Steve. Strictly no drinking, drugs, smoking inside any of the buildings. They must agree to follow Steve's regime to get themselves back into a fit and healthy state, and then actively look for work or further education to get back on track. In return for this commitment they would receive free board and lodging, a reference where required, and that very necessary address to offer future employers. In fact we had actually had drawn up a document for them to sign to that effect so that we would be within our rights to evict anyone refusing to stick to these rules.

We had by this point found the need for extra accommodation, but this was now sorted by the hard working electricians, Dave on the plumbing, Pete on the building and all the labouring forthcoming by so many, to convert the spacious stable block into small one bedroom bungalows of a sort. These we were pleased to offer to those first six who had worked so tirelessly to help get us up and running, though Jez, being a young single chap with hopes still of eventually being able to get back his place in University to finish his degree, decided that he was more than happy to take a bed in the men's dormitory. Perhaps it must sound rather unfair but, by the insistence of all of them, it had been agreed that Steve and I should make the west wing our home! Though I could tell he was a little uncomfortable with taking over such a large part of the house, I suppose it was, after all, his home now. All I could do was hope that the love I felt for this man would be shared by him sufficiently to allow me to make this my home too. Who could tell?

Our friendly constable who we had by now got to know as Jim, had turned up on one occasion with two youngsters, desperate for the help we could offer. Over the course of the next few months we gradually managed to restore and reorganise the main house itself. Before the weather had turned too cold to do so, some of these new residents had to make use of temporary accommodation provided in a collection of wooden pods, the sort we had been so taken with at Stratford not so long ago. We had bought these in a while before our numbers swelled, assuming that they could make a useful addition to our facilities, and could perhaps be rented out in the summer to holiday visitors. By the summer we had planned to build a toilet and shower block, but until then those sleeping there would need to use the indoor ones.

Temporarily though we needed the extra sleeping space that these gave us, and certainly got no complaints from those who, until now, had been reduced to sleeping under cardboard and in doorways or alleys. As we explained when they had the offer of a place, these would just be to sleep in with the addition of plenty of clean bedding provided, and all meals supplied in the dining room of the house itself.

Gradually over the next few months we had completed a renovation of the good size kitchen, putting in a good range of units, a large larder, double sink, dishwasher, in fact pretty nearly anything anyone could need to cater for the number we assumed would be our top capacity!

Next to the kitchen, and completing the length of the rear of the building, was a long narrow dining room. To furnish this we had Graham to thank again. When clearing out the last part of the stable block, one of the larger pieces of furniture we came across was yet another massive, solid oak table, exactly like the one we'd found previously, both clearly made for this very room. Both fitted perfectly side by side, meaning that we could probably now fit twenty to twenty four at a push. (Of course, feeding that many at a time could be pretty hard!).

Our plan, which was gradually coming to fruition, was to completely convert the east wing into two long dormitories, one female, and one male, each with shower and toilet facilities at the end which was the priority with Jez 'roughing it' in the half finished dorm. From the dormitories there would be a landing leading to a staircase going down into the dining room, and another at the front of the house leading down into the entrance hall. Below this were further toilet facilities to serve the main hall itself. Opposite this, on the other side of the entrance hall and tucked away under the stairs which lead up to our apartment, Steve had turned this room into an office from which to concentrate on the running of the business. Strangely, until now, I always thought of him as an action man, but never realised what a good business man he could be too.

From the entrance hall there was of course, the door leading straight into what was fast becoming what must have been a place of sheer elegance! It was this space which, as Josh had suggested, would be perfect for holding social or business functions. Of all the rooms this was the one we put most effort into as we could see the benefits we could gain from the uses it may have. As time went on Josh was to prove correct on this matter.

As soon as the paint was dry, the huge chandeliers, also found under a heap of old sacking in the outbuildings, were hung back where they so clearly belonged. I did put my foot down on this job, insisting that we must get in someone qualified to do this job. I knew that it would only take one false move to send them crashing to the floor, a thing I was sure I remembered seeing in a comedy programme on tv once, and somehow I didn't reckon a couple of ordinary shop bought lights and shades would do the room justice!

We were beginning to get known right across the region, and from time to time private individuals and companies from quite a distance would contribute useful things to us. Things like pots, pans, kettles and the like were given by a local shop. We even had one of the big furniture warehouses in the region supplying us with beds sufficient to fill both dormitories. Another smaller firm provided beds for the four stable bungalows. All we had to do was buy bedding to go on these.

To see Ellen and Bob finally settle into their new home, and so happy to do so, gave me a truly warm feel. After the way their life had been for so long now, they were so clearly feeling as if they now had somewhere they belonged ... somewhere they could settle and feel safe.

Of course, it wasn't just everyone else who was gradually getting the luxury of good beds! The company who had provided the majority of these, knowing what we were trying to do for so many less privileged, took us completely by surprise by including a 'super-king' size bed, especially for us! And I must say this was a real luxury, especially with a well built, six foot-two hunk like Steve spread all over it ... which did mean I had to cuddle up as close as possible to prevent myself falling out! (Well, that's my excuse, and I'm sticking to it!).

We did find ourselves facing a bit of a dilemma on the first occasion we were asked to provide a local business with facilities for their annual do. Though we contacted Josh, who agreed to organise the catering, we suddenly realised that we didn't have nearly enough chairs to seat them all. I had to phone the director of the company to break the bad news. As I said to Steve, this was not a good start. The next day I received a call from the same man I'd spoken to. He said that I should be ready to receive a delivery that day! Later that day a van pulled up outside and a couple of chaps knocked on the door,

"Are you Mrs Lockett?" but before I could get out the word 'no', they started unloading a whole van full of chairs! Ok, not brand new, but all in very good condition. I tried saying that I hadn't ordered these, but was told,

"Nothing to do with me love, we were just told they're for Lansdown Grange. Sign here please missus."

And then they were gone! It turned out that the chap who wanted to use the hall did have a place of his own until recently, but as he no longer had this he was more than happy to donate them.

During the first few months things really took off. Those using our facilities for events, even small local gatherings like our friendly W.I. ladies, certainly brought the place to life, to say nothing of bringing in a pretty good income to help with the running costs. I think it also went a long way towards convincing the doubters that Steve's plans to help, rather than condemn, what many referred to as the 'dregs' of society, was well worth their support. Yes, there was the odd failure who were too far gone to retrieve into normal society, but the harder Steve worked with the majority, the more I could see that it was not just them who benefitted from his work, but Steve himself!

After all he had suffered and all he had lost on a personal level over the last few years, he was quite clearly peeling away the layers of self-protection which he had built up like a defensive wall around himself during that time. He was absolutely in his element when it came to encouraging those able to do so to join his fitness regime.

There was one occasion when we were in Coventry that he had gone into a shop and I went looking for him. As I approached the corner I became aware of a young girl, probably about eighteen years old and quite clearly a rough sleeper by her appearance. As I walked toward her there were two men trying to grab at her, and goad her into a reaction of some sort. She asked them repeatedly to leave her alone, but this just made them laugh and ask why, didn't she like their company!

I looked around for Steve, knowing he would sort this out so easily, but he didn't appear, and I could tell things were escalating. I walked up to them before they noticed my presence and asked the one nearest me,

"Is there something you want from my friend here sir?"

This took them totally by surprise. The one near me turned, leered in my direction, then said,

"Oh look, now we've got one each."

"Sorry," I said, as if I was innocence itself, "I haven't introduced myself, I'm Mel," and as I said this held out my hand.

With a sickly smirk on his face, he glanced first at his mate, then holding his hand out as if to shake mine said,

"Hello Mel, I'm your worst nightmare," grabbing my hand as he did so, but half turning to pull a face at his mate.

Big mistake on his part ... before he knew what was happening to him he found himself flat on his back on the ground, winded and completely shocked! I couldn't resist adding a brisk kick as I put myself between both of them and the young girl, though I was just beginning to wonder just what to do next when the shock of what had happened to him wore off. I needn't have worried. The next thing I was aware of was a pat on the back, making me spin round ready to defend myself against another enemy, just to find Steve standing there behind me.

"Well done tiger, I can see you've taken in some of what I've taught you. I couldn't have done it better myself," and then turning to the bloke on the ground to tell him to, "clear off or you'll have me to deal with … not that she can't cope mind you."

"Are you ok?" I asked the young girl.

Still looking pretty shaken up, and throwing a suspicious glance at Steve, she assured me that she was now they'd gone. I introduced us both to her so that she knew we were not a threat in any way. Steve suggested going into a nearby café for a hot drink and a bite to eat. Still looking just a little unsure of this tall tough looking stranger, but so clearly in need of a good feed, she agreed, but made a point of sitting next to me, not him! Having asked what we both wanted from the menu, Steve went up to the counter to order for us all. As soon as he was out of earshot, Mia, as she was called, asked me,

"How did you do that … with that bloke out there I mean? And another thing, who's this fella you're with? Is he ok? I mean, it's a bit suspicious picking up girls off the street ain't it?"

Well, I don't know what she thought he had in mind but by the time he came back laden with food and drink for us all, I'd convinced her that he was quite harmless, and it had actually been him who had taught me how to do what I'd just done. As I told her, that was though, the first time I'd actually tried it out in real life.

"It worked didn't it? Don't reckon he expected that. Wish I could do it."

Steve was quick enough to have sensed her suspicions where he was concerned, but did just briefly tell her about our place at the Grange. It was left for me to fill in the details of exactly what we do there, and that, no, we were definitely not running some sort of brothel! After he'd finished eating, Steve left us to finish ours while he went off to get something he'd forgotten earlier, leaving me to chat openly with Mia. I stressed that she would be welcome to come with us, or to come another day if she fancied it at some point, but that it was entirely her choice. She asked about the type of accommodation she'd expect, probably worried about the men living there, but I explained briefly the layout of the male and female dormitories, there was therefore no need to worry on that score.

"Anyway, as you can imagine, there's absolutely no way Steve allows any untoward behaviour. The slightest breach of the rules and you're out!"

She sat quietly in thought for a moment. Then, still just a little bit half-heartedly asked,

"So you're saying I can actually come with you right now? And you reckon this Steve bloke can teach me to do what you did just now?"

By the time Steve came back, though still looking just a tiny bit unsure, we had collected Mia's rucksack and dirty looking sleeping bag from where she had it hidden, and were waiting outside to head back to the van together.

Her face was an absolute picture when Steve turned the van into the drive and she saw the Grange for the first time. I'd told her it was a big place, and explained what we were trying to do, but the sheer scale of the place was obviously beyond what she'd pictured! As she climbed out onto the drive, just for a few minutes all she could do was stand and stare, until Ellen came out to see if we'd managed to get the things she'd asked for.

"Oh hello dear, I take it you're another one of us folk with nowhere better to go eh?" adding a hearty laugh before going on, "I'm Ellen. Let me help you with your things, then I'll show you around and introduce you to the rest."

Seeing Mia still looking rather dubious about it all, she gave her an almost motherly smile and said,

"Don't look so worried dear, we've all been in the same boat as you. We were all on the streets until Steve and Mel came along," and then, checking over her shoulder to see Steve was out of earshot, "and I guarantee you can put your future in his hands and know he'll see no harm comes to you."

Chapter Twenty-Nine.

Though I pretended not to hear the conversation between Ellen and Mia, it was so good to know that my trust in Steve was shared by all those he was helping. If I'd ever doubted him before this, I knew I wouldn't do so ever again.

I left Mia in the safe hands of Ellen who took her first to find herself a bed in the female dormitory (actually our first female to use this), and then took her down for a cup of tea, introducing her to the rest of the gang as each of them appeared. Having taken upon herself to undertake much of the cooking, Ellen was particularly pleased to find that Mia was more than glad to help her with the ever growing task. By the end of that day she had clearly realised that no harm would come to her here. In fact, I could see that after talking, in particular to Jez and the other younger members of the community, her view of Steve had changed from suspicion to one of awe! I was beginning to think that if any other girls joined us I may have competition!

Before turning in that night Steve gave his usual pep talk to remind those up to it that he would be outside at eight sharp the next morning for exercises and a 'short' jog! Mia's face was a picture. This was not what she expected, and I believe she was all for giving it a miss until I whispered to her that it was only when he knew you were fit enough, he would let you join the self-defence classes that helped me cope with the bully in town earlier. This was just enough to convince her to agree to it.

Consequently I decided to pop along to her dormitory about seven-thirty, just to see she'd remembered. What a good thing I did! Bless her, after so many nights trying to keep warm in an old sleeping bag outside for so long, she was fast asleep, almost hidden from view under the covers of a good warm bed. I decided to let her sleep. She could start tomorrow, sleep and warmth were her priority right now.

She did in fact turn up in the kitchen just as Ellen and I were beginning washing up from the rest.

"What time is it Mel? Am I in time for the exercise class?"

We both roared with laughter, leaving her with a puzzled expression on her face. When I told her what the time was her first thought was, would she

317

be in trouble with Steve! I was quick to assure her that he had said to let her sleep ... she could join in next time.

"Sit yourself down girl, I'll get you some breakfast. What do you like? How about a good old fry-up?"

Ellen didn't wait for an answer, she could see by the look on the girls face that this was more than she'd dared to expect.

Sure enough, on her second morning Mia was up and outside, eagerly waiting to start work on what she knew was going to transform her life. I really don't think she'd had a steady job of any sort since leaving school, just seemed to have rolled from one to another, never finding anything to hold her interest, and, like so many of our residents, had soon found herself without the funds to pay rent on any accommodation. Watching her over those first few weeks I mentioned to Steve one evening that she did seem to enjoy helping out with the cooking.

"That's handy," he commented, "Perhaps we can help her find a place like the one we found young Josh."

Temporarily it seemed she was pleased to split her days between getting fit and working with Ellen preparing meals.

I was pleased to find that, especially in the case of any female residents like Mia who came to us, they usually found it possible to come and talk to

318

me if they had any worries. The combination of what I'd learnt with my psychology degree, my terrifying experience of living rough (though I did have Steve to protect me), and then watching the long, difficult process of rehabilitation which Steve had gone through following on from that, did put me in a position of understanding how they had come to this position, and what was needed to help them through it. This meant that, whilst Steve could work on getting them fit and ready to get back to a better life, I too could play my part by working on their confidence levels.

By this time the work on the stable bungalows was almost complete. Having made a few changes to our original plans, though still making the two side ones with one bedroom a piece, we did allow for these to be double bedrooms for any couples we might encounter. But the third which ran along the length of the back row, suddenly had to be altered. You see, what we hadn't counted on before was the exciting news broken to us one evening by Ellen and Bob … they were expecting their first baby! Bless her; Ellen even went as far as to suggest that perhaps they should leave, but as we told them, their contribution to what had been done and was to be done in the future, was invaluable.

By this time they had not only brought the decorative flower beds up to a fantastic standard, and with the help of many hands, trimmed the out of shape topiary trees to a pretty fantastic state, but were, now the spring was coming, going to turn over and plant up a huge walled vegetable garden. Of course they had no idea just why Steve had asked them to leave this for some time. I went out around the grounds early one evening looking for him. As a last resort I opened the door into this garden to find him sitting on a bench, alone and deep in thought. I really didn't need to ask what he was thinking of. The bench was outside a shed ... the very shed (no doubt) where his mother had suffered at the hands of Henry Stanwick, and he had been conceived!

I knew that there was nothing I could do or say that would take away the pain he was feeling just at that moment, so all I could do was to sit quietly alongside of him until he was ready to speak. After a few minutes he took hold of my hand in his, turned a pair of tearful eyes to look into mine, and said,

"How Mel? How could he do it? How could a man be so bloody evil?" and then, putting a hand under my chin to look me in the eyes, "You know I'd never hurt you like that Mel, don't you?"

"Of course you wouldn't Steve. I know you couldn't do anything as evil. I trust you completely or I wouldn't be here still. You must know by now that I love you, and if I didn't trust you I would have left you months ago."

An idea struck me. I got up, told him to stay where he was, and dashed indoors quickly before heading back and saying to him,

"Here you are … let's put a stop to this once and for all," and handed him a box of matches, "Go on, set light to that rubbish by the side of the shed, let's burn the damn thing to the ground … sort of a symbol of out with old memories, then get a new one to take its place in making new, happy ones."

As we stood there hand in hand watching it go up in flames I heard him heave one enormous sigh, and felt him physically relax by my side! We stood watching the flames leaping into the air, taking his pain and his mother's shame both up in the air and away in what I hoped marked the symbol of new beginnings for both.

Our moments of quiet contemplation were shortly shattered by the sudden panic stricken shouts of many of the others. They had seen the smoke and flames lapping up over the garden wall, and quite naturally rushed with buckets of water to put it out!

"No, leave it. Let it burn," Steve told them, "We're getting a bigger and better one. Thought it was time to clear that old heap of junk out first."

As a consequence, the next morning Bob and Steve went off in search of a suitable shed. Of course, Steve being Steve, wasn't content with a shed … between them they also ordered a couple of good sized greenhouses. As Bob explained, this would make it possible to give things a good start long before they could be grown outside.

Things were really coming together by that time. Not only had we made a good impression with the local community, but a few of the local businesses had been persuaded to give one or two of our resident's jobs, warning first that this was purely on a trial basis. When they found these to be so much more reliable than they'd expected, most had made these permanent arrangements. One particular lad who Pete had been setting to work helping him with the brickwork of the bungalows, seemed to take to this so well that, after a bit of persuasion, Steve had talked a local builder into taking him on as an apprentice.

Similarly, a lad by the name of Tim was so enjoying helping Graham with the carpentry, on top of which showing a particular flare for carving, that after a week or two on trial, was taken on by another firm.

Young Mia, once she gained her confidence, proved such a great help in the kitchen, and learnt so much from Ellen. After the hassle we'd caused when we first arrived, letting the landlord in the village think we were just a scruffy bunch of tramps, he had now seen his view was purely a misunderstanding, and had therefore offered Mia a few shifts to help out in his kitchen. This, as Steve said, was exactly what we'd done for Josh so long ago, and probably the achievement we were most proud of.

Certainly she had become such a different girl. I was convinced that much of this was due to the exercise and self-defence classes Steve was pleased to see her join in with so keenly. I was never sure if this was her will to be able to defend herself, or her devotion to Steve! Either way, she gradually blossomed into a far more confident and self-assured young woman.

One use we'd certainly not expected our facilities to be put to, took Steve quite by surprise. He was approached one day by a local youth group, who had heard of his morning exercise groups and asked if he could take on a group of youngsters from the area. At first he was rather dubious, thinking they would probably not be prepared to take it seriously, but was gradually coaxed into giving them a few weeks trial. These, once they understood just how strict he was, became particularly popular, though he did draw the line at teaching self-defence to the cubs and brownies, saying that at their age they should be protected by an adult, or kept out of danger in the first place!

By that first Christmas Lansdown Grange was well and truly up and running. Even the building of the toilet and shower blocks for the pods was well under way. This did have to come to a bit of a halt when the weather turned too cold and wet to continue, but by that time the dormitories were complete, so there was rarely anyone out there by then.

Now and again we would have a sort of committee meeting with the two of us, Graham, Dave, Pete and Bob and Ellen. At one of these the subject of Christmas came up, and it didn't take much to agree to the idea of a 'small' Christmas party to celebrate all that we'd achieved there since our arrival.

Though it was originally planned to make this just for our residents, somehow this wasn't to be! Ellen said that perhaps we should invite our W.I. friends after all they'd done for us. Pete said that he thought we should invite Constable Jim and his wife after his support. Though we tried to keep the numbers down as much as possible, I'm afraid to say I added to them by suggesting to Steve that we really should bring our parents up for a visit to show them what we've achieved since we last saw any of them. He was genuinely pleased with this suggestion. Strangely, over the last couple of months, we really had rather neglected to so much as phone them. Of course, that presented the problem of where to put them up as, coming from Kent, my parents would certainly have to stay. Steve said he thought Jamie would probably bring May, but even so it seemed unfair to pack her off home the same night.

I pointed out to him that at the moment there was no one staying in one of the side bungalows, so my parents could use that. As for May, as I pointed out, we had two bedrooms in our apartment, and I could set to and make this very comfortable for her. Besides, as I said to him when we were alone, she may feel a bit uncomfortable coming back here, and would feel happier for being closer to him.

And so it was arranged. Josh agreed to come up and supervise Ellen and Mia in the kitchen. Mum and Dad agreed to take the longish drive up from Kent, whilst Jamie brought May and without asking, included Sally! As it happened this proved a good distraction for May on what must have been, quite a traumatic return to Lansdown after so long. Anyway, it was so good to see Sally again after such a long time, and to hear that she had now finished her course and was a qualified accountant. Due to space, we had agreed to have a special day in the New Year to invite Tom, Margaret and the girls, and Jenny and Alan for a separate visit.

Though I had sent photos to Mum and Dad, I really don't think they'd expected our home to be quite as big. Poor Mum didn't know whether to hug Steve as she had before, or curtsey to him! Bless her, she waited till we went off for me to show them their quarters, then asked me,

"How much of this does he actually own dear? Surely it can't be all his."

I couldn't help letting out a little giggle,

"Yes he does Mum. He owns the whole lot; house, grounds, lake, everything," I so desperately wanted to add, 'plus me', to the list, but thought not to.

I decided that, to save any embarrassment, I would explain something about how Steve had come to inherit the place. Of course I knew they would be careful not to say anything to embarrass May when she arrived. They promised not to say a word. I waited for them to make themselves comfortable, then took them back into the house to show them round, introducing them to those we met along the way. We had not long gone up to our living room when Jamie pulled up on the drive with May and Sally. Steve was first out the door, anxious to greet his mother, and to see she was made to feel comfortable in this place that had held such bad memories for her. We knew that this was our chance to eradicate these once and for all. I was quick to throw my arms around her, knowing how she must be feeling, but it was Steve's big hand that took hers and firmly led her into the hall, then straight upstairs to our rooms. I followed them up. Mum and Dad seemed to understand immediately and, after saying a warm and friendly hello, had taken themselves off downstairs, apparently for a look at the kitchen and a cup of coffee.

I showed May her to room with her bags and then left her to sit with Steve while I took Jamie and Sally across to the dormitories to find themselves a bed a piece.

"Sorry you're in dormitories, but we don't have many separate rooms," I told them both as we went.

I needn't have worried. Both looked perfectly happy with their accommodation. Sally remarked that this was absolute luxury compared with that at the shelter where she'd spent the last couple of years, and it was clear that she soon made a friend of Mia. Meanwhile Jamie immediately clicked with Jez. It seemed they were two of a kind in many ways, meaning that they were more than happy to spend time together. I could tell Christmas was going to be a lively affair at the Grange!

After lunch we both took our respective parents for a tour of the gardens. Mine were keen to see the ornamental areas, particularly the row of topiary trees which had been completely renovated (though still had room for improvement as they grew). At one point, as I looked in Steve's direction, I couldn't help noticing May taking the odd nervous glance in the direction of the walled garden. I whispered in Steve's ear when she was out of earshot about this.

"Ok, you keep yours amused for a bit. Perhaps it's time I got her to face her demons like you did with me."

Without giving Mum and Dad chance to look back I led them off in the opposite direction and, as I did so, saw him take May by the arm and march her off toward the door into the garden!

Not being there with them I can only guess at what he said to her, but they were gone for some time. In fact we were back indoors drinking tea when they eventually caught us up. All I do know is that, whatever went on between them, May came back in with such a relaxed smile on her face, so whatever Steve said or did must have been the right thing. It was clear that the weight she'd carried on her shoulders all these years had most certainly been lifted now.

That evening, while we left the three parents together to chat, we collected all the younger occupants and set to decorating ready for the party of a lifetime the next day!

To our great surprise though, and at first left hidden beneath a swag of paperchains, Graham and Tim had made a particularly poignant gift. They had carved what everyone now knew as the motto of Lansdown Grange, 'Where There's a Will There's a Way' on a plaque which they had fixed above the door to the main hall for all to see! Best Christmas present we could have wished for!

Chapter Thirty.

Sure enough, as we expected, our 'huge' home, suddenly felt so small! It seemed that we'd invited far too many folk, although as they arrived it did seem that I remembered each one being invited … I just hadn't realised how much room so many people took up! Never mind, we did have all those donated chairs, and most of the youngsters, and often, depending on the type of music playing at the time, some of the older folk, there was mostly a good proportion of people spending time either on the dance floor or just walking around socialising.

Although Josh had been organising the refreshments, he had also brought with him the very special guitar Steve had given him, and had somehow coaxed Steve into fetching his and giving us all a good few duets, much to everyone's surprise and pleasure. I think their first piece was a true expression of Steve's feeling of achievement. They gave out a particularly exuberant rendering of

'Don't stop me now' by Queen! As the words said, he was 'having a good time, having a ball!" It was fantastic to see them together, and the words of this so clearly expressed how they were feeling just then.

I made a point of making it my job to see that none of our less confident residents felt left out. After all, this was their home, and had it not been for them and Steve's experience of living their way, this place would never exist.

In fact, though it took a bit of persuasion on my part, I did drag one resident by the name of Paul, onto the floor, to find he was an amazing ballroom dancer! It seemed he did a certain amount of competition dancing some years before ending up on the streets! He was so self-conscious about his scruffy appearance that I really wasn't expecting to find him move that well! Just proved what we'd been telling everyone for some time ... you can't judge a book by its cover! I'm afraid my dancing skills were far below his, so I was pretty pleased when he swapped me for Ellen for the next dance

I watched, hypnotised for a short while, as Dad escorted Mum onto the floor to a particularly beautiful waltz; I don't think I'd ever seen my parents dance before. Most of the youngsters sat this one out to refresh their glasses. I was so deeply into the magic of the moment that I didn't notice Steve coming up to me. Without a word he held out his hand ... lost for words, all I could do was take it. He led me out to the centre of the floor, turned to face me, bowed gracefully, took a hold and waltzed me (at first quite firmly as I wasn't sure where to put my feet!), and then as I grew more confident, so gently that I thought I was floating in his arms!

All I could do was look into those big brown eyes and wonder where this came from. He'd never told me he could dance. Just for a while I felt as if we were the only two people in the room, but as the music faded I was brought back to reality by a huge round of applause. I looked about me to find we really were the only two on the dance floor, and all around had been watching us in what for me was a particularly intimate moment! Embarrassment was barely strong enough word to cover how I felt just at that moment, but through the cheers and clapping we were receiving just then, I could feel so much warmth from all our friends. It seemed at that point that all Steve's inspiration and our hard work over the time we'd been here had truly established us, well most certainly him, as being firmly head of this household!

By the end of the evening, as we saw off all the non-residents, I went back into the kitchen to find Josh, Ellen and Mia collecting up all the glasses and assorted crockery. While the rest collected more and brought it to the kitchen, some began stacking chairs and sweeping up, but then Steve called us all together,

"You've all done so well. I just want to say a big thank you for the work you've put into the preparation, the fantastic way it all went in front of our guests, and I hope you all enjoyed it as much as we did," giving me a particularly warm smile, which was not missed by most!

"Yes mate, we did notice!" remarked Pete, bringing on a huge round of cheers and claps.

"That's enough of your bloody cheek you lot, now I suggest you put the rest of that in the dishwasher, then get off to bed before I kick you out. Don't know about you, but I'm well ready for my bed."

Somehow I wish he hadn't said that. It didn't take much imagination to guess their reaction to that remark,

"We noticed," answered Pete, followed by the wisecrack from Graham,

"Just keep the noise down," looking over his shoulder to see who was listening, "Don't forget you've got your Mum in the next room!"

And so ended a truly special and beautiful evening … well, almost ended perhaps I should say. (It's surprising how quiet two people can be, and how thick the walls of such an old building are!).

Somewhat reluctantly, we said a fond farewell to our parents, Jamie and Sally, though promising to keep in touch more regularly. As we waved goodbye to a far happier May, Steve remarked about the change he'd seen in her over the time she'd been here. I knew just how much this meant to him, but couldn't help thinking in the back of my mind, that this had been a shared change between them both.

I couldn't help too, noticing something it seemed he'd missed. I remarked to him that I'd thought that Jamie did seem particularly attentive to our Sally!

"Do you reckon there's something going on with them then?"

As I told him, with them both in Cambridge area, there was every opportunity after all. I must admit to agreeing with big brother Steve when he said he thought it would calm Jamie down a bit to have the likes of Sally to keep him in order!

This was on the twenty-ninth of December, the day before we greeted our next visitors, Tom, Margaret and their daughters, plus, later in the day, my sister Jenny and her husband Alan turned up to see the New Year in with us. As Steve pointed out, having Tom come in particular, after the help he'd given in securing the ownership of the Grange for his brother, it did seem appropriate for him to see our new start in a New Year with us.

We had left the decorations up, which caused such excitement on behalf of the children, and admiration from the adults. By way of accommodation we gave Tom and family the bungalow which my parents had shared, putting in a couple of blow-up beds for Sandra and Tina. Jenny and Alan took the room May had been in next to ours.

Of course it didn't take so long after their arrival that Jenny did what I quite expected, but didn't get, from our mothers ... a rather tongue-in-cheek remark, strictly behind Steve's back mind you, that I did actually manage to find my way into his bed after all!

"Well, why shouldn't I? I was invited you know,"

I didn't choose to enlighten her that this came about because I nearly drowned in the weir, it was more fun to just leave her guessing.

Though we planned nothing so elaborate as our Christmas celebrations, we did all gather in the hall so that our families could get to know the residents. The kids were desperate to stay up to see in the New Year, but Margaret was worried that everybody else might object.

"Oh, go on, surely it won't do any harm for once," Ellen told her.

Looking around at the others, she could see that most of them were quite happy about it,

"And anyway," Steve told her, "You can't let them miss the fireworks."

Well, the very mention of fireworks excited them so much that their mother could hardly refuse their request.

To be honest, though it didn't surprise me, I genuinely hadn't realised Steve had actually bought and set up a fantastic display outside. Having all they could do to stay awake, the girls followed the adults, all carrying drinks outside with them, into the gardens just before midnight.

Well, I reckon everyone for miles around saw the Lansdown Grange firework display that year, added to the jolly singing of Auld Lang Syne from the mouths of so many truly happy residents and visitors alike.

Eventually everyone tumbled back inside, that bit merrier than they'd been earlier, and most enjoyed making the most of the buffet laid out in advance by myself, Ellen and Mia, to soak up the surplus alcohol before turning in for the night. Of course Tom and Margaret had taken the girls straight to bed when they came in, as they were almost asleep on their feet.

The next morning was a bright, crispy morning and so, to the relief of all those concerned, Steve skipped morning exercise and actually agreed to a far gentler stroll with the family ... well, at least the adult members. Mia and Jez had dreamt up and prepared a treasure hunt in the gardens for the girls, making it possible to allow us chance to catch up properly. Tom was pleased, if not surprised, to hear that Luke Stanwick was finally out of the picture, while both Margaret and Jenny couldn't resist, out of earshot of Steve of course, asking if they should expect wedding invitations before too long! I was quick to assure them that this subject had never come up, and that I was perfectly happy just being here with him. Meanwhile we were more like business partners in the Grange. After all, I told myself, wishful thinking gets you nowhere.

By the time we got back to the house the children were full of excitement, telling us how much fun they'd been having. It seems that Mia and Jez both had a good way with youngsters, and had kept these two well amused. By way of a treat we had arranged a family sized table at the pub so that we could show them a bit of the village. The girls thought that the idea of going into a pub was something they had never been allowed to do before, but they knew that Mum and Dad wouldn't argue if Uncle Steve suggested it! I could sense just a little resistance from a rather reserved Margaret, but with Tom going along with his brother, she knew resistance was wasted. Both girls behaved impeccably though and were more than ready to sit and tuck into their lunch, as were we.

The locals we met along the way, and those who came across to thank us for the good time we'd shown them at Christmas, convinced both Tom and his wife just how well we'd been fitting in with the local community, finally putting paid to any worries Tom had about his brothers plans to take in a house full of homeless waif and strays!

One thing that did come about due to this trip into the village was a piece of useful information passed on to Steve by a chap from the local coach company. It seemed that the company had a small coach, one which carried sixteen plus the driver. He wondered if we had any use for it as the company now needed a newer and bigger one (besides, he also knew we did on occasions, take people hidden in the back of Annie van, even though this was actually illegal!). Somehow I knew straight away what Steve would say. In fact he had mentioned on a few occasions that it would be useful to have such a thing. There had already been times when he'd found work for people to go to and had to dash from place to place dropping them off in different directions. This wasn't so bad if they needed to go to, at the very least, the same areas, but that seldom seemed to be the case.

Of course, by the time we found time to be alone that night he was full of plans for the bus, even though we hadn't even seen it. Apart from the obvious one of transporting residents to any work they were offered, as he said, we could take some on trips to build up their strength and confidence! Having spent the time I had travelling around with him in the past, I could already tell how his mind was going. It seemed I was quite right … before we turned in for the night he was already talking of the likes of the trudge up Snowdon he'd taken me on last year, in fact, even going to the lengths of mentioning this three peak challenge he'd told me of back then! As I tried to tell him, he must remember that quite a number of the residents might consider that rather drastic as I had!

Even so, though our numbers were swelling from time to time, we had managed to keep them within a manageable amount. It was going to be such a help to have proper transport for many reasons. I am pleased to say that by the beginning of the first term of the New Year, mainly due to Steve's drive and determination, Jez had been accepted back into Coventry University to complete his Sports Science Degree. Though we were all sad to see him go we had to accept that this was not a loss at all, this was actually one of our (or should I say, Steve's) biggest success stories so far.

As Steve loaded his gear into the new bus, we all gathered round to say our farewells. Ellen packed him off with a quantity of ready meals to ensure he could feed himself, we'd made certain he had plenty of good, clean clothes, cooking equipment and the like, and we all waved him off. I had already made him promise to phone if he had any problems, as we were always here for him. I knew Steve was going to see he was safely installed into his new digs before leaving him, and had promised to see he had sufficient funds to get started. (What he hadn't told me at the time was that he'd opened a bank account for the lad, in the way a father would for a son!).

It was good to see the way new residents, because that was what we decided to call them, did seem to accept the help we had to offer them. On the whole there were only the odd few that assumed they could move in and just sit back and be pampered. As you can imagine, this attitude didn't sit well with Steve. He explained the rules and purpose behind the Grange to any who requested a place there, and the few who took advantage of his good nature soon learnt that this good nature had its limits! They were accepted strictly on the understanding that we would all help them with any rehab we were able to, those with skills like Graham, Dave, Pet and Bob were happy to help them learn enough to help find employment or apprenticeships where available, and to get them to undertake any of this, Steve put his usual exuberance into their physical fitness, without which they often wouldn't stand a chance.

With Ellen growing bigger by the day now that her pregnancy was moving on nicely, I split my time between helping Steve with his exercise classes (now he admitted I was, at last, up to a good standard!), and helping in the kitchen. I know she did miss being able to help Bob in the vegetable garden, and around the ornamental areas which were really blossoming beautifully now. As I remarked to her one day,

"It's amazing to see you blossoming just when your garden is doing the same. It must be sharing the moment with you."

In fact, now the weather was turning particularly mild the toilet blocks for the pods had been completed, allowing us to open the area they were in for campers. Our next venture was to buy up a huge marquee in which we held the occasional wedding, or any event requiring such a facility. This proved extremely popular with the locals. More often than not we were lucky enough to have Josh volunteer his services as chef for many such events. In fact we were more than pleased one day when he came to us with the news that his employer had managed to replace him, which meant he was free to come to us permanently. It didn't seem to worry him that we were not able to offer him a fantastic wage, as long as he had board, lodging and enough to survive and chance to work with his hero, Steve!

None the less, there were times when I began to feel a little side lined. Steve would often take it into his head to organise a trip to somewhere, usually for the purpose of some sort of challenge, the sort of thing he was so keen to take me on before we settled here. I did ask on a couple of occasions if I should go too, but most of the time it seemed he wasn't particularly bothered whether I did or not. I tried just shrugging it off and walking away, I think expecting him to realise how I felt, but he always seemed so intent on the goals he set each group, it was as if he genuinely either didn't notice or perhaps didn't care, how this made me feel.

With the aim of putting over my point, one day I gathered together the small group of ladies we had at the time, and being a non-working day where no one needed a work bus, waited until we'd sat the men down with their breakfast and, knowing Steve was in his office on a long phone call, we climbed into the bus and took off!

What he didn't know was that I'd arranged for just the ladies to have a scuba diving lesson in a pool some way off! I'd seen it advertised in a magazine a while ago, but when I mentioned it to Steve all he did was laugh at the thought.

"What's the good of doing it in a swimming pool? You do realise you'll never be able to do it for real in this country, waters too murky," and just laughed it off as a joke!

I was fuming! Why should he be the only one to decide what we do … after all, it might be his house, but my money goes into the running of the business as well. I would teach him not to ignore me once and for all! So that was what we did.

Chapter Thirty-One.

We ladies had a really enjoyable time. There were two brilliant young instructors who never questioned us about where we'd come from, but set to and worked hard to make us feel safe, and to feel special, a thing I'd not been feeling so very much of late! After all, it had been Steve who'd shown me that, if I put my mind to it, I could do so much more than I'd ever dreamt of, so why shouldn't I put his lesson to good use and show some independence? Ok, perhaps diving to the bottom of the deep end of an indoor pool didn't offer quite the same risks as some of the things he'd challenged me with in the past, but at least I was using my initiative and trying something new.

By the time we'd finished, showered, and taken ourselves into the café for something to eat by way of lunch, we left there like your average girls outing … smiling, chattering and giggling, all in such high spirits from our little adventure. I'd had to almost prise a couple of the younger girls off our poor instructors, but they really didn't seem in the least bothered, in fact suggested we should come again soon (as they said, to prepare us for any holiday we had planned that year where we could put our skills to good use!). What a hope, I thought, for most of these girls. Perhaps, if they work hard to get back on their feet and earn enough to do so.

"Come on you lot, stop messing about or we'll never get home. Anyone who isn't on here by the time I count to ten, stays behind!"

That did it. Within seconds we were on our way, heading back toward the Grange. Mia sat up near me as we drove back. She was so excited about the experience. It seemed she had always been rather frightened of water, it seemed she had never learnt to swim, but with a rather attentive instructor there, had actually decided she loved it so much that she'd made up her mind to get proper lessons as soon as she had chance.

"Just do it in a nice warm pool." I said with a smile, "Don't go doing like I did and fall in the weir."

She gave me a puzzled look, "You didn't, did you? How did you get out?"

"Steve dived in after me," I told her, but stopped short of going on!

The rest of the drive home I went over in my mind so much of what had happened since that fatal (well, almost fatal) day. We had only come to be here as just another casual stop on our gypsy-style roaming in Annie.

Right from that first day when Steve had been released into my safe keeping as it were, from the military rehab unit, so much had happened. When he first came out of there I believe Paul had hoped that he would by now have settled down to a quiet, normal life. At first I think that was what I'd hoped too, but it wasn't long before I'd realised that this just wouldn't have been Steve … not the Steve I wanted to be with, the one I loved.

So what was it now that I didn't think I liked about him; or was it just because I was having to share him with so many other people? That sounded so unreasonable when I knew from the first time he spoke of his ideas for the Grange that this was how it would be. No, I told myself, I must stop acting like a spoilt child and complaining over silly things. I just can't go saying how much I love him with one breath, and then saying the opposite with the next. I can't expect to monopolise him when he was working so hard to fulfil his dream.

But then, what about me … what about my dream? On the other hand just what was my dream? Did I really dream of having all his attention with the exclusion of all others? No, I must have known right from the start that this would be asking more than he could, or would, give. No, I thought, perhaps he had now reverted to the strong, independent man he'd been before, and would no longer need me around as back up.

By the time I drove back through the village and up through the gates toward the house I had convinced myself that I was being unreasonable in thinking he was showing me any less affection than before. I saw him standing outside the big oak door and told myself that this had all just been a temporary blip; as we pulled up I saw him approaching and just knew that he would greet me with that smile of his and some cheeky remark about me 'pinching' the bus. But I was so wrong; what I actually got as he opened the door was,

"Where the bloody hell have you been? Why didn't you ask first, I might have needed the bus? Or where ever you've been, I might have wanted to come anyway. Just damn well ask next time woman!"

Just for an instant I was torn between bursting into tears or slapping him across the face. By this time the girls had discreetly climbed off and retreated inside, no doubt to tell everyone about the bust-up going on outside. I stepped off the bus and threw the keys at him,

"Why should I tell you, and as for you wanting to come too, you don't bother to ask me if I want to come on the ones you've done lately. Anyway, what makes you think I want you to come with me all the time," then as I turned to go, I looked round to say, "Oh, and don't worry about me spending your money. You might own the Grange, but I've still got plenty of my own you know!"

Speechless for a second, when he did speak, Steve took hold of my arm and looked me in the face. "There's no need for that, you know as well as I do there's plenty in the bank from the Stanwick probate account, and interest from their shares come to that."

I barely knew what to say; he had made it quite clear that he thought I was just being petty, nothing more than a spoilt child! By now I was aware of the odd curtain twitching and knew that we were causing a scene, probably one that would also cause upset to those who had come to look on the two of us as the first stable thing in their lives for some time.

Feeling pretty much as I had the day I was drowning in the weir, somehow I felt that this time he wouldn't rescue me! All I could do was walk away ... all he seemed able to do was watch me go!

It seemed after that neither of us knew what to do next. I had no idea what more to say. I knew that all I really wanted was to turn the clock back to a time when we were so happy together. Perhaps this house has come between us, perhaps after the blight it had put on poor May's life it was now doing the same to mine. And yet why? It was such a beautiful, normally peaceful, place. Since we'd been here it had helped us do so much for so many others; why not us?

For the next week I moved into the spare room and, not wanting to allow our problems to spoil the lives of all those we were trying to help, tried to carry on as if that had never happened. I don't know if it helped me or made me feel worse, to know that Steve seemed genuinely concerned with the way I was shutting him out, I felt I had no choice. You see, all I knew right then was that I loved him too much to let him in! This may seem a strange and confusing way to explain how I felt at that time, but I knew I was too scared to let him in … not into my life, but deeper into my heart than he already was. I knew that, if his depth of love for me didn't come close to mine for him, then I was heading for disaster, a bigger one than I'd ever experienced before.

By the end of that week, unannounced and uninvited, I was just coming out of the shower one night and on my way to bed, when Steve came in from locking up for the night. I wrapped my bath robe tighter round me feeling for some reason, so shy, as if he'd never seen me before. All I could bring myself to do was look down on the floor, say a brief 'goodnight', and scurry away like a frightened schoolgirl! I'd hardly shut the door behind myself before it was pushed open, and there he stood.

At first I couldn't bring myself to look round, but I knew instinctively that he was there in the doorway. Without looking round I threw over my shoulder,

"Yes; what do you want Steve? I'm tired, so if you don't mind..."

That was all I managed to get out, my voice was shaking too much. I knew one more word and I'd not be able to hold back the avalanche of tears which I could feel welling up inside me! No, I told myself, I must be strong. He'd made it clear that he no longer looked on me as more than a business partner, and I had to accept that or ... or what? Leave? Is that really the only solution, I wonder?

I was aware of him still standing there in the doorway, not speaking, making no attempt to move in or out. I took a deep breath to calm myself before turning to face him and repeating my question,

"Well ... what is it you want Steve? I'm getting cold standing here, and I'm tired. So either say what you've come for or get out!"

He took a step forward ... I took a step back. He stopped and looked at me with what I could only describe as a 'lost little boy' expression on his face.

"Mel, you know what I want; it's you I want. It's always been you, ever since the first day I clapped eyes on you last year."

"All I can say is you've got a funny way of showing it lately. It's clear to me now that the novelty has worn off. Perhaps it's best if we keep things on a business basis from now on. Perhaps

348

that way we can survive without hurting one another?"

He stood looking down at me with such a forlorn expression before coming a couple of steps closer. I took another step back, not that I thought he would physically hurt me, but because the closer he came, the more I could feel that terrible, almost unbearable inner pain I'd been feeling all week. This must be what an alcoholic must feel like faced with a drink, or a druggie faced with weed. All I knew was that I dearly wanted to believe him, so desperately wanted him right that minute but what should I do? Believe him or leave him? That was what I had to decide, and quickly; he came another step closer and took my face in his hands to bring my eyes up to look into his,

"Mel, I am truly sorry, please believe me. I'd just got so carried away with everything but I can see now that you were right, I had been shutting you out and I never meant to do that. If you'll give me another chance I promise I'll never hurt you again, never! Please, please my love, come back to me."

"I don't know Steve, I don't know if it's going to work again, or even if you're honest about it, do you really have the will to make it?"

Taking hold of my hands again once more, all he said in answer to this was,

"Well you know what we've always said Mel? Where there's a will there's a way. If you have the will to give things a try, I think we can find a way"

As meek and mild as a child, I let him take me by the hand and lead me back to our room and lift me onto our large, soft bed.

He certainly put his best effort into finding a way this time!

Why, I wondered, do I always let him get round me that way? Obviously because that was what I had wanted him to do. Living at such close proximity, yet having to stay so distant was becoming too painful to bear for much longer. Anyway, I thought at that point that I should give him a second chance to think over just how strong our relationship was before making any rash decisions.

Having made what could be looked on as his best attempt at an apology, we lay together under the duvet, him with a relaxed and satisfied expression and me just so glad to be back there, up tight with his strong arm round me and with that safe, contented feeling he always gave me.

All I could hope was that he had really meant what he'd said, and that perhaps now he would try that bit harder to consider my feelings as I knew I couldn't take what had felt like a rejection from him recently.

Chapter Thirty-Two.

By now it was coming into early May. There was what Wordsworth called 'a host of golden daffodils' around the trees, and there was blossom on the fruit trees in the kitchen garden. Then there were the huge chestnut trees lining the drive and branching out to form a protective woodland around the estate. These too were coming out in full bloom as the days passed by, a truly magnificent sight.

We had already had the pleasure of the snowdrops, followed closely by primroses and bluebells, all scattered, like a multi-coloured carpet, beneath the trees. And then, both on the lake in our park, and along the river by the weir, we had the pleasure of watching the ducks with a following of little ducklings paddling furiously along behind them, and swans with their cygnets proudly showing them off at a safe distance!

Of course by this time our Ellen was also blossoming to the point of feeling particularly cumbersome! She had, so she believed, about another six to eight weeks to wait for her new arrival. She didn't have an exact date, she had refused to go for an anti-natal check-up, and feeling concerned that they might still look on them as homeless and take their child away! Try as I might I could say nothing to convince her that this was now her permanent home, she need never be homeless again.

Since Christmas our numbers had gone up and down quite regularly, due mainly to Steve's efforts to get as many as possible back into the world of work. Some that had found steady employment had found they earnt sufficient to move out into flats or lodgings provided, thus giving us room to take in new residents from time to time. His idea to work simultaneously with their fitness levels and, where he saw fit, a basic course of self-defence, ably assisted might I say by me, had also proved of great benefit to those choosing to take part in them.

Even so, in spite of us previously making up from the rough patch we'd gone through a while ago, somehow I couldn't bring myself to feel totally convinced about his true depth of feeling for me. Yes … he was more attentive and quick to include me in his plans; but since that night when we had brought our relationship back on an even keel with his all-consuming love making, I couldn't help feeling that perhaps I should be asking for more. Perhaps what I wanted was more commitment from him now?

I was so intent on this thought one morning when I was out for a gentle stroll with Ellen (the limit to her exercise now!), that I'd not realised the look she was giving me. Stopping and turning to face me she asked straight out,

"Right you, are you going to tell me what's on your mind, or do I have to shake it out of you?"

I felt myself going red in the face. I hadn't noticed her paying such close attention to me just then when she had her own problems to think of.

"Oh, it's nothing really. Just a little niggle in my mind. It'll go away."

"You know what they say … a trouble shared is a trouble halved. Come on lady, let's be having it."

I must admit that there was just a little something on my mind, just a very little thing I couldn't get off my mind. Logically speaking I knew it was probably too early to even consider the thoughts that have been going on in my head over the last couple of weeks. But now Ellen could tell there was something troubling me, and I had a strong suspicion she had some idea what it was.

"Come on, out with it. I thought you and Steve had made it up since your bust up the other week?"

I was quick to assure her that we had, and that he'd been fantastic lately. Her next remark quite took me by surprise; she was always careful not to overstep the mark, even though she could be pretty blunt on occasions,

"So what you're saying is that he's been a bit too 'fantastic' eh? And now you're worrying about the consequences?"

All I could do was throw her a shy little nod of my head.

"How late are you then? Have you told him yet?"

Ok, as I told her, I was only a bit late, but I have never been at all before. But I certainly have said nothing to Steve, I was too scared of upsetting him … even more scared of losing him! I know she just couldn't see what the problem was. I explained to her that, since the first time we'd got together in that way, I had made it my duty to take necessary precautions. I explained to her about what had happened to his little son Sean, and just what a wreck he'd been following this. I had decided right from the start not to put him in that position again. In fact, the only time I'd let this slip was for the week when we'd slept in separate bedrooms, and that first night when he'd coaxed me back into our bed, I didn't stop to give it any thought. If I was right about what I was thinking, that must have been the time it happened!

Anyway, it had felt good to be able to share my worries with Ellen, and I promised to think over her words of well-meaning advice. We walked on in silence, enjoying the smells and sights of spring around us, and commenting as we strolled back up the drive on just how much it had improved since the time we all squatted in, what was then, an almost derelict house, with a drive you could barely see for moss! Now the drive was pristine, and the house was well on the way back to being fully restored to its former glory. Who back then would have thought for one moment that this would turn out to actually all belong to Steve! Personally, in my mind, I couldn't think of anyone more deserving of this. He was possibly the only man who would inherit such a place and, instead of lording it over the locals, or using it to make money as Luke Stanwick had planned to do, would convert it into a place to do so much good to so many in need. All I could think of was just how on earth did I get to be with such a man?

Even so, this niggle in the back of my mind just wouldn't go away. I was pretty sure I was right about that. I just couldn't shift it, neither could I bring myself to tell Steve.

I was genuinely way out of my depth and finding it hard to cope with my thoughts and no one to share my concerns with. I didn't want to say anymore to Ellen, she was in no state to take my troubles on her shoulders right then. I thought of rushing home to my parents, but I didn't want to upset them. Though they had learnt to accept the fact that we actually lived and slept together, they were still of the generation that believed that marriage should come before babies! I thought of May, but instinctively knew that would be the last thing she should have to hear, having just come to terms with the loss of Sean. Of course there was always Jenny, but somehow asking for relationship advice from my big sister seemed a last resort, and anyway, her and Alan had been unable to have children, so this would be a cruel thing to do. And anyway, other than May, there was no one who knew Steve well enough to speak to about our problems. No, there was no one I could think of who knew us both well enough to understand where I was coming from. Or was there?

A couple of days later we had arranged to take a bus full of our younger folks to visit Chris's leisure and climbing centre. It was a fair drive to get there, but it would be good to see Chris again. We had kept in touch fairly regularly, in fact he had made it his business to come for a visit, as Steve said, 'just to be bloody nosey', and invited us to take the odd group to his place now and again.

I liked Chris. He had such a relaxed, familiar, way about him, and it was easy to see the close connection the two men had … an unbreakable link, presumably formed by their military days. This must certainly have been the case as, every time I tried to ask them just what action they'd seen together, all I got was.

"Nothing you'd want to know about," and, if I was quick I might catch a wink or grin pass between them!

Somehow I always felt that whatever part of their service was spent together, this was not to be spoken of, either to me or anyone else! I'd very soon picked up on this and had therefore respected their silence. Even so, this closeness between them did make me think that perhaps Chris just may be someone I could speak to about my worries. After all, it seemed he'd know Steve for so long now, I believe since the both joined up at eighteen. If anyone knew how my suspicions would go down with Steve, it would be him.

When we arrived there Steve was keen for the two of us and Chris to give the others a quick demonstration of just how easy it was to shin up that dirty great wall he'd got me up the first time we'd gone! As you can imagine, that was the last thing I wanted to do. I made a compromise, going up one of the smaller one instead. Of course, I got mock jeering from both Steve and Chris but, as Steve told the others,

"Take no notice of her; she's been up it many times. Just doesn't have much of a head for heights!"

I left them to it and sat in the café while Chris got a few of his staff to help the youngsters with Steve watching on. I'd not been sitting there many minutes before Chris came across to join me with two cups of coffee. This could be my chance, I thought, but dare I? Would he repeat what I told him to Steve I wonder? I didn't have long to ponder on this before he looked across the table and asked,

"So Mel, how are you and my old pal getting along? Last time I came over I thought there was a bit of tension between you, was I right?"

Of course this was just before our brief bust up as far as I remembered. I was quick to reassure him that this had only been a temporary blip, and that we'd certainly made it up since. I could already see the saucy grin on his face, and knew the sort of response to expect,

"Um, don't think you need to go into details. I reckon I know what Steve's idea of 'making it up' would be. You can safely leave that to my imagination! So, everything is ok between you now then is it? Then why I aren't I convinced you're telling the truth girl?"

Of course, this came just as I had decided not to say anything after all. Now I felt that, if I didn't, he would speak to Steve to find out, and that was the last thing I wanted! All I could do was pour out the whole story (well, as much as you can tell a man about these things!), and wait for his response.

"So, you think you're pregnant? Haven't you told him yet?" I shook my head, "Why Mel? You have to; it's not just you that did it you know. He must have been the cause in the first place?"

"Of course it was him," I was horrified to think he could even think otherwise. He must know I wouldn't do that to Steve!

"No Mel, I didn't doubt you for a minute." And in an attempt to lighten the mood, he added, "anyway, if he thought you had he'd have thrown you out long since!"

I could see through the window that it wouldn't be too long before the climbers would be packing up ready to leave.

"Don't you see what I'm getting at Chris? I'm frightened that he might not cope with the idea of a baby; not after what happened to Sean. And at least he was married to Beth ... he's not interested in marriage since then, so why would he want another kid?"

He squeezed my hand, looked me in the eye, and just said,

"Listen, you've got to trust him Mel. At least tell him, talk it over and give him a chance. He might be fine with it ..." but before he could finish what he was saying Steve's voice interrupted from the door,

"Hey mate, you can put her down, she's mine!"

Throwing a wink my way, Chris got to his feet and took my hand to help me up from my chair,

"Are you sure of that pal? I reckon I could take her away from you if I had a mind to, what do you say Mel?"

Just for the briefest instant they squared up to one another as if they were about to kick off; then in the next they broke into hysterical laughter!

"What's so funny," I asked, "doesn't it matter to you two who I'm with?"

Steve pulled himself together and put his arm round me,

"Yes of course it does Mel. You're with me ... and he knows it, that's if he values his neck, that is!"

I couldn't help, after seeing the way they'd squared up to one another, even in gest, which one would have come out on top if a fight had broken out between them? They did look surprisingly aggressive, leading me to think that it would have been quite a scrap. Bearing how tough and scary Steve had been last year in his dealings with his arch enemy, Morgan. Whatever sort of training they had received they certainly were a formidable bunch that worked together in whatever their role was.

On the way home I began mulling over what Chris had said, but soon found myself distracted by the high spirits of the others. It seemed they had thoroughly enjoyed the challenge put before them. Although some had preferred to stick to the smaller walls, there was about six or seven who did actually get to the top of the bigger one, and even then, only one who froze as I had and had to be rescued by Steve!

Alongside the climbing area, Chris also had a gym, boxing ring and a firing range. Though Steve agreed to take them back at some point to try the gym and boxing ring, he was reluctant to agree to the firing range, feeling that self-defence was one thing, but after living rough for some time, perhaps it would look bad to be teaching them to use firearms. I could quite see his point on this matter as the last thing we wanted was to gain a reputation for turning out gunmen!

I couldn't help watching the way these youngest members of our community were looking on Steve as a sort of father figure, and in return he treated them as one big family. He seemed complete now, no longer a man looking for his roots. Yes, he'd lost his first family … now it looked to me as if he was content with the new one, the one he'd built around himself to take their place.

What I had to tell him could so easily smash all of this; take him back to how he was before! I don't think I dare risk doing that to him. He means too much to me. I'd hoped that by the time I'd spoken to Chris I would have made a clear decision as to what to do. Instead of that I believe I was by this time, even more confused than before!

Whatever I was going to do about it, I would have to think long and hard. I couldn't risk getting it wrong, if not for his sake, then certainly for mine. Chris had said trust him, he might be fine … but what if he wasn't? Where would that leave me, and even more important, just what would it do to Steve?

I really had no answers to either question that night. As I lay there alongside him, watching him sleeping so very peacefully, it broke my heart to think that I might very well shatter his newly found peace if I made the wrong decision, and after all he had done for me, this thought was unbearable. Try as I might, sleep just wouldn't come that night. All I wanted to do was lay quietly by his side, listening to his steady breath, and wonder if anything, what dreams were passing through his mind, and was I there in any of them?

Chapter Thirty-Three.

By the following night I still hadn't made any decision as to how to tell him, or indeed if I should do so. It was tearing me apart knowing that whatever choice I made, I most certainly would be the cause of him being upset. The big question was just one of which decision would hurt him the least? For the first time since we met last year, I began to think that perhaps, for his sake, it might have been better if we'd not met at all.

I knew that I'd dithered long enough now. I knew that the longer I left it the harder it would be. Yes, in the back of my mind I think I'd always known I would have to go. If I go now perhaps he need never know why. It was clear to me now that, apart from the hurt I would cause him, I had to accept that I could not expect to keep both him and the baby! If I stayed with him I would need to lose the baby. If I wanted to keep the baby, his baby, I must leave and build a new life somewhere on my own. Somehow I just couldn't face losing his baby, and had no intention of bringing up his old wound by trying to replace Sean.

The next morning I made an excuse to get out of helping with the exercise class. As he did by then sometimes get Josh to stand in for me when I was busy, this didn't make any difference. While he was gone I dashed back upstairs and fished out my old rucksack from the back of the wardrobe. Packing it with what I thought I might need and a bit more besides, I ran back down and put it into Annie van. I knew Steve would be using the bus after breakfast, so wouldn't need her today. By the time he came back with his class ready for a hearty breakfast, I managed to face a bit of banter that he always came up with, but as we sat together with everyone eating it was almost more than I could do not to burst into tears and rush out the room!

"You don't need Annie this morning do you Steve? I just want to pop to the village and see the W.I. ladies about something they asked me a while ago. They've got a committee meeting this morning."

"No, all I need is the bus to get a few of these lazy beggars to work! Go for it girl and I'll see you later. Perhaps we'll get a bit of time to sort out some paperwork?"

As he got up to leave the room he bent over and gave me an affectionate peck on the cheek. That was almost more than I could bear; how I managed to stop myself throwing my arms around him and letting go the flood of tears waiting to burst the dam that had held them back over the last few days, I shall never know!

I looked away from him and back to the table. Ellen and Josh were just beginning to clear the breakfast things away. I picked up a tray and set to helping them until Ellen stopped me in the doorway,

"Are you alright Mel? You look a bit off colour this morning. Leave this to us and go and rest for a while," and then, in a quiet whisper, "Have you told him yet?"

Lying through my teeth I told her not yet, but would do so as soon as he came in this morning, or failing that, when I came back from the village. She knew we were supposed to be doing some paperwork later, so she accepted that answer, even though she didn't see why I hadn't done so sooner! Anyway, just to cover my tracks I reminded her I was going out in a while, but would rest first.

Of course the next problem was going to be just where to go? I knew he would look for me; I had thought to leave a note telling him I didn't want to be with him, and not to look for me, but just couldn't bring myself to put such a lie on paper! No, I decided that I would drive away in the van to throw him off my scent as it were. Annie was pretty hard to hide, being such a distinctive red and white, so I thought that if I parked her in the village at least it would look as if I was there somewhere meeting someone, or shopping. It had been known for me sometimes to drive into there and then catch a bus to Coventry, so perhaps that would give me a little more time to get further away before he knew I had actually left.

How I managed to drive there through the constant curtain of tears streaming down my face I shall never know. It felt that, the further away I was going from him, the stronger the pain inside me was. If I had means to do so at that minute as I parked in the carpark on the edge of the village, I believe I would quite willingly have taken my life. Perhaps I should have gone back to the weir and finished what would have happened if Steve hadn't saved me that day. Yes, perhaps that would end this pain for good … but then, what about that innocent little life growing inside me! I knew I couldn't do that, not to his baby.

No, I knew that I had to go away, as far away as possible, and let him forget he'd ever known me. After all, he was happy now, he'd built a new family around him. He had a purpose in life. Yes, he would feel hurt, perhaps angry at first, but he would recover … I knew he would, but he must never know the true reason I left for fear of opening up old wounds.

I climbed out of Annie, put my rucksack on my back and set off. We always hid the keys inside the petrol cap cover if we were splitting up anywhere, so that we could both get back in when we got back, so that was what I did this time. I was just in time for the next bus heading to another village about ten miles away, not very far, but that would be a start and, as it was not in the direction we went usually, I thought it might slow him down for a while. How long it would be before he gave up looking I couldn't say, but I was sure he would eventually assume I'd gone for good.

By nightfall I was tired, hungry and scared. This was the first time I'd been without his protection except when I was at home with my parents. Though he'd taught me so much, and I know I should be able to look after myself after all he had taught me, I'd not felt so lost and alone since I found myself with no name, no memory and no idea where I was last year. It had been Steve who'd come to my rescue, and now I was walking out on him and taking myself almost back to the situation he'd found me in then! Once again I wasn't entirely sure where I was, I'd just got off the bus and walked until nearly dark. And then, having remembered to bring just a small amount of cash, I booked into a small B&B just for a night. As he always said, if you don't want to get noticed, keep moving.

Over the course of the next two days that was what I did, kept moving. I had no plans as to where to go. I did think to take my phone with me, but kept it switched off. I couldn't bear to hear his voice if he rang, or see his face which I had as the wallpaper. I did actually switch it on very briefly on that first night as I tried to sleep in that strange bed, and there was that face I longed to see …

those deep brown eyes laughing at me as they did when I took the photo. But then I could see he had been ringing me, in all fourteen times since he must have gone looking for me and found the empty van. It seemed he'd just let it ring at first, but by late the first night he'd left messages, desperate messages, begging me to answer and speak to him! He was clearly clueless about why I'd gone, or where I was. By early the next morning he sounded genuinely panic stricken and close to tears. Oh God ... if I could just go back to him, fall back inside his arms and never let go again!

No ... I must try to resist his pleas. I'd thought this all out and now I must be strong enough to carry it out somehow. I switched the phone off and put it to the bottom of my rucksack.

On the third morning I was walking through a village, not even knowing where I was or where I was heading. I was becoming aware of a car coming up behind me, and as I looked round, thought that I was sure this was the same one that had already passed me a few minutes ago. Had I been in a different frame of mind I would have been more cautious of this, but to be honest, I really didn't give it a second look.

But then, there it was coming up from behind me for a second time. I remember thinking that they must be as lost as I was feeling, and would be no use asking me for directions. They pulled up alongside me and the passenger got out. Before I had chance to realise what was happening, I found myself being bundled unceremoniously into the boot! I tried screaming, kicking the boot lid, anything I could to gain attention, but to no avail! I had no idea what was happening or why. Even less so, who these men were or what they wanted with me, but all I knew at that moment was that I was terrified.

We were obviously going along a pretty rough road as I was getting shaken up and in such pain. An idea came to me, perhaps I should ring Steve, but then how would he find me? Even so, I needed to hear his voice right then. With difficulty I fumbled around in my bag for my phone, but of course, being inside this car boot there was not sufficient signal to connect. I was just trying it again for the third attempt when the car stopped. Still unable to connect, I lay there quietly listening and wondering what to expect next.

A few minutes later I heard voices approaching and the boot opened. To my horror I found myself looking straight up at Luke Stanwick!

"Ah, Mrs Lockett I believe, allow me to help you out," and held out a hand.

"No actually, I am not Mrs Lockett, I'm Miss Melanie Cook if you don't mind; and no thank you, I can get out without your help."

With a struggle that was what I did. As I turned to retrieve my rucksack, my phone dropped to the floor and before I could do so, one of his men had grabbed it and handed it to him.

I could see I was in trouble. Just what he had in mind to do with me I had no idea. I knew I was in a pretty vulnerable situation just then, and without my phone, no way of calling for help from Steve or anyone else.

"Bring her in and chuck her in the back bedroom." He told one of his men.

Two things flashed through my mind hearing that. The first was the natural fear of being in some blokes' bedroom; the second was, if there was a window, would I be able to climb out of it! As it happened I needn't have considered either. There was no furniture in the room, not even a carpet, so little fear of being molested; and as for the window, there was no hope of climbing out as it was boarded up.

I sat myself down in a corner of the room on the rather worn out looking lino. I felt battered and bruised from my ride in the boot of that damn car! What was going on downstairs I had no idea. I listened hard, but though I heard their voices, there was no chance of hearing what was being said. Perhaps the only thing stopping me from being as scared as I knew I should be just then was the fact that I had somehow turned my fear into sheer rage! What makes them think they can treat me like this … and just what exactly do they intend to do with me now they've got me?

I guessed it was somehow to get revenge of some sort on Steve; but what they don't know is that I've left him, and by now I expect, three days after leaving him, he will have stopped looking and got on with his life. Probably by now he would have thrown a tantrum and decided that, if that was what I wanted to let me go! Why, oh why did I do this? He always said, though mostly in jest, that I wasn't safe without him to look after me; now I'd proved him right in a pretty spectacular way. I wished I could turn the clock back; not just to the day I left, but to the time I allowed myself to fall pregnant.

Too late for regrets now. I could hear voices and footsteps on the stairs. The door opened and there stood Stanwick, followed by one of his men carrying a tray in one hand and my old sleeping bag over his other arm.

"Got you worried have we Miss Cook? Never mind, you won't be here so long. Just until that man of yours signs over the Lansdown estate to me to get you back."

As he said this I'd stood up and stared him straight in the face (as Steve always said, never show fear!), and took a step toward him,

"Well, you've left it a bit late for that. We've split up, and he wouldn't give a damn what happens to me now, so you've got no hope!"

"Come now, I'm sure he wouldn't leave you to suffer, even if that was the case. Perhaps he may need a little more convincing if you're to be believed, but I can be very persuasive when the need arises. After all, I am my father's son ... and you know what a way he had with the ladies. I'm sure your chap wouldn't like to think of you suffering the same fate!"

As he said this I could picture the pain in poor May's face as she poured her heart out to us that day, and in particular, the way she described how Henry had thought it was his right to treat her that way! I could feel my temper rising at the very thought that his son shared his complete lack of respect for women. As I stood there with these thoughts rushing through my mind, I could feel my temper taking away any fear that was left in my mind and replacing it with sheer hate for this low life in front of me. Without hesitation I instinctively lashed out, slapping him across the face, and while he grabbed my wrist to prevent a repeat, just for good measure and because he'd pulled me in closer to him, took the opportunity to bring my knee up as hard as I could for maximum effect! I would have followed this up with an even more effective move Steve had taught me, but his man stepped in to grab me. He was of too bigger build for me to handle under the circumstances. I found myself pushed back against the far wall and had all I could do to stay on my feet.

"Oh yes, I think I can see what that Lockett chap sees in you. Like me, he obviously likes a challenge eh? We'll have to see which one of us gets that pleasure when this is over. Anyway, keep that strength up till then. Here we've brought you something to eat and drink, oh, and this in case you get cold ... or of course my bed's warm if you fancy it ..."

"No thank you, I prefer a real man, not an excuse for one like you. And as for your food, I don't want anything from you," and as I said this, I grabbed the tray his man had picked up, and threw it at him, tipping the contents across the floor as I did it!

Without another word they left the room, at least leaving me with my sleeping bag to soften the hard floor and give what little warmth it could offer. I had no watch on to go by as it had recently stopped working and I'd not got round to replacing it. I hadn't been in any rush as, like so many these days, it was as easy to go by the time on my phone, but from what I could tell peering through a tiny crack in the boards across the window, it was pretty dark outside so it must have been quite late. I could hear no voices, leading me to believe Stanwick must have turned in for the night. I began to wish I hadn't sent the tray flying ... I had just realised I'd not eaten all day, and was desperately thirsty!

A thought crossed my mind as I was peering through this tiny crack at the window. I had caught my hand on a loose splinter of a board. I went back to it and gently wriggled it until it came away. Just maybe, I thought, I could use it to pick the lock on the door; pretty vague hope I know, but I gave it a go anyway! The key was obviously still in the other side … perhaps I could turn it? But no; what actually happened was that it dropped out with a clatter on the floor!

Now what, I wondered? I heard footsteps, and then the door opened and in came the ape-man (as I called the big chap!).

"Ok, the boss says, if you give me any bother I've gotta tie you up."

It was clear there was nothing to tie me to, so what he chose to do was to tie my hands behind my back. Then he tied my ankles together, just for good measure! He left, locking the door behind him again. The only other time in my life I've been tied up like this was last year when Steve did it to fool Morgan into confessing to three murders.

If you've ever tried getting into a sleeping bag with your hands tied behind you and your ankles tied together, you'll know it's pretty nearly impossible! All I can say is that this would make a good party game, but I really wouldn't recommend it!

I spent a very cold, very uncomfortable, and extremely lonely night that night.

Chapter Thirty-Four.

Meanwhile, back at the Grange the day I'd left, Steve had apparently carried on as normal, assuming I would be home in time for our evening meal. I believe he did actually ask Ellen if I'd said what time I was coming home, but quite truthfully, she had said no. I'd thought it wouldn't be fair to involve her in my plans as I didn't want to get her in trouble.

By late evening Steve was really worried. He took Josh, Bob and Pete along with him in the bus to ask around the village to see if anyone had seen me, or even seen me get on the bus to Coventry, but the answer to both questions, wherever or whoever they asked, was no. He had no reason to expect I'd gone in a different direction, in fact, no reason to have expected me to go anywhere without telling him where I was going!

Eventually he contacted Constable Jim and reported me missing, though was not impressed when he was told that he couldn't count me as a missing person until I'd been gone for twenty-four hours. Jim told him that, in spite of this, he would start inquiries anyway, but to go home and stay near the phone in case I rang. He explained that he had been trying to ring me but it had just gone to voice mail. Anyway, he had no choice but to go back to the Grange and hope I would make an appearance.

This didn't happen of course. By the second day, he was apparently storming about, constantly trying to get me to answer my phone, and bellowing at anyone who dared attempt to make comforting suggestions, in fact anyone who dared even to speak to him at all! Some of them, some who obviously hadn't know him long enough to know better, tried to distract him by getting him to work with them on their self-defence; bad idea ... apparently, one chap argued with him over a pretty minor matter causing him to lose it during the session, throwing them about like a collection of rag dolls, and then marching off to drive back into the village to start another search!

So I heard much later, he went off driving all over the district, covering as wide an area as he thought I could have gone by then. Of course, by that time he knew I had taken my rucksack, sleeping bag and assorted clothes, but hadn't thought to ask anyone if they had any idea why. It was not until the third day, the day I'd been picked up by Luke's men, that it seems he went to see Ellen in her bungalow. She was taking the opportunity to leave Josh in the kitchen and put her feet up for a bit. Steve tapped on her door and called out,

"Ellen, it's me, Steve. Can I come in for a chat?"

It seems she answered him in quite a sharp tone of voice which came as a bit of a surprise to him as they'd always got on so well together. Even so, he was at his wits end, and had decided that, if anyone knew anything, perhaps she might.

"How are you getting on today," he asked, trying to show his caring side to soften the rather sharp tone he'd picked up in her voice.

"I'm fine. More important, how are you, and what are you doing about that poor girl?"

He was totally astonished by her tone, but even more so by her question!

"Pardon; I'm not with you Ellen. What do you mean, 'what am I doing about' her? I take it you mean Mel?"

"Of course I mean Mel. I know they say you're rushing about looking for her, or so you say; but if it wasn't for you she wouldn't have gone in the first place. You can't treat her like that just because you've had a bad experience in the past. Sounds to me as if you've just been stringing her along for your own pleasure all this time. You've certainly not shown the poor kid much commitment have you...?"

"Whoa there! Hang on Ellen. You obviously know more about this than I do. For a start, what's this about how she wouldn't have gone if it wasn't for me? And another thing, what's it have to do

377

with my past experience come to …, oh my God! Are you telling me she's pregnant?"

"You know she is. She said she told you the day she left; she did, didn't she?"

"No, honestly Ellen, that's the first I've heard of it. Why didn't she tell me? Losing her is the last thing I want, even less our baby. Did she say where she was going?"

Ellen explained that she had no more idea than Steve as to where I was going, but just that I was scared of opening up his old pain of losing Sean. The day I'd left, as far as she knew, I was just going to see the W.I. ladies, and just assumed I'd be back. When it became clear that I'd packed a bag and left, she'd assumed we must have had a row. Now, although he now understood why I'd gone, Ellen had no more idea of where to suggest he should look for me.

It was on the fourth day that Steve received a video call to his phone. It came through just as he had gathered together the group he had been so rough with that time, feeling that he owed them an apology. In fact it seems he had by then gone from being out of control, to being (as Ellen told me later) a truly pathetic excuse of a man!

Now, this was where he found that sometimes the particularly young members of our team who he was now having to apologise to, had come into their own. A while before all this had come about one of them had been showing us some technology new to us both. He had downloaded an app onto both our phones which recorded video calls between us. At the time we had said this was something we probably wouldn't need, but this proved to be just the occasion when it came into its own. As his phone rang, he pulled it from his pocket and starred at the screen,

"It's Mel. Thank goodness, at last," and was about to answer it when the young lad who'd set it up grabbed it from him quickly! Steve was about to shout at him until the lad, having tapped something on it, gave it back saying,

"Go on, answer it now. It's recording."

"Hello Mel, where are ...." At this point he stopped and starred in horror at what he saw! It was at this point that he could see I was not alone. He saw straight away that I was sitting, tied to a chair, with my ankles still tied together and a bag of some sort over my head. I'd been dragged there, extremely roughly, by a couple of Stanwick's men. Where I was, I had absolutely no idea, but all I knew for sure was that I could hear Steve's voice.

"Steve, where are you? Are you here?" yet I could tell as I said it that the voice, his voice, was too distant to be as close as I wished it was right then.

The next voice I heard was certainly not his; it was Stanwick. He was telling the ape man to take the bag off my head.

"You see Lockett, I think you'll recognise this pretty little face here,"

As he said this, just to taunt Steve, he bent over and took my chin in his hand to point me to the phone. After the treatment I'd had from him so far, I felt the need to fight back. I spat in his face, taking him completely by surprise, but all I got in return was a hard slap across my face!

"Leave her alone Stanwick. Try picking on someone your own size if you've got the guts to try," Steve challenged him. "Where are you, or are you too cowardly to meet face to face without a woman to hide behind?"

All he got in return was a sarcastic laugh and the remark,

"Seems you do care after all. She tried telling me you'd split up, and that you wouldn't give a damn what happened to her."

I could tell by the tone of Steve's voice that he was already beginning to let his temper rise up a notch, though he was hiding it well from anyone who didn't know him as I did. I thought I should say something to throw Stanwick off course,

"I've told you, we had a row and he kicked me out. What makes you think I'd go back if he asked me? Now let me go and get on with my life while you men sort out your differences between you!" I yelled at him, hoping that would keep him from thinking he could use me as bait.

Unfortunately this didn't work, in fact, all this achieved was to bring from Stanwick just the remark which I knew would only have the effect on Steve of making it ten times worse!

"Oh well then girl, if you're right he won't mind if I find some use for you before I do let you go will he?"

As he said this, still holding the phone for Steve to see, he ran one hand round my face, sending a shiver down my spine, and said to the ape man,

"Ok, she clearly wants you to put her back in the bedroom. Sorry Lockett, you've left it too late; looks like I've got more pressing business, if you get my meaning?"

"You touch her Stanwick, and that'll be the last thing you do! Ok, you've got my attention. Now, what the hell is it you want?"

"Ah, that's more like it. Now, what I want is for you to get papers drawn up to say you're handing over Lansdown Grange and its land to me. Then we can do a swap, her for my inheritance … sounds fair, I think you'll agree?"

By this time he'd turned the phone so that I couldn't see Steve anymore. I tried shouting to him not to do it, but found myself stopped by a huge hand across my mouth. I bit it … but just got another slap, this time from the ape man's much bigger hand!

I heard Stanwick give Steve instructions as to where to meet one of his men. He was told that he would then be brought here (wherever here was) blindfolded, where they would exchange me for the documents. He also said that Steve must come alone or he wouldn't see me again. I couldn't help feeling guilty, knowing that by leaving him I would be the cause of him losing the Grange, unless of course he decided he'd sooner lose me. At least, as far as I knew just then, he knew nothing about the baby, but I desperately wanted him to refuse Stanwick's demand to sign over his dream after the work he'd put into it, and the good he had already done for so many.

I took one last chance to shout out to him not to do it, by this time barely able to feel one more slap, before hearing Stanwick tell Steve not to try tracing or ringing back on my phone, and watching as he dropped it on the concrete floor and smashed it into pieces!

All I managed to glean from what I could see around me was that this place was some sort of disused factory. There was a pretty big open and empty space, and I'd been sitting on a wooden box right in the centre. There was what looked like a narrow walkway around the top, but I didn't see any stairs to get down from there, except a space where I assumed they used to be some time ago. Other than the door which I was obviously taken in through, there were no other signs of access. That was as much as I saw in the brief minutes before the bag was put over my head once more.

As I was carted back and thrown back in the room I was in before, I wondered just how I would endure another two days here. I still had not had food or drink since throwing their first offering on the floor, so when the ape man came in with another tray and suggested I make the most of it this time, I reluctantly gave in. At least he untied my hands so that I could do so, but then stood by the door watching until I'd finished before tying them up again! For the next two days that was my life … sitting on a hard floor with just my old sleeping bag; hands and feet tied, and the odd bit of food and drink once, sometimes twice, a day. I also had to suffer the indignity of being escorted to the toilet and have my guard stand outside the door!

I don't think I barely slept during that time. All I could think of was the trouble I was causing my Steve. Perhaps I should have been straight with him after all and not assumed I knew what he would have wanted, but now I knew it was too late, and that by this time I was probably going to be the cause of so much more hurt than if I'd taken that risk. Would I ever forgive myself, or more importantly, would he ever forgive me … I was sure that the answer to this was no!

Chapter Thirty-Five.

It seems that this call from Luke Stanwick stirred Steve into a real frenzy by all accounts! Apparently he spent some time after this playing the recording of it over and over, desperately searching for the smallest clue as to where they had me, but could find none. It was obviously some empty factory somewhere, but it gave no clues as to where this was. One thing he did pick up from this was that Stanwick had at least three men with him, all, especially the one who was being so rough with me, pretty tough looking.

He was still sitting at his desk looking at this when Dave tapped on his door and asked if it was safe to come in! He could tell the frame of mind Steve was in and had learnt enough by now to know it was best to tread carefully at such a time.

"Steve, will you have a chat with these two chaps? I think they could have some light to shed on your problem."

Steve, though looking a little impatient, said to bring them in.

"Ok, what can you tell me about this then? You'd better not have anything to do with Mel's abduction or ..."

They didn't give him chance to finish his threat, clearly already knowing better than to risk his wrath.

"No mate … I mean, no sir; it's just that we heard Dave talking about an old factory building, and, well, we squatted in a couple last year. One got demolished, but the other one we got kicked out by a couple of blokes. Big brutes they was too!"

Steve wasted no time in showing them the recorded conversation he'd had, and it took them barely a minute to recognise the place!

"And anyway, that's the big brute we said about … the one who smacked her one! What you gonna do boss?"

"Well, first you're going to tell me where this is, and then I'm going to get her out of there. Is it near here?"

"Not so far really. I reckon it was just outside Bromsgrove. They were talking of building on the site sometime. We can take you there and show you. Then how about us getting a gang together to come with you and sort them out?"

Steve said he was happy for them to go with him that same day to show him where it was, giving him chance to check it out before having to meet Stanwick there, but was adamant that none of them could go on the day he had to meet the gang there.

"That's all well and good," Dave had said, "but you can't expect to handle that lot on your own. You could hand over this place and still end up dead!"

But Steve had insisted that this was handled his way. Realising that he wouldn't be able to get in there without the documents demanded of him, he first rang Dean & Son to ask they be drawn up. Mr Dean was amazed that he was apparently giving up on the place so soon, but agreed to do so as Steve was extremely insistent. Having organised this he took Dave, Bob, and the two lads who had given him the information, and set of for Bromsgrove in the bus.

When they got within about a mile of the place he'd been told the factory was, Steve parked up on the outskirts of a nearby village, and went the rest of the way on foot. It seemed that they had been right in their description of the place, and he could see that it was quite possibly the one I had been in when Stanwick had phoned. He told the others to stay well out of sight and keep a watch on the gate while he sneaked in to do a quick recce of the place. As it happened, apparently that day, there was nobody about. Having done what he felt he needed to, he returned to the others and they went back to the bus and drove home.

Of course, he could see they hadn't actually been holding me there, so assumed from the remark about putting me in a bedroom that

Stanwick must have a house of some sort around the area, but he knew that if he went around asking questions, this might get back to them. As a consequence he had to be content (well, as content as a bear with a sore head!) to wait until he was contacted.

It seems from what Ellen told me much later, that during the time he was waiting, first for Mr Dean to send through the papers, and then wait for the call with instructions as to where to meet Stanwick's men, he had spent some time locked away in his office on the phone. Nobody knew who he spoke to, nor dared ask, but on what I thought was the second day after he'd contacted Steve, though by then I was losing track of time, it seemed that Steve received another call from Stanwick with instructions as to where to meet his man. It seems that Steve relented sufficiently to allow some of the men to go with him, but strictly on the understanding that they were to get out of the bus before he got to the meeting place and stay well back. As he told them,

"You're all getting your lives sorted now, and if there's trouble, and you get in the middle of it, the police will get involved and you'll all be back to square one! Now, just do as I say, do you understand me?"

Though they were all obviously worried about Steve going in alone, there were none brave enough to argue when he laid the law down to them so firmly. So that was what they did. He dropped them off a bit before arriving at the appointed place leaving Dave with the spare keys and drove on, meeting two men who were waiting for him a short way off.

Without any argument or resistance Steve stood passively, allowing them to tie his hands and blindfold him. They were within walking distance of the factory, and when Steve heard Stanwick's voice he knew they had brought him to the right place. He stood still and quiet, taking in any sounds around him, and waiting to have his blindfold removed. When he finally did, the first thing he did was look around him, at first for me where I sat on the box with the ape man keeping a firm hold of a rope tied around my waist, and then I couldn't help noticing him casting a swift another glance around the place, I assumed to see how many men Stanwick had there.

As it happened, I knew there were five more as well as my guard, so seven altogether if you could count Stanwick as much of a man! Whatever made Steve come on his own? Surely, after all the work he'd put into teaching so many folk from the Grange how to defend themselves, he could have brought some with him? Perhaps he's got them outside keeping out of sight till he tells them. But no; he was showing no signs of putting up any resistance at all! In fact I couldn't help feeling how down he looked, standing there in the middle of these bullies with no chance of beating them.

"Did you bring the papers then?" asked Stanwick.

Steve put his hand in his pocket and produced a bundle of legal looking documents. Stanwick looked at them, at first with a smile, then turning to the back page said,

"This is no good Lockett, you know it isn't. You haven't signed them!"

Steve took out a pen from his pocket and held it, poised,

"You know what the deal was ... you hand the girl over, and I'll sign your damn papers."

Just for a minute or so there was a standoff between them. Steve obviously had no intention of signing, and Stanwick knew he would have no leverage if he let me go. I could tell by Steve's expression that he had something up his sleeve, but just at that point could see no safe solution to the position he was in right now. After all, I've seen him in action before and quite honestly knew just how tough and how scary he could be, but to tackle all six of these brutes at once would be asking a lot of any one man!

Stanwick called on ape man to leave me for a minute and stand over Steve, to see he was as good as his word, while Stanwick himself came to stand guard over me, obviously trying to look the big man he wished he was!.

And then all hell broke loose! A shout came down from the walkway above,

"Catch number one," and as I looked up a large knife (the same type I'd experienced Steve using last year), flew through the air, straight into Steve's hand.

Simultaneously, four men in balaclavas followed it down, sliding down ropes attached to the railings! As the ape man glanced up in complete shock as to what was happening, Steve caught him a hard blow in the stomach and, as he bent double to deal with this, followed it up with a double fisted blow across the back of his neck, sending him reeling on the ground in pain!

As these hooded men got stuck into the task of dealing with the others, Steve turned his attention to Stanwick who was still standing nervously behind me. He pulled me to my feet as if to use me as a shield against Steve's ever encroaching knife! The expression on Steve's face at that minute left me in no doubt as to how he was feeling about this man ... I knew him too well, and knew that he would show no mercy to the target of his fury this time if pushed too far. I knew I had to do something to prevent him from falling back to his previous days of the PTSD which had led him to being taken away for months' worth of rehab the last time he'd lost it and attacked Morgan with a knife like that one!

Perhaps I was worrying unduly as he then came a step closer, saying to Stanwick,

"Let her go; let me cut her loose then I'll put this down and we can sort this like men."

By this time the hooded men had rounded up the others and got them sitting in a bundle on the floor, standing over them with similar knives in their hands. Stanwick could see he was beaten, and so let Steve step forward and cut me loose. Just for an instant Steve looked over his shoulder to those on the ground, but as he did so Stanwick took the opportunity to move a step toward him, a pretty stupid move bearing in mind what Steve still had in his hand!

Now, I thought, is my turn to get my own back on this low-life! He put his arm out to push me out of his way ... I grabbed it firmly by his sleeve, swung myself round and with all the force I could muster, threw him over my shoulder, landing him hard enough on the concrete floor to knock the wind out of him, then rolled him over and jumped on his back, putting him in an arm lock!

Shouts of, "Go girl, go," and howls of laughter came across the place to me. One of the masked men strolled across, patted Steve on the back and said, "You've still got it mate!"

I thought I recognised the voice ... I certainly recognised the wink he gave me as he relieved me of my prisoner to tie up with the rest of his gang.

And having secured the whole gang, they vanished as quickly as they'd appeared!

All of this happened so quickly that I was left feeling bewildered and completely drained. Bewildered by not knowing where all of this left Steve and me, and drained through the events of the days since I'd left the Grange, and the fact that I'd been hungry and drastically thirsty since being in Stanwick's capture!

I looked up at Steve standing beside me, wondering what he was thinking, until he put his hand down to help me to my feet, but as I tried to stand my legs gave way under me.

"Oh my God Mel, what the hell has he done to you?"

As he said this he scooped me up like a rag doll and carried me to the box I'd been sat on.

"I'll be ok Steve, I'm just a bit dehydrated. He's not very generous with his refreshments at his place." I said, in a feeble attempt to make light of it.

It seems that the next thing he did was to call the police to pick up Stanwick and his men, giving them a brief account of what had happened, but saying he would speak to them as soon as possible as he needed to get me to hospital. As the ambulance was going to be quite a while arriving, he had said not to bother, and that he would drive me there!

All this I only had on hearsay later as I apparently passed out before he made these calls. He rang Dave and got him to pick us up to drive us to the hospital, after checking first to see the prisoners were secure!

The first thing I knew was when I came round in a complete daze, not knowing where I was or how I came to be there. Just for a second I felt myself going into complete melt-down, thinking I was back in Stanwick's place; but then I heard a voice I knew … Steve's voice, speaking gently to me, and felt his hand holding mine.

"It's ok, you're safe now Mel."

As I opened my eyes I found myself looking straight up into those big brown ones I loved so much.

"You're in hospital my darling. You needed to be checked out and rehydrated. The doctor says we can take you home tomorrow."

'Home,' he said we can go home tomorrow. So perhaps he really does want me back. But then, what about the baby? I haven't told him that yet. What will he say when I do?

I thought I could avoid it no longer,

"Steve … well you see, there's something I haven't told you."

"No, I know, you silly fool. You mean about the baby I take it? You don't need to, Ellen has told me already, and a right good telling off I got from her too when she thought I'd kicked you out because of it! Why on earth didn't you say something?"

"I didn't want to upset you. I didn't want to upset you after … after Sean. And I'd always been so careful until then. I'm so sorry Steve."

He stood up from the chair he was sitting on and moved onto the edge of the bed to put an arm around my shoulders.

"Now, just you listen to me; I couldn't be happier. I never got chance to get to know Sean, but now I'll really get chance to know this one. We can really be a proper family."

And then, as he managed to peel his lips off of mine, he had an afterthought,

"I suppose we should get married first though … that's if you'll have me my love?"

I don't think I need tell you what my answer to that question was!!

As Steve had said, I had to remain in hospital for another twenty-four hours. During this time the doctors checked me out thoroughly to assure us that the baby had come to no harm because of the trauma I'd suffered. Steve was like an old mother hen, flapping about, quizzing the nurses about every little thing and refusing to go home, even for long enough to freshen up. He did, however, phone the Grange and tell them I was safe and would soon be home.

However, we did get a visit from the police during that time, wanting our version of the whole incident. Steve explained it all from his side of things, carefully forgetting to point out Chris's input into the affair! The police were apparently bewildered as to the story from the gang of being attacked by a group of men in balaclavas with big knives! Steve stuck rigidly to his story that this was their way of covering up for being overpowered by one man! None the less, just to make it sound just vaguely feasible, I couldn't help hearing him having a quiet word in the ear of their inspector, and could swear I overheard the initials SAS mentioned, away from the hearing of the lower rank officers! Nothing more was said on the matter by the police, but I couldn't help wondering if this was in some way related to the photo of him he'd not wanted me to see before! When we were alone later that evening I decided to ask him outright, especially if we were going to be married. Though rather reluctant at first, he did open up and explain to me that, although he was actually in the paras, there were occasions when the SAS seconded those they considered up to dealing with certain, more difficult circumstances. Apparently both he and Chris had been picked for certain missions. When I asked if there would ever be need for them to call him again, he heaved a sigh and said that this was ruled out since the PTSD had hit.

"But then," he said, "I'll have my hands full using my skills keeping you out of trouble now I reckon."

When the police came back in later it was to question me as to where they had taken me. Although I only saw the house once, on the occasion when they pulled me out of the car boot, I did my best to describe it, saying that they would find my sleeping bag in a back bedroom if they found the house. Going by the minute details I could think of, it seems that they did actually find it and later returned my bag.

It seemed that Stanwick and his gang were being charged with abduction, false imprisonment, assault and blackmail. We were assured that there was no chance of them, Stanwick in particular, seeing the outside of a prison for some time to come. Somehow I felt that it was extremely unlikely they would risk getting back in Steve's bad books again!

When I was finally given the all clear to go home, Dave turned up to drive us back. I don't remember ever feeling so happy to leave anywhere, not that the hospital staff hadn't been fantastic, but because I was finally going 'home', our home! Home was a good word, but now there was something special about it. It was 'our home', it was where I belonged with Steve, where we would raise our child!

And to top all of that, as we drove back up to the house, the whole place was decked with banners saying 'Welcome Home Mel', and all the residents (all our friends), were there outside to greet us! Just to top that, there was Josh with his guitar striking up a tune and all joining in to sing the old Peters and Lee song, 'Welcome Home'!

Chapter Thirty-Six.

From this time onwards things at Lansdown Grange seemed to revolve around wedding plans. With Steve fussing around me and Ellen tending to my every need as if she hadn't too far go to her own big day, I had never felt so pampered! Of course the first thing we did was to ring our respective parents with the news. Mum and Dad asked us to book a hotel for them when the date was set, but every one of our residents made sure we had the two side bungalows available, saying that they would move temporarily into the dormitories so that my parents could stay in one, and Jenny and Alan in the other. We said that May should stay in our spare room as she had previously, and that perhaps Jamie could sleep in the dormitory. We were about to ring Sally with the news and an invitation one day when we did actually receive a call from Jamie.

Steve answered it, and as he listened to what his brother was saying, he burst into fits of laughter, and I heard him say,

"Mel said as much. You crafty devil. I suppose you're hoping to get it for nothing? Ok, I'll see what she says."

When he got off the phone, he came back in the room with a broad grin on his face,

"Guess what? You were right about that brother of mine. He only wants to get in on the act and have a double wedding. Reckons him and Sally were thinking about it anyway so why not share the expense! You know what that means ... big brother pays for it!"

"Well, we do have the venue here, and the marquee if we need it. And Josh has a few budding chefs helping him with the catering. Yes, why not. It'll be fun. Sally can sleep in the dormitory till the day, and then, if we're going away that is, they can use our room for a few a few days."

Ok, I suppose so. So, Mrs Lockett-to-be, where do you want to go for a honeymoon? Florida, Cyprus, Thailand, you choose?"

"No, I don't want to go anywhere like that. Let's just jump in Annie and go, like we did before?"

As far as he was concerned he said we could go anywhere I chose to go.

And so it was arranged. The wedding was to be the second week in June (as I didn't want to have too much of a bump showing), It would be a double wedding with Jamie and Sally. All of our families would be there, with Sandra and Tina (Tom's girls), as flower girls to walk in front of us all up the aisle. Tom was to be Jamie's best man, and of course (as I sort of knew he would be!) Chris would be Steve's.

Though we knew we'd never fit the whole village in the marquee, we did tell them that anyone was welcome to pop along to the do in the gardens after the ceremony. One of the ladies from the W.I. had a portable organ which she had transferred for the day, and Josh arranged music for the reception.

To add to the excitement, Ellen gave birth to a beautiful baby girl who they named Lily, two weeks before our big day, which meant that she was feeling decidedly more mobile by then

The night before the big day, Chris turned up with a small bus load of their old army chums.

"Well, poor old chap's got to have a stag do hasn't he? You can't tie him down without letting him taste freedom one more time Mel!"

Somehow I knew it was useless saying anything, besides, we did owe him for helping me out of the mess I was in.

"Ok. But just make sure you bring him back in a fit condition tomorrow, do you hear?"

"Yes Ma'am, orders are orders eh? Don't you worry about us, we'll look after the old man."

I hadn't realised they were taking Jamie and Tom along, or I might have had more to say, but I just had to watch them go and hope!

The next day turned out to be a beautiful, bright and sunny day. Everyone gathered in the grounds. The residents had moved the chairs and arch of roses into the grounds, leaving the marquee for the evening reception.

Then Jenny and Margaret, each acting as our maids of honour, helped Sally and I dress and made certain we were fully prepared. The two girls could barely contain their excitement. The Mum's both came up to wish us luck, ending in tears of joy at seeing us looking, as my Mum said, so amazing.

We went down, assuming everyone would be there ready to begin. The vicar and congregation were all in place, and just as we came out the door, the bus turned up with Jamie, Tom and some others who were attending.

Jamie and Tom were quick to walk up to stand near the vicar, the poor lady with the organ sat ready to strike up the music, but then I realised there was a problem … where on earth was Steve? I looked round at the bus and saw Chris, smartly dressed for the first time since I've known him, getting out of it. As he came up toward me I grabbed him in sheer panic,

"Where the hell is he? What've you done with him? He should have been here before now. He hasn't changed his mind has he?"

"Stop panicking girl. Of course he hasn't changed his mind. Just fancied another form of transport that's all. He'll be here."

So saying he walked off up the aisle to stand with Jamie and Tom!

Just as I was working myself into a real frenzy I heard a noise, quite a deafening noise, and it was getting louder. I, like all those around me, looked up to the sky to see what it was.

It was a helicopter, and as I looked at it hovering above us I saw something falling from it. It wasn't until a parachute opened that I realise this was Steve!

Well, I didn't know whether to scream at him or laugh, but at that moment I wouldn't have been surprised to hear a James Bond theme to strike up!

He landed, so casually, undid his parachute, patted himself down, grinned at me, and walked up to stand by Chris as if this was the most natural thing in the world to do ... but then, I suppose for him perhaps it was!

As Sally and I walked down the aisle behind the flower girls, past our friend's family, and half the neighbourhood, all I could see was my Steve waiting for me. I'd never dared believe this day would ever come. I'd come to accept we would never be more than friends, perhaps lovers, but here I was walking up an aisle with him waiting for me; and to top this I was carrying his baby ... our baby. If this was a dream, I thought, please don't ever wake me up!

We could have been the only two people on the planet except the vicar as, right through the ceremony we couldn't take our eyes off one another. Not long after this we all moved to the

402

dance floor in the marquee and Steve led me into the centre where we drifted around to the tune, 'Unchained Melody', feeling as if we were the only two people in the room!

By the time we dragged ourselves away from the crowds of family and friends to jump into Annie, I was so happy, I felt I'd burst! We drove off down the drive lined with well-wishers, all waving us off and laughing at the noise of the empty cans tied on behind!

"Ok Mrs Lockett, where to now?"

"As long as we're together, I really don't care, Mr Lockett!"

As it happened, unknown to those back at the Grange, we spent our first night back by the weir … where we had first come together. Well, I thought, where else but the place he'd first had the will to find a way!

P.S. When we finally returned home to continue with all our plans for Lansdown Grange, we managed to find different ways to turn it into a successful business, as Steve looked at it, to take them in, sort them out, and ship them out, even packing a few off to join the army!

But my biggest achievement came in the middle of January, on a cold snowy day, when I presented Steve with a healthy baby boy.

Oh; so you want to know what we called him? We called him Will of course!!

Printed in Great Britain
by Amazon

70470795R00234